# CAPTAIN JACK

*A honeymoon they never forget, if they survive...*

Newlyweds Jack and Alice Stratton are determined not to let something like a hurricane upset their honeymoon plans. But the storm's winds and churning tides unearthed a secret long hidden beneath the turquoise waters of the island paradise.

A local tour boat captain discovers the mystery and offers to sell the location to a man known only as the Dyab—the Devil. The captain is murdered. The police suspect Jack and Alice and confiscate their passports. Trapped between the Devil and the deep blue sea, the handsome young detective and his blushing bride have nowhere to turn and everything to lose as they set out to prove their innocence and find the real killer.

Also by Christopher Greyson:

WALL STREET JOURNAL BESTSELLING AUTHOR
# CHRISTOPHER GREYSON

# CAPTAIN
# JACK

**A HONEYMOON THEY'LL NEVER FORGET, IF THEY SURVIVE...**

*This book is dedicated to my grandmother Ma,*
*a woman with a gentle spirit and the heart of lion*
*who showed me so much love.*
*(and molasses cookies!)*

A ndres fidgeted in the passenger seat of his beloved two-toned 1986 Ford Courier. "Why we gotta wait 'til we on da boat?"

Ramon flashed his gold-toothed smile. "Patience. I tellin' you, Dre, dis surprise gonna blow ya mind."

As Ramon sped toward Lucaya Beach, Andres stared out the window at the fleeting parade of run-down shacks, rubble, and broken trees. Hurricane Axel had left its mark on the Bahamas a couple of months ago.

Ramon seemed oblivious to the devastation as he whistled and strategically swerved to avoid potholes and debris. It was clear that he did a better job avoiding trouble behind the wheel than he did in life with his constant scheming and illegal ventures. Ramon was handsome, tall, charismatic, and lucky. It almost didn't seem fair that he was so blessed while his little brother missed the boat in all four categories.

"Because it's a surprise. Look, I really appreciate ya lettin' me stay with you and dis my way of sayin' tanks."

"No need, bro. Dat's what family for." Andres cleared his throat. "Speaking of which..." His mind flashed to his three-room bungalow in Bain Town, which was too small for him and Irene. And now with a baby on the way, Irene was anxious for Ramon to leave. So was Andres. "Um. I was wondering when you were tinking 'bout, you know, maybe heading back to your place in Abaco? I hear dey are rebuilding."

"Ha! Nuttin' to rebuild. Erryting is gone! Da only ting dere now is rats and gulls."

Andres slumped in his seat.

Ramon parked by the dock where the *Dive Into Paradise* shack had stood defiantly through the hurricane. The little truck shuddered when he shut off the engine.

Andres got out and stared at the dancing waves. His brother had taught him to swim in these waters, to fish, and how to flatter the girls on the beach. Besides his uncle Victor, Ramon was the only family he had left. How could he throw him out?

Ramon pointed toward the sun as he swaggered down the ramp to the dock below. "I tellin' you, Dre, today's da day!"

Andres's hope rose along with his brother's cocky grin. Ramon had girlfriends all over the islands. Surely one of them would take him in?

With Ramon whistling in front of him, Andres pulled the cover off the *Azariah*, a thirty-foot dive boat named after their mother. He folded it neatly, while Ramon untied the lines.

A canvas tarp covered a small pile in the stern. It looked like a large mound of laundry that Irene had covered with a sheet. But that pile wasn't there last night when Andres moored the boat. A puzzled look crept across his face as he stepped toward it.

Ramon immediately grabbed his arm.

"Not yet, Dre." Ramon's voice took on a sing-song tone. "It's a surprise."

Andres chewed the inside of his cheek. There could be anything under that tarp. Bait fish or gear that Ramon had traded for booze. He wouldn't even be surprised if Ramon had hidden a stripper under there who'd leap up any second just like they do in the movies when they jump out of a cake.

"Just wait 'til we're at our spot. I show you den." Ramon flashed his signature smile and wiggled his eyebrows.

"Is it Kalik?"

Ramon chuckled and started the engine. "Kalik? A pile dat big would be six cases! Not even Uncle Victor could drink dat much beer in a trip."

The propeller churned the water and the small boat pulled away from the dock. Ramon steered the boat due south out of the harbor. The bow skimmed across the surface and the salt air swept the worries from Andres's mind. He was going to be a father! It didn't matter if it was a boy or a girl. There were so many things he wanted to teach his child. With all the wonders of the island and the sea he didn't even know where to begin.

Ramon checked the GPS and shut the engine off.

Andres tossed the anchor over the side with a splash.

Ramon hurried to the back of the boat, grinning from ear to ear. "Bro, watch, our lives are never gonna be da same."

"Ramon, stop ya foolishness. If you gat gyals under dere, you gotta tell Irene I knew nuttin' 'bout this."

"Dis is even better!" Ramon laughed and yanked the tarp off.

Lying at the bottom of the boat was a pile of old ceramic vessels and pots. Some were whole but most were broken beyond repair. Caked with dirt and clay, the bottom of the boat was turning a muddy brown.

"Why you bring dat crap on my boat?" Andres moaned. "Now I gotta wash it again before we bring out da newlyweds."

Ramon lifted his chin and touched his chest. "I 'bout to show you how we're gonna turn dis crap, as you call it, into cash. Like Midas. Dis stuff gonna be gold."

"All that rum rotten out ya brain. Dat junk isn't worth nuttin'."

"It's gonna be worth something now." Andres lifted up a clay pot with a hole in the side. "We're gonna toss some crap into da sea, take dem tourists out to dive, and let dem 'find' dey phony treasures."

Andres thought for a moment. At least once a week, someone diving came across an old, rusted piece of metal, then came rushing to the surface, hoisting it high overhead like a victory cup as if it were from a pirate wreck. "But how's dat gonna make us money?"

Ramon tapped the side of his head with his forefinger. "That's da genius part of my plan. I'm gonna tell dem dey suppose to report any antiquities dey find so dey could be returned to da rightful owner, das if dey could find da owner. Dey gonna ask how long dat's gonna take. I'll say, 'Oh, after five or so years, you'll probably get ya treasure, but you're gonna have to pay taxes on it, and dat tax bill gonna be real high.' I'll give dem a few seconds to let dat sink in, den I'll tell dem most people prefer to do it da 'island' way. Dey greedy face gonna brighten up—especially dose Americans, boy." Ramon wheezed with laughter. "Two minutes later, dey offering me money to keep my mout' shut so dey could take dey junk home with dem. Erryone gonna be happy!"

Andres glared at his brother. That was *not* the island way. That was Ramon's way.

Ramon shot back a sidelong glance. "Relax. Ya gat nuttin' to worry 'bout. I have all dis figured out. We're doing nuttin' illegal anyway."

Andres shook his head as Ramon started putting on his diving gear. Andres remained silent as he strapped on his own gear and checked the air supply.

Ramon grabbed a few pieces of junk from the pile. He waved at Andres as he did a backward flip off the dive platform.

A knot was starting to grow in Andres's stomach. Ramon might believe the plan was legal, but Andres had his doubts. Even if it were, it was most certainly morally wrong.

Ramon's head broke the surface and he bobbed in the water, smiling. "Hand me dat pot and grab some stuff, too."

Andres picked up a rusted vase from the deck and gave it to him. "I gat a bad feeling 'bout dis, bro."

"Chill." Ramon winked. "We need da money. You're gonna tank me tomorrow."

"What if dey go to da police? We don't want no vibe with CDU."

"Dey not gonna do dat. Look, if dey say something, blame it on me," Ramon said. "But dat's gonna mean we splitting seventy–thirty."

Andres picked up his own mask and sat down on the dive platform, his feet dangling in the warm water. Cheating tourists went against everything Andres believed in, but everybody knows it is bad luck to have a disagreement on the open water. He couldn't speak here; it would have to wait till they were on land.

"We selling dreams." Ramon spat into the inside of his mask and rubbed it to keep it from fogging. "Just like Disney. Da sucker who buys into dis fantasy gonna feel like Indiana Jones. Besides, dey balling, man. Dey gat money to burn. Tink about how much dey blowin' here anyway! You tink dey gonna miss a few dollars? 'Memba now, dey da ones breaking da law—not us!" Ramon laughed and readjusted his mask. "Come on!" He popped his regulator into his mouth and disappeared beneath the shimmering waves.

Andres pressed his mask to his face, grabbed a moldy pot, and dropped backward into the water. The warmth and pressure of the ocean wrapped around him like a heavy blanket. Instantly he was calm. Things were so much simpler beneath the surface.

The waters had finally returned to some of the clearest in the world, with visibility up to a remarkable two hundred feet, but how much damage Hurricane Axel had done to the slow-growing coral was unknown. The powerful storm had dredged the sea bottom like a giant washing machine with a load of rocks. By some miracle, the south side of the island had been relatively protected—not like Eleuthera and the Abaco Islands, where their uncle Victor was, if he was still alive.

Andres followed Ramon's trail of bubbles down. Ramon had already reached the buoy he'd left yesterday as a marker and was looking for a spot to plant his vase. Andres swam away from him, following the reef toward a sandy undersea hill. Stopping near the crest of the slope, he floated over the sand and reached down to dig a small hole in order to partially bury the pot, when his hand hit something hard and flat.

Puzzled, he brushed away more white sand. The water became momentarily cloudy with sediment, but as it settled, he clearly saw a metal panel and gasped, sending bubbles streaming out from his regulator.

A shipwreck? After all his years of diving, had he finally discovered a real hidden treasure?

Casting the pot aside, he began sweeping the area with both hands. Everywhere he moved, he revealed more rusted metal. Glancing up, he began to believe that this huge mound was hiding something beneath it.

*If a boat rolled over when it sank, dis would be da bottom of its hull ...*

Ramon was suddenly at his side. Behind the plastic of his mask, his eyes were wide and he grabbed hold of Andres and shook him with excitement. Together they cleared more sand away, until flaked red paint showed through beneath their hands. Andres swam upward so he could see the entire emblem they had revealed—the red hammer and sickle of the former Soviet Union.

*He'd just found a Russian submarine.*

# 2

Jack and Alice approached the shed where a large man stood in front of the homemade sign for Williams Town Paramotor Tours. He smiled from ear to ear and loudly called out, "Welcome to da Bahamas, Mr. and Mrs. Stratton! My name is Kevin." The paramotoring instructor's English accent was as thick as his toned muscles. "Will you both be takin' a tour today? Would you like to try a tandem?"

Jack cast a hopeful look at his new bride.

Alice crossed her arms and shook her head.

"Come on now, little lady, you must try once," Kevin encouraged her. "It is free to go up."

"Free?" Alice's voice rose skeptically.

"Yes! And only a hundred and fifty dollars to come down!" Kevin's rich, booming laugh made them both chuckle.

"Are you sure you don't want to give it a try?" Jack asked. "The motor does most of the work." He was eager to try paramotoring because he loved paragliding, and the motor would allow him to get even more elevation and control over the flight. When he saw there was someone offering tours right next to their resort on Silver Point Beach, he couldn't pass it up.

"Not a chance. I don't even want *you* to do it."

"It's perfectly safe, and I'll be right behind you."

"Then you'll be on the ground." She pointed at her feet. "Because this is where I'm staying."

"Chicken," Jack teased.

"Bock-bock," Alice clucked, sticking her thumbs in her armpits and flapping her arms.

Jack leaned down, kissed her a little longer than he should in public, and flashed a roguish grin. "I'll be right back, Mrs. Stratton."

"I'll be here. And you'd better come back in one piece, Mr. Stratton."

Jack gave her a wink and turned to catch up with Kevin.

She cupped her hand to her mouth and called after him, "If you hurt yourself on our honeymoon doing these crazy stunts you call fun, you will miss out on the *real* fun!"

He looked back over his shoulder and flashed a reassuring smile. Alice had good reason to worry for his safety: Jack had a habit of pushing limits.

Kevin and Jack jogged over to the center of the huge field, where the equipment was laid out for a flight. The paramotor rested back onto its huge fan and two yellow harnesses were hung from the wing.

Kevin grabbed a harness and handed it to Jack. "Dis is a fine way to plunge into your honeymoon."

"I agree—but don't use the word *plunge* in front of my wife."

Kevin laughed. He glanced over his shoulder back at Alice. "She may be nervous, but I can tell she wants *you* to be happy. She is very much in love, my friend. Her smile for you is bright as da sun."

Jack hadn't stopped smiling since they'd finally said *I do* three days ago. But he knew that while Alice was smiling on the outside she was still reeling at the death of her great uncle—especially considering that it was her own cousin that killed him in order to protect Jack. Right now, Alice didn't want to discuss any of it. He was hoping that the vacation would enable her to process finding out her grandfather was still alive and move beyond the tragedy.

"I am very glad you chose da Bahamas for your honeymoon," Kevin said.

"I thought we should change plans since the hurricane caused so much damage, but Alice had her heart set on coming here. I'm glad we did. The islanders we've met seem to really appreciate the tourism."

"We do!" Kevin said cheerily. "Dere were many losses, especially on some of da uddah islands. But we will rebuild. Bahamians are resilient."

Jack stared down the green slope to the shimmering turquoise waters that filled the whole horizon. "It's so beautiful. I can see why you fight for it."

"Careful, Mr. Stratton." Kevin checked all the hooks on the nearest paramotor and pulled on his harness to make certain it was securely fastened. "Many who come to da Bahamas love it so much dey stay, and dose who don't, dream 'bout it for da rest of deir lives." He handed Jack a helmet and helped him strap into his harness. "Dis being your honeymoon, however, I imagine you're dreamin' of uddah tings."

Jack chuckled good-naturedly, but the truth was, the newlyweds had yet to consummate their marriage. Alice had expressed her desire for him but was struggling with being intimate. She had been molested as a child, and the emotional scars ran deep. He wouldn't rush her. He'd waited this long for her; he could make it a little longer. But he hoped he wouldn't have to wait too long.

Kevin ran down a list of instructions and showed him how to operate the throttle and the brake pulleys, much of which was familiar to Jack from paragliding. Jack listened intently. An avid learner, he forced himself not to interrupt every time a question popped into his head, but patience paid off. Kevin was a good instructor, and Jack didn't have any unanswered questions at the end of his spiel. After checking their equipment a final time, Kevin strapped the paramotor to his back, a large circular metal cage with a spinning prop in the center. He reached forward and attached the back of Jack's harness to the front of his own for their tandem flight.

"Are you ready to fly, Mr. Stratton?"

Jack nodded. "Always." He looked back at Alice and waved. She gave him a thumbs-up.

His heart began to race with the start of the paramotor's engine—from excitement, not fear. The thought of sailing into the blue sky made him feel like Superman. The huge wing billowed out behind them, large enough to support the weight of two grown men. Together they ran a few steps, and with a single leap Jack found himself taking flight up over the grassy field. Warm, salty sea wind kissed his cheeks and filled his lungs as they flew not far over the ground, the grass beneath them streaking by like waves alongside a boat.

"Want to go a little higher?" Kevin yelled.

Jack shouted back, "You bet!"

Using the handheld throttle, Kevin increased the thrust and the pair soared like two eagles. Kevin leaned and the glider responded and turned slightly east, toward a beautiful building with a blue roof and turrets.

"Dat's Cooper's Castle!" Kevin called out.

Jack nodded. The story of the Reverend Dr. Harvard Cooper, his faith, and his rise from rags to riches had caught his eye, though the internet pictures failed to capture the grandeur of the building and the compound. It was privately owned by the Cooper family, but they gave tours—Alice would probably enjoy that.

Right now, Jack wanted to explore the sky. "Can I try it now?" he called out.

Kevin nodded.

Jack gently pulled on the levers attached to the glider above him. Like a skilled captain steering a ship, the craft responded to his commands and gracefully turned toward the beach.

Jack shifted his weight further back. The glider climbed higher and streaked upward, giving him a breathtaking view of the archipelago. He let out an exuberant cheer as they put Freeport behind them, setting their faces to the sun and water.

Kevin tapped Jack's shoulder. "Maybe not so high!" He adjusted his weight and the glider leveled out and headed back to the coast.

Jack glanced over at the instructor. "How do we dive?"

"Slowly!" Kevin laughed. "Tip da nose down. I can show you."

"I think I got it," Jack said.

Kevin raised a nervous eyebrow and nodded.

Jack's lips pressed together. Trying to ascend while flying felt a whole lot easier than the decision to aim toward the ground. He took a deep breath, pulled forward, and angled the nose down. Like a hawk diving for a mouse, the glider rocketed forward. The salty sea breeze stung his cheeks as their speed increased. They waved at the swimmers and sunbathers, coming in about thirty feet over their heads, then the sand gave way to grass, and the grass rushed closer.

"Slow!" Kevin reached out and tapped Jack's arm, his hand moving toward the wing's brake toggles.

Jack shifted his weight once again, changing the angle of approach and cutting speed. All too soon the grass was under his feet. Jack pedaled his legs and he and Kevin ran to a stop.

"That was awesome! What a rush." He whooped again as Alice raced across the field toward him.

Somehow, she managed to smile and give him a cross look at the same time. "You went *way* too high and came down *way* too fast." She stopped and faced Kevin. "Do newbies normally fly like that?"

"*Seasoned professionals* don't fly like dat." Kevin chuckled. "I'm sorry to inform you, Mrs. Stratton, but your new husband likes to live on da edge."

"I knew that when I married him." Alice wrapped an arm around Jack's neck and pulled herself close to him.

"Be careful, Jack," Kevin said. "Da Bahamas are very beautiful, but dere are many dangers, especially for people like you."

# 3

ndres sat at his desk in the office while Ramon paced the wet floor. The sea water ran off their wetsuits and gear they'd hastily tossed in the corner. Andres wanted to throw the windows open so the sea breeze could sweep away the musty odor that hung in the air, but he didn't dare. He felt like a rat, hiding below deck on a ship at sea. "We should tell da government what we found."

Ramon stopped pacing and pointed at Andres. "You crazy, Dre?" Ramon hurried over, glancing around like the walls had suddenly grown ears. "Den we wouldn't get nuttin'."

"You don't tink dey would give us a reward?"

"Reward?" Ramon scoffed. "You know what dey would do? Shut us down. Or block off da coast 'til dey raise da sub! Or strike some deal and turn it into a memorial and ban diving dere altogether—permanently. You know just how dey go."

Andres rubbed his forehead with the palm of right hand. Why was life so complicated? "Planting fake treasures for tourists to find is one ting but hiding a sunken submarine gonna get us sent to jail. And for what? Scrap metal?"

Ramon's hands pressed against the table so hard the veins in his forearms stood out. "You know what dat sub is?"

Andres shook his head.

Ramon shoved him aside and took his seat. He typed quickly at the keyboard and the old monitor flickered to life. "Soviet Union. Alfa-class. Only seven made. I tink it be dis one." He pointed at the Wikipedia page he had pulled up. "Less dan thirty in da crew. It went missin' in 1990. Look."

Andres's pulse sped up. "The *Red Star*?" Together they read in silence for a minute. The article said most of the information was all highly secret and classified on both sides, but the United States had publicly accused Russia of trying to deliver a nuclear warhead to Cuba. Russia claimed all the crew had deserted and the sub was scuttled near the Arctic. A small-scale, very hushed, search was conducted for five years by AUTEC off Andros Island, but it was defunded in 2001. The Russians couldn't conduct a search of their own, at least not publicly, since they said the sub went down in the Arctic.

When they were done, the brothers looked up from the monitor, their eyes wide.

Andres glanced out the window at the harbor. "Das da marine biologists dat were diving off Andros ..."

Ramon turned back to the computer and switched to another page. "I was wonderin' da same ting. Look. Dis dey boat—*The Refute*. Registered in Greece. What you know 'bout dem?"

Andres shrugged. "Dey been here near a year. Dey go diving almost erry day. Dey captain is a man named Demetrios. Big guy. *Real* big. Even Chooch is scared of him."

"You talk to da captain or any of da crew?"

"Nuttin' beside da tide and wedduh. Dey keep to deyself. Lilly and some of da gyals tried but dey told dem to mind dey own business. All Lilly say is…" Andres's mouth flopped open. "Lilly say da mean looking one, Vadik, spoke Russian not Greek."

Ramon scoffed. "Marine biologists studyin' da native dolphins. Ha!"

"I bet you dey looking for da *Red Star*!"

Ramon walked over to the safe drying out on the table in the corner. It was small, the kind that would hold a handgun, some cash and important papers, but made from a surprising light metal. It had taken them three days to get into the shipwrecked sub and remove it from the captain's quarters.

"Or maybe dey was looking for what's in here. We should open it."

Andres shook his head. Something about this whole business scared him down to his core. "No."

Ramon glared at him. "It must be waterproof. No water comin' out and nuttin' sloshin' round inside. Whatever's in dere must be still dry."

"If whatever Demetrios is looking for isn't in dat safe, he's gonna tink we took it," Andres said.

Ramon looked thoughtful. "If we don't open it, how're we gonna know how much of a reward to ask for?"

"Even if you open it, you aren't gonna know! How much is an old sub worth? It may gat no cargo. For all we know, dey was heading to Cuba for cigars."

Ramon's eyes lit up. His chuckle slowly built into a laugh. "For a fool you's a genius."

Andres raised a puzzled eyebrow.

Ramon laughed even louder. "It's much closer to Freeport and to Florida dan to Cuba. Dey probably had a warhead on board. Maybe more than one."

"A warhead?" Andres swallowed with an audible gulp. "Nuclear?"

"Yes, Dre."

"Den we have to tell da police. What if it's leaking? It could damage da ecosyst—"

Ramon shot foreword and slapped Andres hard across the face. "Das da last time you're gonna mention going to da police." He jammed a finger against Andres's chest. "Ya understand me?"

Andres nodded miserably. Ramon had always had a temper, and now that Andres was a target of it again, he was scared, just like when they were boys.

"Dis change erryting." Ramon smiled and squeezed Andres's shoulder. "You know what we got now? A bidding war!"

Andres's head spun. "Ya need two customers for a bidding war. Who else's gonna want da sub?" He was going to ask if Ramon was thinking of selling the location to the government, but his cheek was still stinging.

"We go to da Dyab. He'll pay."

Andres felt like Ramon had punched him in the gut. "You crazy, bro?"

"No." Ramon scoffed. "The Dyab buys and sells erryting. Drugs, weapons, anyting."

"But who dey gonna sell a warhead to? If da wrong people get ahold of it ..."

"What do we care? We gonna be long gone."

Andres gasped as he found a flash of hope that he could bring this insane talk to an end. "But we don't even know how to find da Dyab."

Ramon crossed his arms. "Chooch knows."

Andres pressed his eyes closed before opening them and glaring at Ramon. "You lost ya mind! You wanna run talks with Chooch now? Ramon, if Mummy was alive ..." He could only shake his head. This was going from bad to worse. "Chooch's crazy. Even Aunt Naomi say his head's no good."

"Chooch works for da Dyab. He says he handles business for da top brass. Da pickup spot is always da same store. I'm gonna leave word dere."

Andres swallowed and stared at the door like it might open at any moment. Mothers told stories of the Dyab to scare their children into obeying. The Dyab was feared throughout the Bahamas. It was rumored that he lived in Nassau, but no one knew for sure, and it didn't matter, because his net was cast over all of the islands, and the Dyab could tighten it at will, or send his minions wherever necessary on a fast boat, plane, or helicopter. Few had seen him, but even the white people who felt snug and secure in their mansions and gardens knew that the Dyab—said to be as black as coal and slim as a snake—only tolerated their presence in his dominion.

Andres shook with the effort of holding back his thoughts, and from the desire to throttle his big brother right now, get him out of his life. Thinking quickly, he saw his only option was to let Ramon hang himself by his own rope. Let him test his crazy idea in the open market and he would quickly become the target of either ridicule or invite someone to beat some sense into his head—but Andres had to stay as far away as possible, minimize his exposure.

Andres shook the tension out of his shoulders and said calmly, "No one goes directly to da Dyab. Go to da men in da market. Go to da West End. Deal with dem. Not da Dyab himself."

"Da uddah men don't know how to handle a deal dis big, dis sensitive. Besides, dey gonna want dey cut, too. Dat'll cut my profits."

"You can't spend money if ya dead."

"I'm not gonna just bust in. I'll leave instructions. I'll get one of dem burner phones." He leveled a threatening finger in Andres's face. "And you're not gonna tell no one. Especially Irene. Your wife likes to run her mout'. Ya understand?"

Andres nodded and choked back the rising bile in his throat. The truth was, he was afraid of what Irene would do if she found out what Ramon was thinking. Even before the pregnancy test, she'd changed. What did she call it? Nesting? With the baby coming, Irene was determined to make a stable and safe environment for the child. If she found out, she'd kill him.

Andres hung his head. As he stared at his hands, his gaze traveled to the desk. It was cluttered with bills stamped with large red warnings: PAST DUE. He needed some money but could any good ever come from a deal with the Devil?

"Relax, Dre." Ramon's sharp white teeth flashed. "Dis perfect. Dis like eBay! Dey bid against each uddah, we get da highest price, and walk away rich." He laughed. "We don't have to worry about shipping, we just give dem da location. Dey won't even know who we is."

Andres placed his shaking hands in his lap. Thank goodness their mother was not alive to see the depths her sons were sinking to. She would have shaken them senseless for even speaking of the Dyab. "I don't like dis at all."

"You gatta do nuttin' else, bro." Ramon smiled. "I'm gonna take care of erryting. All we gatta do is go 'bout our normal routine. It'll be all right, you'll see. You take the dive tour today and I'll take the uddah one tomorrow. And after dat, who knows, we might retire!"

Andres felt his heart racing, but he knew he had to hide any sign of fear or weakness—from his own brother. "I'll take my tour to da usual spot."

"Take dem somewhere else—up north, to Crab Key." Ramon roughly shook him, forcing Andres to look into his eyes.

Andres nodded. "All right."

Ramon released his grip on Andres's shoulder. "We need to act like nuttin' happened. We don't want to raise suspicions."

Andres wanted to run, but of course he couldn't. Now his legs were shaking, too.

Ramon jammed his finger down on the pile of bills on the desk. "Keep it together for just a few days and we be rich. I'll make all da arrangements. All you need to do is take out ya tour today and I'll take da dive out tomorrow; business as usual. Who am I taking?"

Andres looked down at the desk. "American couple. Dey just get marry. The Strattons."

*t last, a real lead!* For the first time in Dimitri's life, as *The Refute* sliced through the sharp blue waters toward Grand Bahama, he felt hope. The decommissioned patrol boat was a huge step down from the massive Greek salvage ships Dimitri was used to commanding. But for this mission, he had chosen speed over size. At eighty-seven feet with two diesel engines, they could reach any of the islands quickly— and Cuba and the Florida Keys as well. Endless choices, and many risks.

Dimitri stared at the sea as it parted to let him pass. Their cover as marine biologists was good as far as it went, but he was running out of money to pay the crew, and they would have to return home to their real jobs soon. All these years, he had burned with the quest to clear his father's name, and now, finally, it was within reach.

His beard was shot with gray now, and the good life had cushioned his powerful muscles—did he still have the strength to turn back history and fulfill his promise to his mother? His brother Boris had also died on the *Red Star*, only twenty years old.

Vadik—his oldest friend, and the son of his father's lieutenant on the doomed voyage—banged open the desk door, pulling a pouch of tobacco out of his pants pocket. Vadik seemed never to have evolved from the angry teenager Dimitri had said goodbye to on the Odessa docks when they were both young. Dimitri had made his fortune and reputation in Greece, enjoyed women, good food, and sunshine, while Vadik stayed behind in Russia, standing in bread lines only to be turned away, doing odd jobs for shady characters, playing cards all day and drinking all night with the other poor souls huddled against the cold, six or eight to a room. Such was the fate for most of the *Red Star*'s families. They were all tainted by their fathers' treasonous actions.

But the official Soviet story was a lie. Dimitri had once believed the propaganda himself until he ran into the old mechanic who was supposed to be on the mission but sliced off three of his fingers the night before they left the dock. Drunk and rambling, the old man insisted Dimitri's father was no traitor. Dimitri had grabbed him by the throat and demanded proof. The man offered one word—Cuba.

Since that day, Dimitri had pieced together the facts. Tracking down every lead. He was so close now, but he wouldn't share this new information with the crew of four men and two women. Their hopes had been dashed too many times before.

Vadik strolled up behind him, puffing on his hand-rolled cigarette. "Where are we going, Dimitri? We aren't usually in such a rush," he said in Russian.

Vadik's gratitude for saving him from his misery was a never-ending resource. Still, Dimitri sometimes feared that Vadik's hard life had damaged his brain a little.

"Can't you learn to call me Demetrios? And speak English. Especially when we get back to Freeport."

"I will try." Vadik nervously tapped on the railing. "So, Freeport? Do you really believe they found it?" Vadik's brown eyes twinkled.

Dimitri frowned and stroked his beard. "The man said he had proof they located the *Red Star.*"

Vadik grabbed the railing and shook it. "Is it possible? Did he say what this proof was? Who was this man?"

"He would not give his name. Our policeman friend traced the call to a small tourist diving operation out of Lucaya Beach."

Vadik was pacing up and down the deck, running his hands over his freckled bald head. "Divers?"

Dimitri nodded. "The hurricane may have uncovered the wreckage. I believe this man is telling the truth." He scowled at Vadik. "He is well aware that we are not marine scientists, by the way."

"What does it matter now? We couldn't ask for better news!" He clapped Dimitri hard on the back but stepped back hesitantly when he saw the expression on Dimitri's face. "Right?"

"He wants me to make him an offer for the coordinates." Dimitri knew he could trust Vadik. His fierce desire to disprove the lies about his father almost matched his. "He also said that there was another buyer making a bid for the information."

"Who?"

"Again, he would not say."

Vadik took a long drag off his cigarette. "The only ones with a legal right to the salvage are the Soviet Union and the Bahamas, with proper submission to the minister."

Dimitri met Vadik's stare with an even darker one. "Don't quote the Abandoned Wreck laws to me. We are the only ones who have a right to the *Red Star*. The Soviet Union is gone. It was a Russian sub with a Russian crew. The Soviets turned their back on our fathers. Branded them deserters. Are we going to abandon them, too?" His life's mission had been to find that sub, and now that he was so close, the thought of someone toying with him made a fire burn in his chest.

"Nikogda." The tip of his cigarette glowed as he inhaled deeply. "Never." Smoke poured from his mouth with his pledge.

Dimitri turned back to the sea. "I will go and meet with this man and I will... what is that American movie you like so much?"

"*The Godfather?*"

Dimitri nodded. "I will meet with this man and make him an offer he cannot refuse."

# 5

Chooch's blindfold was ripped off his face and he stood in a grand hallway, his body swaying with his thundering heartbeats—and this was the calmest he'd felt since he'd been roused from a sound sleep by two burly thugs, hustled into a car, then into a helicopter, then into a car again and driven here blindfolded, while his captors never said a word.

He'd seen the two huge enforcers before, though, around the seedy parts of Bain Town and Grant's Town. When he'd asked who they were, he was told that they were royalty in the Bahamas' black market, the personal guard dogs of the Dyab himself.

Chooch had a role in the black market, too, on the lowest level—as a courier. Not only that, he worked the West End, which had always been a poor earner, and actually closed down after the hurricane. But even before, the West End had been the weakest faction. In the organization, Chooch was the mold beneath the bottom of the rum barrel. Why would the Dyab want to see him? This had to be a mistake, but judging by the rudeness of his seizure, and the opulence of the neocolonial mansion he'd been taken to, he was in the very house of the Devil.

Chooch pulled up his jeans. He'd had to dress so fast he hadn't put on underwear, let alone a belt. Standing between the two large armed men, he was sweating profusely. What had he done to cross the Dyab? Maybe a little gambling on the side. And one or two weekends when he drank too much and was a little late with a delivery.

Could they have found out about the prostitute, too? All these things were violations of the oath he had taken as a new recruit, but he was a man, after all, with desires that needed to be quenched.

The door in front of him was opened by another brute, who waved his Uzi to motion Chooch into a small study. A bookcase, filled not with books but with antiques and curios, took up one wall, except for a closed door opposite the one they'd entered. The only furniture in the room was two leather chairs, a small side table, and a reading lamp, all exquisite, and huge potted plants, some with vines reaching up to the ceiling, others fanning out. Chooch felt like he was in a little jungle shrine. It looked so real he imagined venomous snakes lurking in the dangling vines, watching him.

"Arms out," the man with the Uzi ordered.

Chooch had already been searched by the men who picked him up, but he wasn't about to argue with a man holding a submachine gun pointed at his chest. The man roughly patted him down, then motioned him over to one of the chairs.

Chooch sat down and stared at the closed door on the opposite wall, as the man holding the Uzi walked over to it. His breath caught in his throat as a slender, elegant man walked in without a sound. Chooch had never seen him before, but he knew. Barefoot, but immaculately dressed in a silvery gray business suit and white silk shirt with no tie, the Dyab strolled across the Turkish carpet and stopped beside the other chair. The man was no more than six feet tall and slim as a whip, but his mere presence was enough to make the man holding the Uzi look at his feet.

Chooch jumped up, and the Uzi was immediately leveled at his chest.

"Forgive me." Chooch froze, his breath coming in ragged puffs.

The Dyab motioned for the man to lower the gun. "You are Charles Knowles?" His voice was a deep rumble from his chest.

Chooch nodded. It was indeed his birth name, but not even his mother called him Charles anymore.

"Sit." The Dyab waited until Chooch sat down before he took the chair opposite him. His ebony features were cast in shadow, while Chooch had the light in his eyes and blinked nervously. "You must be wondering why I brought you here."

Chooch couldn't trust his voice and nodded, then looked down at the small table between them. He had never seen anything quite like it—it was a mosaic made of different types of wood, outlined in fine brass wires.

The Dyab's rumble interrupted his thoughts. "We received an anonymous letter last night." He reached into his inside pocket, removed a folded piece of paper, and flicked it onto the table.

Feeling like he was being given a live spider, Chooch's hand visibly shook as he took the paper and opened it.

*We have something that you may find very valuable. Does the name* Red Star *mean anything to you? We have proof and another interested party. Submit your bid.*

At the bottom of the page was a phone number. Chooch carefully set the paper on the center of the table. He badly needed to go to the bathroom.

"What is da *Red Star*?" he asked cautiously.

"Don't you know?" The Dyab seemed amused, though he certainly wasn't smiling.

"I never heard of it." Chooch looked from the Dyab to the man holding the Uzi. "Do ya want me to deliver a reply?" he asked hesitantly.

The Dyab arched one eyebrow. "No. Right now I am more curious as to who thinks I would be interested in a Russian submarine carrying a nuclear warhead."

Chooch's eyes widened.

The Dyab lifted up the letter, folded it with his slender fingers, and tucked it back in his pocket. "You are here because I want to know exactly how much you told your cousin Ramon about us."

The man with the Uzi shifted his stance, turning slightly so the barrel was pointed at Chooch's chest.

Chooch felt the front of his jeans dampen. What could he say? Ramon had called him a few hours ago but they didn't talk about anything, really. Ramon asked Chooch to meet him on the docks in the morning. He was taking a dive tour out but wanted to speak with him first. Chooch thought about lying, but what if they had his cousin in the next room? What if Ramon had already told them that Chooch had told him he worked for the Dyab?

Chooch shook his head as if he was watching a tennis match as he spoke. "I didn' tell nuttin' important ... I was drinkin'. I was happy ... proud dat I was accepted by ya. Ramon was so drunk. He called me worthless. I told him I wasn't worthless, because I worked for da most powerful man in da islands now."

The Dyab nodded and sat forward in his seat. "You need to calm down and clear your mind. You told your cousin more than that because he knew where to send this message."

Chooch's whole body was shaking. "I ..." He closed his eyes and imagined the Uzi lifting up to point at his head as he admitted the truth. "He didn' believe me. I told him I was gonna deliver a package da next day ..." Chooch knew it didn't matter what he said. He'd already said far too much.

The Dyab folded his long fingers in his lap and twisted the large signet ring. "You are the cousin of Ramon and Andres Knowles."

Chooch didn't say anything; there was no need to. The Dyab raised his hand, and the man with the Uzi stepped back and knocked on the door by the bookcase. After a few seconds, an older, small man with thick glasses wheeled a cart covered with electronic equipment into the middle of the room and began to press an assortment of buttons and switches. Whatever the machine was, it whirred to life and a little cooling fan in the back blew a gentle breeze across Chooch's face.

As Chooch shifted uneasily in his chair, he was startled to see someone standing in the corner whom he hadn't noticed before. The man was tall, thin, and dressed in dark black slacks with a gray shirt. He had close-cropped gray hair and a weathered face. Chooch couldn't tell the man's nationality—it was hard to tell with white men—but the man's eyes drew Chooch's gaze. Gray and cold. Dead eyes in a live body, eyeing Chooch like a wolf contemplating whether the small lamb under his paws had enough meat on his bones to be worth the effort of killing him. How long had he been standin' dere?

The Dyab spoke to the dark, short man with the electronic equipment. "Is everything ready, Bashir?"

Bashir nodded.

"I am going to call this number now," the Dyab said coolly to Chooch. "You are to do nothing but listen. Do not move or make a sound. When the call is done, you will tell me if you recognize the voice. If you do, your transgression will be a thing of the past. You will have helped me, and I will be grateful. Do you understand?"

Chooch nodded rapidly.

Bashir dialed the number. The line rang and someone picked it up before it rang a second time.

Ramon answered. "Hello?"

*Da stupid fool.*

Bashir spoke. "We wish to discuss your offer. We will meet you at seven o'clock tomorrow evening at the end of the Port Lucaya pier. Wear a red shirt with a blue hat. Do you understand?"

"Seven tomorrow. Blue shirt, red hat, Port Lucaya," Ramon incorrectly repeated the instructions.

Bashir looked questioningly at the Dyab, who waved his hand dismissively.

"Until tomorrow," Bashir said and disconnected the cell phone from the machine.

The Dyab turned, his expression a neutral mask. Chooch knew he was waiting for an answer. Ramon was a fool if he thought Chooch would risk his own life to protect him. "Dat was Ramon."

"Are you certain?" the Dyab said.

"One hundred percen'."

The Dyab smiled. "Excellent. And you are positive that he mentioned nothing to you about a submarine?"

"Nuttin'. He's a loser."

The Dyab nodded softly, then smiled, and Chooch sat up in his chair. The Dyab was known to be ruthless—but also very generous with the people who helped him. Chooch knew he had done the right thing and the time had come for his reward.

His head was roughly yanked backward by the gray man who had been standing in the corner. Chooch hadn't heard him walk up behind him. The man's expression didn't change as he raised a long knife and plunged it into Chooch's chest, but his eyes sparkled like diamonds in dust as he twisted the blade.

Though the pain was intense, Chooch was now only a spectator in his own body. He couldn't draw a breath to scream. He wanted to run, but his legs just twitched in response.

The Dyab stood up, not even glancing at Chooch. He addressed the man who had stabbed Chooch. "Go and pick up the cousin in the morning, Alaire. Before you speak with him, bring him to me."

"It will be done."

The Dyab left the room as quietly as he had entered.

Now, instead of pain, Chooch felt nothing. It was like he was falling asleep. Everything was clouding up in a white haze.

Alaire stroked Chooch's cheek with the back of his hand.

As Chooch gurgled his last attempt at a breath, the ice man leaned so close, his mouth was only inches away. Alaire inhaled deeply and smiled. Chooch felt as if he gazed into the eyes of death himself. His bladder let go.

"Close your eyes, Charles," Alaire whispered. "And don't forget to say hello to my real father."

6

Jack woke up but kept still. Alice's head rested against his chest. Right now, her scent and warm breath on his neck, were stirring his senses into a dizzying whirlpool. They had fooled around a little last night, but Alice always tensed up before he started to make his move. He found himself in uncharted territory and unsure what to do. He didn't know if he should wait and let Alice move forward at her own pace or help her along somehow. His vote was for helping things along, but what he wanted didn't matter. It had to be right for her.

But maybe with the right encouragement…

Jack pulled her close and kissed her.

Alice passionately kissed him back. Her fingers ran through his hair and down his neck as she pulled him to her.

His desire revved up into sharp need, but the vivid memory of trying to disarm a mine came rushing back. The gruff Staff Sergeant teaching the explosive class normally had a voice that sounded like he chewed rocks for breakfast but when he was walking you through the process which could save your life, his voice took on a fatherly tone.

*Slow. Gentle.*

Jack forced himself to move tenderly. Carefully. His fingers caressed her face and glided down the side of her chest.

*Easy, soldier. If you feel resistance, wait.*

Alice's breath hitched.

*Double check.*

Alice moaned softly.

*Proceed.*

Jack's fingers traced down her side and stopped on her hip.

Alice relaxed in his arms.

Jack's smiled broadened. He rolled her over on her back and suddenly her whole body tensed. Her eyes closed as if she was bracing herself against an attack. She was clearly terrified and trying to fight it.

*Boom. Abort mission.*

Jack stroked the side of her face. "I'm not ready."

Alice's emerald eyes slowly opened. "You're not?"

"No, not till you are. I've waited this long; I'll wait forever for you." Silently he prayed that wouldn't be the case.

Alice pulled him close and laid her face against his chest. "It's not you. I trust you, it's just ... every time I close my eyes, I see *him.*"

Jack gently lifted her chin and smiled at her. "You could try not closing your eyes."

They sank into another kiss, and Jack was thinking they were getting that part right when Alice's alarm blared to life, and she sat up straight. "Oh, shoot! We're gonna be late."

"We're on our honeymoon. How can we be late for anything?" He tried to pull her back down under the soft cotton sheets, but Alice kissed him and slipped out of bed. "I booked a scuba diving tour. That's the one thing you said you really wanted to do."

There was something he'd like to do a lot more than scuba diving, but he wasn't going to pressure Alice or seem ungrateful about her booking a dive. He forced a crooked grin on his face. "Sounds great."

Alice glanced over her shoulder as she headed into the bathroom. "Who knows, maybe we'll find some lost treasure!"

***

Only a few exhilarating miles up the coast from their resort, Jack pulled in at the Port Lucaya pier and pointed out the dive shop.

Alice grinned. "I am so pumped for this."

"Promise you'll stay with me, okay? Ocean diving is a big step up from the pool."

She reached out and squeezed his hand. "I know you won't let anything happen to me."

He kissed her, moaning a little as he tasted her strawberry lip gloss. Even before the wedding he'd had a hard time reining in his passion, and it wasn't getting any easier, with Alice only inches away and her sun-warmed skin glowing. Opening one eye, he glanced around the deserted dock and debated about making a more definitive move.

"Don't tell me you're even considering making love to me for the first time in the front seat of a rental car," Alice scolded.

"Of course not!" Jack held up his hand in a Boy Scout salute. "I was thinking we could get in the *back* and —" He leaned forward and kissed her again.

Alice's green eyes narrowed, but she was laughing, too.

"Okay." Jack sat up. "You can't blame a guy for trying."

Alice fluttered her eyelashes flirtatiously, and his heart almost leapt out of his chest. "Cool your jets, big boy. Someone's coming."

A man about thirty-five years old, in shorts, a floral shirt, and sandals came strolling down the dock toward the car. "Morning!" He smiled widely, showing lots of white teeth and one gold one. "I'm Ramon. Ya must be da Strattons!"

"We are." Jack and Alice got out of the car and introduced themselves.

"Welcome to da Bahamas, where da water is warm, and da breeze is cool. Ya know how to dive?"

"Yes," Jack said, and Alice added, "This is my first open-water dive, but I've been certified." She held up a folder. "I have the docs here if you need them. The man I spoke to said I should bring them."

"Excellent. You spoke to my lil' bruddah, Andres. He's very careful 'bout all da details. I'll make a copy of dem at da office. I'll also need ya to fill out some paperwork. Liability. Just a formality."

Jack and Alice followed Ramon down to a little shed at the end of the dock. Alice was documenting their honeymoon with photographs so both she and Jack posed in front of both the dive boat and the shack.

Inside, the office looked more like an equipment room. Piles of various diving, fishing gear and miscellaneous stuff surrounded a desk with a computer and printer.

Ramon gave them forms to fill out and made a copy of their dive certificates, whistling and making small talk. After fitting them out with gear, Jack and Ramon carried the equipment down to a small boat equipped with a dive platform.

As Jack stepped over the side, he almost stabbed his leg on the tip of a spear gun. "Hold up," he cautioned Alice, picking up the gun and handing it to Ramon, who was in the middle of a story about the luckiest day of his life, when he caught five huge bonefish right near where he was taking them diving.

"Would you like to use da gun on your dive?" Ramon asked casually.

Not wanting to make a scene, Jack just said, "No thanks," and helped Alice into the boat, checking her seat before letting her sit down.

"Where we're heading, da water is especially clear after da hurricane." Ramon smiled and his eyes darted to the dock, scanning the pier.

"I've seen the pictures of the destruction," Alice said. "It's amazing how fast you're rebuilding."

Ramon nodded. "A hurricane destroys, but it also brings new life. And we are many islands. Not all were affected."

"We were hesitant about coming," Alice said. "We didn't know if it would make people feel worse that we were vacationing after a tragedy, but then I read that tourism would help the economy recover."

"True, true. We love tourists. Without ya, we'd go outta business." He turned and bowed to Alice. "I tank ya."

Jack thought Ramon was overdoing it a little, but Alice smiled, and he was grateful to Ramon for trying to make Alice feel at ease.

Ramon cast one more glance back at the pier, frowned, then started up the engine. "I believe that one's actions come back upon demselves." He winked at Alice. "Because of ya kindness, perhaps ya find someting on ya dive, maybe pirate treasure."

Alice nodded excitedly. "I agree with you. You reap what you sow."

Jack did his best not to make a face. The odds of their stumbling on pirate treasure were about the same as getting hit by lightning, if not worse. But Alice was so excited, and she looked so incredible in her purple one-piece bathing suit, the last thing he was going to do was steal her lollipop and tell her the odds.

Ramon continued to smile, but Jack noticed the warmth had left his eyes. They were dark now, almost black. "Sometimes fortune favors da brave!" He walked over and cast off the line from the dock. "As dey say in da navy, anchors aweigh!"

Ramon took a swig of his beer as he leaned against the side of the rocking boat. He stared into the water at the silhouettes of the two American tourists as they explored the coral reef far below. The newlyweds couldn't seem to keep apart. Like blue tangs, they would slowly drift apart as they zigzagged across the ocean floor only to dart back to each other, embracing then slowly circling each other before continuing on.

"Fools." Ramon spit into the sea, the dark spittle dissolving almost instantly.

An unwanted image of his ex-wife flickered in his mind, but he brushed it away as he wiped the sweat from his face with his hand. Love was fleeting. Money is what mattered. And now he was about to come into more of it than he ever dreamed of.

He pulled out his phone, scowled and stuffed it back into his pocket. Of course, he had no signal out here, but the fact that Chooch had failed to meet him at the dock still bothered him.

His cousin was brainless, but Ramon had said he wanted to talk to him about making easy cash and if money was involved, Chooch was as guaranteed to show as gulls on chum.

But he didn't show up this morning and he wasn't answering his phone.

The sound of an approaching boat made him peer over his shoulder. He cupped his hand to his brow and stared at the small boat as it moved closer. It was a pleasure boat. Smaller than his with a broad canopy that cloaked the driver in shadow.

*Probably some rich tourist out fishing for marlin.*

Sweat rolled down Ramon's back. He turned back to check on the Strattons. It was nearing the end of their dive and he hoped they were paying attention. The last thing he wanted to do was put on his gear and go after them. He threw his beer toward their silhouettes but undershot the throw. It drifted beneath the waves and quickly sank.

The key dangling from the elastic around his wrist glistened in the sun. He pulled the bright elastic band off and kissed the cold, metal key. It was the key to his future. But the wait was killing him. Both the Dyab and the Russians agreed to meet. He wouldn't bring the safe with him. It was why he hid it. He didn't even tell Andres where.

*Andres.*

He promised his brother half. But why? Ramon was taking all the risk. It was his plan, too. So what if Andres found the sub. He wouldn't have even been there if it wasn't for Ramon. Besides, Ramon would have found the sub if Andres hadn't. This was his golden ticket. He should keep it all for himself.

It was time to leave the Bahamas anyway. He could always go to Vegas. Or LA. He'd have the money to live anywhere now.

Something slammed into his back and his hip bashed against the side of the boat. He grabbed the rail to avoid falling over and the key tumbled from his hand and into the sea. He reached for it but too late. The brass flashed briefly before it disappeared from sight.

The slight pain in his back erupted. What initially felt like a hard punch now burned like fire. It was difficult to breathe. His knees wobbled and he slipped to the deck, landing on all fours.

There was a loud bump and the boat rocked.

Ramon's arms shook and he collapsed face first to the deck.

Footsteps slapped against the wet deck behind him.

The fisherman. Maybe he saw Ramon fall? Maybe he knew what happened?

Ramon opened his mouth to speak but no sound came out. Instead, his mouth filled with something that tasted like metal. He gagged as darkness clouded his eyes then everything went black.

Footsteps drew nearer and stopped. Someone grabbed his head and lifted it up. He tried to open his eyes, but his lids felt as if they had been sealed shut.

A person spoke but their words sounded far off. There was something familiar about the voice, but he couldn't place it. It was soft. Was it a woman?

They spoke again. Like a song played from a distance, he heard only the tone.

Something sharp sunk into the burning area of his back and then twisted. The pain was unlike anything he had ever felt. His mouth sprang open to scream, but only an odd gurgling escaped his parted lips.

It hurt so—

8

Although Jack knew that the weight of the sparkling turquoise waters swirling all around would crush him if he were on land, he felt weightless and the happiest he'd ever been, swimming within arm's reach of his beautiful bride. Her mouth was hidden behind a regulator, but he could tell Alice was smiling because bubbles seeped out around her mouthpiece as a school of yellow fish with bright neon blue stripes swam past.

They'd been cavorting among the corals and sponges and other undersea wonders for about twenty-five minutes before a large shadow passed over their heads, and another boat pulled toward Ramon's. Jack glanced at his diving watch. Alice swam on, unconcerned, but Jack kept looking upward and watched as something fell into the water from Ramon's boat, briefly flashing a reflection of the sun before spiraling down to the sandy bottom.

Jack scowled. All boats have to stay at least one hundred yards from a diver-down buoy. It was probably another diving group getting ready to start, but a boat propeller could kill you. Ramon should have warned them off.

Alice swam back to him, and he pointed at the second boat above them and patted the top of his head. She gave him a thumbs-up, blew him an underwater kiss, then grabbed a rock outcropping and shot forward like a torpedo to go explore the other side of the reef. Jack had to kick hard to catch up with her. What was the thing that had fallen from the boat? He wanted to look for it, but Alice was as fast in the water as a hummingbird in the air. Twisting her lithe body around, she'd search a sandy area for a moment before zipping over to another.

She was longer than usual in one spot, and he was able to catch up to her. She looked like a mermaid, beckoning him to her, with her hair drifting around her shoulders. In three powerful strokes, Jack reached her and wrapped his arms around her waist. Desire flamed once again as he caressed her body. The shadow over them shifted and the water became brighter. They both looked up and saw the second boat leaving. Jack checked his watch and made the agreed-upon sign that they should start back up soon.

Alice pointed to her underwater camera, a present from Jack's parents, and motioned him to move back. She swam up and over him taking photos of Jack's goofy poses, but suddenly she lowered the camera and frantically pointed beneath him, her eyes wide behind her mask.

Jack spun around, thinking a shark or barracuda was about to take a bite out of him, but the water was clear all around and there was nothing there. Alice shot past him and grabbed something off the ocean floor. She momentarily disappeared in a cloud of sand. When it settled, she was holding something in one hand. Jack swam toward her. Alice excitedly pointed at the object, which looked to Jack like a broken pot. He shrugged. Alice pantomimed drawing a sword and holding it high.

Bubbles trailed from Jack's mouthpiece. He couldn't help but chuckle—the broken clay pot looked like something you'd find in someone's backyard, but why diminish Alice's excitement at her "*pirate* treasure"? He gave her a big thumbs-up and glanced at his watch. Time to go. He tapped his wrist and she nodded.

Probably the best part of the dive for him was holding onto her as they swam to the surface. She certainly didn't need his help, but he loved feeling her muscles move beneath his hands.

The moment their heads broke the surface, Jack took his regulator out and Alice did the same. "It's pirate treasure!" She awkwardly held up the pot as she treaded water.

Jack kissed her. "Sure, it is."

"It is!"

Another salty kiss cut her off. "I'm agreeing with you."

"You're agreeing with me just so you can kiss me."

"Exactly." Jack pulled her close and held her for a moment before she wiggled free. "Let's see. I'll ask Ramon."

*I'm sure he'll be a completely impartial judge,* Jack thought as he swam over to the boat. He grabbed onto the ladder, pulled himself halfway up, and froze. Their charming tour guide lay slumped face first on the deck, a knife protruding from his back.

"Stay in the water!" Jack called out. He looked around and saw a sailboat and two pleasure fishing boats too far away to make out any details.

"Take a picture of those boats," Jack told Alice.

"What? Why?" Alice lifted the camera to her face but quickly lowered it. "It's an underwater camera. There's no zoom. What's going on?"

Jack climbed over the railing and into the boat. "Ramon's been stabbed."

Alice swam over and Jack helped her up onto the diving platform. "Stay back," Jack cautioned. He didn't see any footprints, but he wanted to preserve the crime scene as much as possible for the authorities. He hurried over to Ramon. The body was still warm but there was no pulse. The huge pool of blood on the deck told him the man was dead.

Jack fired up the engine and turned on the radio. The screen flashed to life, but Jack couldn't see the microphone. He glanced around and noticed it lying beneath the chair. He lifted it up and the springy cable bounced around in the air, bare wires at the end shining.

"I take it we can't call for help," Alice called from the stern.

"Do me a favor," Jack said, "take some pictures of the crime scene before we get moving."

Alice's face had a greenish tinge to it, and Jack worried that he'd asked too much of her. Being a former cop, he was used to crime scenes. Alice wasn't.

"On second thought, I can do it, babe." He held out his hand. "Toss me your camera."

Alice shook her head. "No, I got it." She raised the camera and started snapping away from different angles and levels.

Besides the radio, everything else on the dashboard seemed to be working. He put a hand on the throttle and turned back to Alice. "Those will be fine. Get in." He glanced at the blood mixing with the water on the deck. "Why don't you sit down in the back and keep your feet up?"

She nodded and sat down, lifting her feet up on the seat as she eyed the pool of blood spreading her way. She suddenly sat up straighter and scanned the horizon. He could see the fear in her as she tensed. "Can you get us back to port?"

"Of course I can." Jack squared his shoulders. "Why do you think Chandler used to call me Captain Jack?"

The Dyab strolled along the rooftop deck of his massive villa letting the warm breeze of the sea wrap around him. Everywhere he gazed was his. If he didn't already possess it, he could simply take it—such was the power of the Dyab.

The bitter taste rose in his mouth. The Devil was never a title he'd sought out in his youth. His grandmother used to tell him and his brother stories of the Dyab. Tales going back to the age of lawlessness. The era of pirates.

"Is the Dyab eternal?" his brother had asked.

His grandmother nodded. "In some ways, child, he is. Dyab is a title that has lasted for hundreds of years."

"Like a king?"

"No." She trembled and so did they. "Kings pass on their titles to their sons. The title of Dyab must be taken. The new Dyab must be bathed in blood."

The Dyab stared at his hands. So, it was for him. He had ripped the still-beating heart from the last Dyab's chest, and that act had secured his power. Now he reigned over all the Bahamas. He reached out and laid his hands upon the imported Italian marble railing. He'd had the whole Roman villa dismantled and moved here. In some ways, the grand home, a fortress—a palace really, was as much of a prison for him as the people locked far below in its cellar. He stared at the blue waters shimmering in the distance and tried to recall the last time he had plunged beneath the surface. *Years? Decades? Probably.*

The last time he recalled swimming was with Samuel. That was the also the last time his brother had seen the sea. Now he was in the basement with the others. Closing his eyes, the Dyab tried to embrace the darkness, but bathed in the splendor of the Bahamian sunshine, his world was not truly black—not like Samuel's.

His eyes flashed open, and he glared at the sun and the sea. He'd curse both if he could. He had many times before, but the dawn still rose, and the tide still flowed. But the sea would yield its secret to him. There were many people who would pay an extraordinary amount for the location of nuclear warheads. *Who cares what they do with them?*

*Let the world burn.*

"Sir?" Bashir called from the penthouse doorway. "A moment?"

The Dyab nodded but did not turn around. "Speak."

"I've been monitoring the police radio. It may be an ill report, sir."

The Dyab's eyes narrowed, and he turned around.

Bashir stopped halfway across the deck. He swallowed, his large Adam's apple bobbing up and down adding to his resemblance to a turkey—long necked and fat bodied. "The police and an ambulance have been summoned to the docks. The call was about an emergency on Ramon Knowles' boat."

The Dyab waited impatiently for Bashir to continue but the little man stood there nervously wiping his hands together.

"What was the nature of the emergency?" The Dyab strode forward.

Bashir took a step back. "Ramon has been stabbed."

The Dyab felt the familiar burn of hatred deep within his breast. The Frenchman had a thirst for violence, but he'd given Alaire specific orders not to harm Ramon until he spoke with him personally. If he had disobeyed him, there'd be the Devil to pay. "Where is Alaire?"

"He's headed to the docks now. He was on his way to pick up Ramon as you requested."

The Dyab turned back and glared at the sea. It shimmered in the sunlight as if it were taunting him. Its secrets still safe beneath the waves. "Find out what happened and if Ramon is still alive. Do you know who called the police?"

"An American. Jack Stratton."

"Tell Alaire to get there now. And find out everything you can about this American."

# 10

The dive boat bumped the old wooden dock and the smell of diesel hung in the tropical air. A crowd was already starting to form. Jack had called out to a few boaters to radio ahead to the police when they entered the harbor, and word must have spread like wildfire.

Alice bounded over the side, rope in hand, and searched for a cleat to tie off to. As she forced the rough rope into figure-eights, the group of gawkers shuffled and bumped their way down the pier like seagulls chasing down a French fry.

A tall man in a Hawaiian shirt dashed toward the approaching throng and swung the chain-link gate closed, blocking the crowd at the end of the dock. As the group protested at being held back, he hurried over to Jack and Alice. "I heard the call on my radio and gave the police a bell. They're on their way," he said in the prevailing British-accented island lingo. "Is that Ramon?" He gasped and covered his mouth with his hand like he was trying to cut off a scream before it could start.

Jack had to admit, the bloody scene looked like something out of a horror movie. The saltwater spray from the ride had diluted the blood and spread it everywhere, so the inside of the boat was now bathed in blood.

The man swallowed and stepped back nervously. "What happened?" His eyes shifted back and forth between Jack and Alice.

"I don't know," Jack admitted. "We were diving and when we came up, we found him like this, dead on the deck. Did you know him?"

"Not well." The man shook his head. "We were competitors." He held up his hand, palm out. "It's really Andres's operation—Ramon's brother. We got on all right, we just didn't fraternize." He pointed at his boat, *Permanent Holiday*. "I operate a dive tour too. Name's Oliver Rolle."

"Hey! Open this gate." Two policemen had pushed through the crowd and stood at the locked chain-link gate like prisoners wanting out.

Jack and Oliver walked over and when they opened the gate, the crowd surged forward.

"Is it Andres? Let us through! Is it Ramon?" random people called out one after another.

"Get back!" the older of the two policemen bellowed, shoving against the crowd.

It took all four men to keep the crowd at bay and close the gate. The older policeman walked down to the boat and stopped. The younger man took one look in the boat, and ran over to the opposite side of the dock and threw up.

While the older policeman reached for his radio and called it in, Oliver said his goodbyes and headed for his boat. Jack waited on the dock with Alice, who was very pale. He wrapped a protective arm around her, gave her a reassuring squeeze and tried to shift her attention away from the boat, pointing out sights along the harbor in the distance.

There was more commotion at the gate as additional policemen arrived. Cutting through the crowd was a group of five officers who had difficulty getting the people to move out of the way on the cramped dock. Once they reached the chain-link fence, Jack saw that there were six officers in total. The one in the middle of the group was very short.

The five larger officers wore the uniform of the island police: crisp white shirts and blue pants with a red stripe. The short man was dressed all in tan, indicating his higher rank. The younger police officer with the squeamish stomach opened the gate for the rest to get through. The policemen gathered at the side of the boat and spoke among themselves for a moment. The older officer pointed at Jack.

The short man in charge approached. "I am Inspector Renard of the Royal Bahamas Police Force. Perhaps it would be best if we spoke over here." Renard placed a gentle hand on Alice's elbow and led them over to the shed for privacy. "You found the body?"

Jack nodded. "I'm Jack Stratton. This is Alice Cam— Stratton. We just got married."

Renard nodded but didn't smile. "Congratulations."

Jack continued. "Ramon had taken us out for a dive. When my wife and I returned to the boat, we found Ramon slumped on the deck, dead."

"I see. How many other divers were on this charter?"

"None. It was just me and my wife. But another boat approached Ramon's during the dive."

Renard was taking notes in a flip-top notepad. "What did this other boat look like?"

"I just saw its shadow," Jack explained. "We were underwater, diving. I assumed it was another dive group ready to start or someone Ramon knew. The boats came together for only a few minutes and then the second boat left. I didn't think anything of it until we returned to the surface and found Ramon. We saw three boats when we surfaced." Jack pointed at Alice's camera. "Alice took pictures, but they were too far away for any type of detail. I also had her photograph the crime scene."

Renard appeared surprised. "That was very insightful of you."

Jack inhaled. Explaining that he was a *former* police officer usually triggered speculation about why he was no longer on the force. And, technically, he was still deputized by Sheriff Morrison ... "I'm a detective with the Emerson County Sheriff's Department."

"Please accept my apologies, Detective Stratton. Had I known, I would have addressed you by your professional rank."

*This guy is really old-school.*

"Think nothing of it," Jack said—the most courtly reply he could think of. "I didn't expect to get involved in a case on my honeymoon."

Alice opened the compartment on her camera that held the memory card to remove it, but Renard stopped her, saying, "We would prefer to bring the entire camera with us." When he saw the hesitation on Alice's face, he added, "I will personally ensure its safety."

Alice slipped the camera strap off her shoulder but hesitated. "It's a wedding present from Jack's parents."

"It will be fine." Renard snapped his fingers, and the older policeman came over. He whispered something to him and handed over Alice's camera. While they were talking, Oliver sauntered over with two bottles of water. "Excuse me." He nodded politely and held out one bottle to Alice and one to Jack. "I thought she could use some water."

"And you are?" Renard asked rather gruffly.

"Oliver Rolle. That's my boat over there. I'm—"

"Did you see anything?"

"No."

Renard beckoned the young police officer over. "Send him back to the other side of the gate and secure this scene."

The young officer blanched. "Yes, sir." He saluted and grabbed Oliver by the arm.

"Thank you!" Alice called after him as the police officer led him away.

Oliver gave her a wink over his shoulder. "My pleasure."

Jack stepped closer to Alice and wrapped his arm around her shoulders.

Renard's lips pursed together. "How did you know Ramon?"

"I met him this morning."

"And you, Mrs. Stratton? Did you know Ramon or his brother, Andres?"

"No. We booked the dive over the internet."

The crowd at the gate suddenly got very loud, heralding the arrival of more emergency responders. Renard frowned and tucked his notebook in his shirt pocket. "I'd like to continue gathering information in a less chaotic environment. Would you both agree to continue this conversation at the station?"

Jack nodded.

"Excellent." Renard snapped his fingers again and the team of officers surrounded him. He spoke with them for a moment before turning back to Jack. "I need to finish up here, but I will follow after you in a jiff."

The group of officers broke into two groups. Several stayed with Renard and five others surrounded Jack and Alice. The officer with the most stars on his shoulder applet held out his arm toward the gate. "Please follow us." He smiled, but Jack knew it wasn't a request.

Jack took Alice by the hand. "Stay beside me." She didn't look frightened, though. If anything, when she stepped next to Jack, it reminded him of his military days with a fellow soldier at his side.

The police marched forward and the crowd at the gate started yelling questions. With all the pushing and shoving that ensued on the narrow dock, Jack was surprised no one ended up in the water. They jostled their way through, only to see another crowd waiting for them on the pier.

The police hustled Jack and Alice up the ramp leading from the dock to the pier. When Jack reached the top, he noticed a man turn and jog away from the crowd. "Do you see that guy?" Jack asked the lead policeman, but he was too busy shouting orders to hear Jack. "Hey!" Jack grabbed the cop's arm and pointed in the direction of the fleeing man.

"What?" The policeman glared at Jack's hand on his arm.

"That's the only guy running away. Why?"

The policeman called another officer over, but the crowd pressing in around the car made it impossible for Jack to hear what they said. When they finished, the less senior police officer ran after the fleeing man.

Alice climbed in the cruiser but wouldn't let go of Jack's hand. "Get in, Jack!"

Jack stared in the direction the man had fled and couldn't see him anymore—only the policeman jogging down the street after him. Jack got into the police car and tried not to scowl. From the way Alice was stroking the back of his hand, he was doing a miserable job of masking his frustration.

When the lead officer got in and locked the back doors, the hairs on the back of Jack's neck started to rise.

*Are we witnesses ... or suspects?*

# 11

ndres's heart thundered in his chest as he raced down the crowded street with the policeman not far behind. The policeman's whistle pierced the air. The pedestrians stopped and hurriedly got out of the way as Andres dashed along the sidewalk.

The years of swimming had toned his muscles and with his long legs he started to gain distance from the policeman who was now shouting at him to stop.

Maybe he should? He'd done nothing wrong. But his legs had a mind of their own. He ran, blinded by grief and a fear he'd never known. He always believed the stories of the Dyab were old wives' tales but now he sprinted as if the Devil himself was behind him.

The policeman's shouts faded in the distance.

Andres cut right down a side street and darted toward some dumpsters along the wall. There was a chained gate next to the dumpsters, but he managed to squeeze through. He hid in the alley behind a trash can as the policeman ran past. Cowering amongst the garbage and stench of urine, Andres wanted to scream in terror.

How had it come to this? Ramon was dead. Tears ran down his face. In spite of all the stupid things Ramon had done, they were brothers. He pictured the boy he'd gone fishing with; his huge smile when they caught a shark or when they fixed up the old dinghy and first headed out to the deep sea.

Now Ramon was gone, and Andres didn't know who had killed him. He doubted it was the Americans, but it might have been the Dyab or those phony scientists. Representatives of each camp had been on the dock when the American brought the boat in, covered in Ramon's blood. They were watching the office. He'd seen Gregory, Chooch's co-worker, and the Greeks or Russians or whatever they were—all huge, incredibly mean-looking, and of course white—were easy to pick out.

*Did Ramon tell whoever killed him da location of da sub? Or did Ramon refuse?* Andres's heart sped up. *Is that why they killed him?* He pictured his brother's defiant stance. His stubborn streak. He used to say that if he ever met the Devil, he'd spit in his face. Maybe he did, and maybe the Devil spat back his poison.

Whoever it was, if they didn't know where the sub was, they would come looking for the person who did. Him. That's why they were at the office now.

Andres's breath caught in his throat, and it felt like he was deep diving and his oxygen failed. He tried to breathe but nothing happened. He gulped in the foul air of the alley. Coughing, he stood there in the muck, hot tears streaming down his face.

What had he done? He'd only caught a glimpse, but the memory of Ramon sprawled on the bottom of the bloody boat brought more tears to his eyes. Ramon had always protected Andres, looked out for him in his own misguided way.

Andres clamped his eyes shut. He had to call Irene. He reached for his phone and swore. It was still in the office. So was his wallet. He'd only gone out for a few minutes for a quick smoke, but by the time he got back, the dock had been surrounded.

Andres started down the alley and stopped. He couldn't go home. They could be watching his house too. *Stupid! Stupid!*

He interlaced his fingers and put his hands behind his head. The police! His eyes lit up until he remembered Sergeant Mateo. Everyone on the docks knew to give him a little money. Even if you were doing nothing wrong, you'd give him some cash just so you wouldn't find your tourists' cars ticketed or equipment missing or damaged. Andres had not been able to give Mateo his extra share lately and had been avoiding him. And then there were the rumors that Mateo worked for the Dyab.

He couldn't go home or to the police. No money. No phone. Nowhere to go. He wouldn't go to any of his friends and endanger their lives, too.

*Uncle Victor!*

The old man was like a pirate. He certainly acted like one. He'd been around, too. He'd even been in jail. He'd know what to do.

Andres dug into his pockets. How could he make a phone call? He tried to calm down. *Tink. What would Ramon do?*

*No, you idiot! Ramon's tinking got him killed and me in dis mess.*

What would Irene do?

He closed his eyes. He pictured his pregnant wife sitting on the couch, cradling her growing belly with tears rolling down her cheeks. She'd be rocking back and forth, close her eyes and… Irene would pray.

Andres closed his eyes too but right now the words wouldn't come. He was guilty. Ramon's death was on his hands. He could have talked Ramon out of it—done something—but now it was too late. If Irene was here, he'd beg her to pray for him. Beg her to go ...

*To da church!* They would help him. They would at least let him use a phone. They could get a message to warn Irene!

Andres started walking. It wasn't far. He'd stick to the side streets and head straight there. He'd call Irene and then he'd call Uncle Victor. He'd know what to do. But within a block, once again his hope had chilled as if a cloud had passed over the sun.

What could his uncle do? Andres was stuck on Grand Bahama without a boat; his uncle was on the Abacos, if he was even still alive. Andres slowed to a stop and stared out at the ocean.

He was truly trapped between the Devil and the deep blue sea.

# 12

laire smiled as the police cruisers pulled away from the pier. Tourists. Even better, *Americans*. He hated Americans. He took out his cell phone and moved away from the crowd. The stupid locals were all aflutter like vultures vying over a dead squirrel on a busy road. Each time a policeman walked forward they scuttled away, but as soon as the policeman turned his back, they moved in again.

Alaire stared down at the screen. The Dyab was not someone to take lightly. In fact, he was the coldest man Alaire had met in all his travels. It was a quality he admired, and it was why he'd agreed to work for the Dyab, but it was a double-edged sword, nonetheless.

The Dyab met even perceived weakness or failure with certain death. The Dyab's zero tolerance kept Alaire quite busy. He enjoyed the work and the lucrative pay, but his boss's impulsive tendency to order a person's swift end not only instilled fear in the black market workers but made Alaire himself cautious. It was abundantly clear that the only life the Dyab valued was his own.

Even so, being timid was not in Alaire's nature. He was primal, instinctive. He dialed the phone. Someone picked up the other end.

"There's been a complication," Alaire said. "Someone killed Ramon before I could reach him."

"Explain." The Dyab's unmistakable growl.

Alaire's eyes widened with excitement. He had expected Bashir to speak. The Dyab never spoke personally on the phone. He must be upset. The line was considered secure but still, Alaire hesitated to say Ramon's name. New technology was being developed every day that enabled the powers that be to listen to communications. But, on a small island, news travels fast. Word of Ramon's murder was certainly already circling the island like a hurricane.

"His boat arrived at the dock with Ramon face down on the deck with a knife in his back. There were two Americans aboard. The police brought them down to the station for questioning."

There was a long period of silence.

Alaire waited. The Dyab was just being dramatic, he reasoned. A bead of sweat rolled down the side of his face. He lifted it off and stared at the water droplet on the end of his finger like it was an alien substance. He never sweated.

But as the silence stretched on, he found himself glancing over his shoulder.

"Who took them in?" The voice was now Bashir's, but Alaire knew that the Dyab was feeding his puppet what to say.

"Renard."

"Are they suspects?"

"From the way they were handled, yes. The locals seem to think they were responsible too."

"Ramon has a brother. Bring Andres to me—*unharmed.*" Bashir read off an address.

"Understood."

The call disconnected. The lack of closure had the intended consequence on Alaire—it left him wondering what the Dyab was going to say if he were to fail. A thousand tortuous ways to die flipped through his mind. If it were someone else's death he was contemplating, he would have smiled, but the last way he wanted to die was slowly.

But that kind of death wasn't his destiny. He was promised more.

Still, it was a very dangerous game he was playing. But wasn't that what life was all about? It was chess with living pieces—each one having their own thoughts, desires, motives and moves. That's what made playing so interesting. That and the high stakes being life and death.

Alaire turned and walked back toward the dock and the two men keeping their eye on the tiny dive shack. The office had been cordoned off by the police, but it would be no difficulty to break in later, if they needed to.

"Gregory, you and Miles stay here and stand watch. Anyone comes by, you call me. Understand?"

Gregory nodded rapidly.

As Alaire walked away, he overheard Miles whisper to Gregory, "Where's he going?"

"Shut up," Gregory whispered back.

They feared him. As they should. Alaire spoke only as much as necessity dictated to those beneath him, but he would have gladly answered that question. He was heading out to engage in one of his favorite pastimes—hunting human prey.

# 13

The Central Police Station was like nothing Jack had ever seen in the States, more like a large house with a veranda, painted a minty green. As if there weren't enough palm trees outside, potted palms and houseplants cluttered the main reception room and many of the desks. But the small interrogation room was straight out of an '80s TV police drama: plain green walls, cement floor, large two-way glass mirror, and a metal table with two metal chairs on either side. Jack sat waiting in one of the uncomfortable chairs. He suspected that Inspector Renard was in the observation room, discussing with his superiors the circumstances of two American tourists finding Ramon dead.

Alice was in the adjacent room. It was standard procedure to separate witnesses for interviewing, but Alice hadn't been pleased about it. And neither was Jack. This was their honeymoon, after all. But a man had lost his life and finding out who took it was far more important to Jack than working on his tan. He sat at the table waiting as patiently as he could while the minutes stretched out to close to an hour before the door finally opened.

"My apologies for the delay, Detective Stratton," Renard said as he stepped through the doorway. "As you witnessed, the scene at the dock was quite chaotic."

The inspector was an extremely short man and somewhat stout. Not so much thick in the middle as through his back and shoulders. Still, with his glasses and small mustache and immaculately pressed uniform, Jack would have pegged him for an accountant or a pencil pusher rather than a detective. He sat down opposite Jack and pointed to the half-full bottle of water in front of Jack. "Would you like something else to drink?"

"No, thank you. But can you please have someone check on my wife and make sure she's okay?" Jack asked.

"I looked in on her personally before coming in. She's fine. I'd like to ask how you chose the *Dive Into Paradise* tour."

"My wife picked it. She knew I loved scuba diving, so she compared a dozen different dive tours before settling on that one."

"A dozen?"

"She's very thorough in fact-finding via the computer."

"So, you had never been to the business before?"

"No."

"But you had spoken to Ramon?"

"No. I never spoke to anyone. My wife booked it, but not with Ramon, with his brother, Andres." Puzzled, Jack raised an eyebrow. "You're not going to write any of this down?"

Renard grinned and tapped his temple with his finger. Jack kept a poker face. Unless this guy was Sherlock Holmes, he would need to record the facts. Jack didn't need to look around the room to know there were no cameras inside. He crossed his arms and forced himself not to glance at the two-way glass. He was relatively certain now there was a camera in there and it was recording.

"When did she speak with Andres?"

"A few weeks ago. He described what the tour would entail, and the cost, and she booked a forty-five-minute dive and the gear to do it. And the boat," Jack added.

"And the cost?"

"I don't know. Alice didn't tell me. It was kind of a honeymoon surprise."

Renard's lips pressed together and he hmphed but didn't press him. "So, you only met Ramon today?"

"Yes. We showed up at the dock a little before nine, met Ramon, grabbed the gear, and got in the boat. He took us out to the reef."

Renard held up his hand interrupting Jack. "Who else was at the *Dive Into Paradise?*"

"No one. Just Ramon."

Renard stiffened. "Did you go into the office?"

Jack's gut tightened. For some reason Renard had pinged on Jack's answer to who else was there. It didn't show on his face, but the inspector was no longer relaxed. He was trying to appear so, but with his feet planted on the floor, Renard was in the midst of a fight-or-flight response. And since this was his house, Jack assumed it would be the former.

"We went in the main building to sign forms and grab equipment."

"And you didn't see anyone else inside?"

"No."

"And just you, your wife, and Ramon got into the boat and left the harbor?"

"That's correct."

Renard leaned forward. "Did anything happen on the way out to the reef?"

"Are you asking if anything happened between Ramon and *me*?"

"No, Detective." Renard smiled politely. "I'm wondering if you noticed anything out of the ordinary. Another boat? Did Ramon get a phone call? Anything."

Jack shrugged. "Nothing. The ride out to the dive spot was beautiful."

"Since you brought it up, *did* anything happen between you and Ramon?"

Now it was Jack's turn to stiffen. Of course, any policeman would have to have some suspicion about whoever found the body, but still, Jack didn't care for being a suspect, even for a second. "No. Ramon was very friendly."

Renard nodded understandingly. "To you and your wife?"

Jack bristled at the implication and realized it showed on his face by the way Renard's eyes widened slightly. "Ramon was being a pleasant tour guide. That's all."

"That's what I am trying to determine, Detective." Renard smoothed his mustache. "So, Ramon drove the two of you out to the dive location. What happened next?"

"Alice and I went into the water. We were down for about thirty minutes when I saw a boat approach Ramon's."

"So, you first saw this boat when you were under the water?"

"Yes. I could only see a silhouette."

"And you didn't surface at that time? You didn't think it was odd that another boat just happened to come out to Ramon's?"

"Not at all. The harbor was crowded, I figured Ramon must know a lot of the other boat owners. I thought it was someone saying hi or maybe it was another dive about to start. It was a little surprising that he came so close."

"And why was that?"

"Vessels must maintain a distance of at least one hundred yards from a diver-down buoy. Boat propeller injuries are a nasty business."

"It's been years since I last went diving. But you are correct, Detective." Renard took a cloth handkerchief out of his pocket. "How long did this second boat visit with Ramon?"

"They stayed for less than five minutes and left."

Renard removed his glasses and began cleaning the lenses. "And then?"

"Alice found this old pot—"

Renard sat up straighter. "What kind of pot? An antiquity?"

"No." Jack chuckled. "It looked like something from a backyard potting shed, actually."

"Where is this pot now?"

Jack shrugged. "No clue. I think she dropped it when we surfaced."

Renard turned to look at the two-way mirror and then stared at Jack. "You are aware that it is a serious offense not to turn over antiquities to the Bahamian authorities?"

"I am." Jack put his left hand down on the table and met Renard's gaze. "But it wasn't an antiquity, it was a broken common garden pot. And Alice didn't take it. She dropped it when I found our dead tour guide."

"So you say."

"So I say?" Jack repeated, his voice rising. "That's what happened. I came out of the water, climbed up the ladder, and Ramon was lying on the deck with a knife sticking out of his back. Keeping track of a stupid pot wasn't a high priority at the moment."

"And instead of you radioing for help, you took pictures of the body. Were you planning on selling them, Jack?"

"What?" Jack sat bolt upright. "We're on a first-name basis now? No more Detective Stratton?"

Renard calmly placed his glasses back on. "Why would you take pictures of the body?"

"To help you catch the bad guy. Where I come from, the police help each other."

"That's not my impression of American policing. The local police *always* reject outside assistance."

"On *TV.*" Jack scoffed. "In real life, we work together. That's why I took the pictures of the scene. Evidence would be lost by the shifting sea water in the boat before you had a chance to photograph it yourself and the boats would be *long* gone by the time you got out to the area. I figured you would appreciate the help."

"None of the pictures of the boats provide enough detail to identify them."

"I told you that. Alice's camera had no zoom feature."

"Yet you didn't chase them down?"

Jack shook his head. "What was I going to do? Chase three boats heading in three separate directions? One of which could have a killer and I had no weapon, my wife onboard, and a dead body onboard?"

"Why didn't you just use the radio?"

"It was broken. The mike was ripped right off the cord."

"I find that odd. Are you aware that another captain said he spoke with Ramon this morning before you headed out? The other man was heading out to sea and Ramon called him over the radio."

Jack shrugged. "This morning, Ramon was alive and able to speak, until someone killed him. Chances are the killer ripped the cord out so no one could radio it in, giving him more time to get away. That's what it looked like to me. When I picked up the mic to call for help, the connecting wires just dangled and the ends were bare. And I got the attention of other boats on the way in and yelled for them to call ahead. I did the best anyone could have."

"And you insist that neither you nor your wife spoke with Ramon's brother Andres this morning?"

"Neither of us did. He wasn't at the dock."

"Hmmm." Renard leaned back in his chair and studied Jack for a moment. "Andres's truck is still parked at the pier. His wife said he went to work this morning. She's very worried about her husband. She can't reach him by phone and she's expecting their first child. Could you alleviate her fears and tell me where Andres is?"

"I can't because I don't know. I've never seen or spoken with Andres."

Renard frowned and smoothed his mustache as if in thought.

Jack fought back the frustration growing inside him. The inspector was playing the sympathy angle for Andres's pregnant wife hard but there was nothing Jack could do for the woman. He had no idea where her husband was.

Jack spoke before thinking it through. "You don't find it odd that Ramon ends up dead and his brother goes missing too?"

"Yes I do, Detective Stratton. That is why we are here. And there is another thing I am curious about. This pot your wife found. Are you certain that she didn't take it with her?"

"*Positive.*" Jack crossed his arms.

"How can you be so certain?" Renard asked, leaning in a little.

Jack exhaled. "We're getting a little heated here and I don't want this to sound insulting, but think about it. The police came the minute we pulled up to the dock. We were transported by them straight here. And we were frisked upon entry to the station. Where could we have put it?"

"Fair enough." Renard nodded. "Although she could have dropped it over the side so you could go back and get it later. Or you could have given it to that other boat. Is that why you fought with Ramon? Or did he say something to your wife?"

"You are way off base, Inspector. I didn't fight with Ramon, and I certainly didn't kill him."

"Then why are you lying to me, Detective?"

Jack froze. "What are you talking about?"

"We received a report of a missing person this morning. Charles Knowles. He is Ramon's cousin, and he was supposed to go out with him on the boat today."

"No one was with Ramon when we showed up at the dock and only the three of us went out on the boat."

Renard pulled his chair closer to the table. "You are a former soldier, are you not?"

Jack nodded.

"Ramon was killed with an American military-style knife. The killer twisted the blade. That is a technique you learned in your armed forces training, is it not?"

"It's taught by armies around the world." Jack left off the fact that it was the most efficient way to make sure someone you stabbed died. "There was *no one else* on the boat. Just Ramon, my wife, and me."

"WHAT?!" Alice's muffled cry from the room next door brought a smile to Jack's face. It sounded like Renard's partner was following the same script for Alice's interview and had just told her that Ramon's cousin was with them and was now missing. "That's not true!"

"Your wife sounds upset," Renard said.

"You're saying we're lying about a murder. How would you react?"

Renard nodded. "Well put, Detective. But you do understand the position I find myself in, yes? You two left the harbor with Ramon and came back saying that an unseen killer murdered him at sea. Now I have a report that the victim's cousin is missing, and he was supposed to meet with Ramon at the docks this morning. Yet you claim he never showed up. What would you do if you were in my place, Detective?"

"Give me a polygraph," Jack said without hesitation.

Renard lifted his chin. "You would submit to one?"

"Yes."

"That will take some time to arrange."

"This is my honeymoon, so while you arrange the polygraph, are we free to go?" Jack's heart sped up as he waited for Renard's reply.

"For now. But I am going to hold onto your passports."

*Then we're not really free.* That was a punch to the gut. Without their passports, they couldn't get out of the Bahamas.

"I am extending a professional courtesy to you, Detective Stratton. This is a serious matter. You and your wife say one thing, but the facts are painting another picture. I hope, for your sake, what you say is true. If additional information comes forward, such as someone seeing Charles leaving the harbor on Ramon's boat with you, and my men are canvassing the harbor for witnesses as we speak, I will have no choice but to arrest you."

# 14

Inspector Renard stood at the window overlooking the parking lot, watching the Strattons get into the back of the police cruiser that would return them to their car, which was parked at the pier.

"I'm surprised that you let them go."

Renard turned and came to attention. "Good afternoon, Chief Inspector Fletcher."

Fletcher waved his hand like he was chasing a fly. The chief inspector ran a very tight ship, but he was making small changes to the military-like structure of policing. Besides, he had been Renard's mentor and considered him a friend.

But to Renard, John Fletcher was still the chief inspector and his supervisor. He couldn't bring himself to act casual around him.

"Do you not agree with my decision, sir?" Renard asked.

Fletcher shook his head. "I do agree with letting them go. So far you only have the missing person's report versus the word of this American detective and his wife. Have you read his file?"

Renard nodded.

"All of it?" Fletcher strode over to the window and looked out as the Strattons were driven away. "He's a decorated soldier. Back in the States, he solved a number of high-profile cases."

"Something bothers me about Stratton," Renard said quietly. "Did you hear my questioning?"

Fletcher nodded.

"He was nonplussed. If another man found himself suspected of murder, how would he react? Would he not offer more denials? Wouldn't he be shocked and outraged that I had the audacity to accuse him?"

Fletcher slowly nodded but said nothing. He reminded Renard of a teacher, using silence to force his student to think of the answer himself.

"Hmmm." Fletcher's thumb stroked his jawline. "Is that how you would behave?"

Renard scoffed, till he realized he'd walked straight into his mentor's trap. Of course, he wouldn't think that way. "No, but ... Stratton was calm. Did you see his hands? Not even a tremor. Who remains like that under pressure? A sociopath? Or a guilty man."

"Or a man hardened by life."

Renard shook his head. "He is twenty-six. How hard could his life have been?"

"That is why I asked if you had read his *whole* file." Fletcher crossed his arms. "Stratton was raised by a prostitute until he was six. Then he was placed in foster care. He served a tour in Iraq where most of his unit was wounded or killed including his foster brother. He was awarded three medals and returned to the States to become a police officer. He was wounded rescuing a kidnap victim, left the force and now is the youngest detective in his state. That is a determined young man who was been hardened by pressure."

"You talk about him like he's a diamond," Renard said. "He is a suspect. Do you really think another boat operator or fisherman just happened by, stabbed Ramon, and left?"

"It *is* odd," Fletcher admitted. "I do not claim Stratton is innocent. Only that he does not fit the profile of someone who would commit this act. And Ramon Knowles was no angel. Neither is his missing cousin. Has your canvassing found any witnesses that report seeing Charles at the dock or on the boat?"

"Not yet."

"You mean no."

Renard nodded respectfully. "We are still canvassing the pier."

"Until you get some evidence to the contrary, I have to say that I am more inclined to believe the testimony of an American detective and his wife."

Renard nodded. Normally he would agree with his mentor, but this time, he could not. There was something about this whole case that screamed there was more to it. He was certain there was something hidden beneath the surface, like moray eels within the coral reefs, and he was determined to find out what secrets Jack Stratton was hiding.

# 15

The crowd at the pier parted as Dimitri and Vadik marched toward the *Dive Into Paradise* office. Women stared. Men murmured. All got out of their way.

Dimitri was used to it. The beefy salvage expert was an intimidating man, and he knew how to use his size, his booming voice, and encyclopedic knowledge of international maritime law to get what he wanted. He glanced at Vadik. His shorter comrade was the opposite of him physically, but his sinewy muscles were still strong, despite his former life of poverty and hardship. It was Vadik's quick temper that made him ill-suited for command but also made him an excellent enforcer and second-in-command. People moved out of Vadik's path, too. Perhaps they sensed that if they got too close, he would bite.

Dimitri grinned. He kept Vadik on a short leash. He had to. But his old friend was invaluable in a fight. And as they got closer to the dive shack, and the crowd got larger, Dimitri had no idea what he was walking into. His police contacts had traced the call to the dive shop. Andres Knowles, the owner, had been out on a dive when the call had been made. It must have been his brother, Ramon, who called.

Dimitri stopped at the closed chain-link fence blocking off the end of the dock from the rest of the pier. Emergency services were loading a body bag onto a stretcher. The police had gathered up their equipment and most of the entourage was heading toward the gate.

Officer Mateo marched at the front of the group. His eyes widened as he met Dimitri's stare. Dimitri nodded. He and Vadik stepped to the side to let the stretcher and police pass.

Before Mateo could close the gate, Vadik grabbed hold of it, keeping it open for Dimitri and himself to slip through.

Mateo closed it after them and secured the lock from inside. The crowd murmured but no one dared say anything as Dimitri and Vadik followed Mateo further down the dock and away from prying ears.

"You should have waited," Mateo snapped.

Dimitri ignored him. The man had been a useful patsy, but now that Dimitri was within sniffing distance of what he wanted, there was no time for the niceties. "Give me the details," Dimitri barked.

"A local matter." Mateo's voice lost its early bravado. "A tourist killed a dive tour operator."

"The name of the operator?"

"Ramon Knowles. He was stabbed."

Dimitri fixed him with his blue eyes. "Why do you say a tourist killed him?"

"They were the only ones out in the boat with him. It's obvious."

Dimitri nodded to cover his impatience. The waters around the Bahamas were surprisingly crowded, and most everybody knew each other. But Mateo was a fool, so it was pointless to argue. "I need to get inside the office."

Mateo chuckled, but when he realized Dimitri was serious, the smile disappeared from his face. "That's impossible. I don't have the authority." Mateo shrugged. "I don't even have a key."

Dimitri cracked his neck. The noise was both loud and unnerving. When he was young, on one of his first ships, he had rushed up a ladder and knocked himself out on a closed hatch. Ever since the injury, his bones cracked like this. It had been embarrassing at first, but he found that he could sow the seeds of fear with it, so now he considered it a blessing in disguise. Dimitri handed Mateo a thick, sealed, plain envelope. "Go down to the other officer at the boat. Walk very slowly with him to the end of the pier."

"But—"

Vadik took a large step forward. Had this been two years ago, when Dimitri first located Vadik and convinced him to help in the search for the *Red Star*, Mateo would have found himself dazed and bloody on the dock a moment after Mateo hesitated but even Vadik had mellowed after a couple of years in the warm island sun.

"You will make more money during your short walk than you have all month," Dimitri assured Mateo. "Just be sure to take your time."

Mateo smiled and nodded. "Yes. Thank you." He turned and ambled down the pier.

"The man is a moron," Vadik said in Russian and laughed.

Dimitri shook his head. If Mateo was smart, he wouldn't be so easy to control. He doubted Mateo ever wondered why a marine biologist would need police information, but in his world, everybody had their hand out and wanted their palm greased. So Dimitri paid well for the man's stupidity.

Mateo waved the other officer over to him. Once they were on their way, Dimitri turned his attention to the dive shack. Living on the sea for months on end forced one to become a master of many trades, and Dimitri was somewhat of an expert locksmith. He pulled his army knife out and had the door open in less than thirty seconds. Dimitri hit the timer on his watch. He estimated they'd have less than ten minutes before the police returned—eight if they played it safe.

The office was a mess. Dimitri scowled at the haphazard stacks of bills and receipts, the smelly dive equipment and fishing reels. He headed for the two old desks that faced each other. One had a small, outdated computer on it.

"Take the hard drive out," Dimitri instructed Vadik, opening drawers and looking for maps. On a table near the window, he found a stack of charts. He didn't have time to go through them now, but he could process the information later with his high-res camera. He started snapping pictures with his phone.

Vadik held up the hard drive. "Got it. What's our cover? There's no hiding that it's gone."

Dimitri frowned. The police would be suspicious if they found the computer without a hard drive. He snapped his fingers and grabbed a Post-it note off the desk.

HARD DRIVE DIED. GETTING FIXED.

He slapped the note on the monitor and said, "We'll leave the unit open." Vadik grinned approvingly. Dimitri checked his watch. "We need to get going..." His voice trailed off as his gaze fell on the corner of the desk. Partially obscured by papers, a piece of metal caught his attention.

The engraved words made his breath catch in his throat. He seized the metal and held it up.

Vadik gasped. "A hatch handle."

Dimitri pointed at the Russian manufacturing stamp. "From a Russian submarine."

"Then they really did find the *Red Star*."

Dimitri nodded. He suddenly felt lightheaded at this amazing news, but now was not the time to celebrate. Stuffing the handle into one pocket and the hard drive into another, he marched to the door. Both men slipped outside, locking the door behind them.

No police were anywhere in sight, and the onlookers had dispersed, but as they approached the gate, a man hopped off his boat and waved them over. When he came closer, Dimitri recognized him.

"Oliver," he muttered to Vadik.

Oliver waved and rushed over to cut them off before they reached the gate. "Demetrios, I have not seen you in a very long while." The man's polite smile and British accent grated on Dimitri, but both he and Vadik stopped. "Did you hear the news?"

Dimitri decided to play ignorant. "No. What happened?"

Oliver frowned. "I saw you go in the office, so—"

"You don't know what you saw." Vadik jammed his finger in Oliver's face.

Oliver staggered back and almost fell off the pier.

Dimitri grabbed Vadik's arm and pulled it down. There was no use denying what the man had witnessed with his own eyes. "We were looking for Mr.—uh—Knowles." He pretended to make an effort to recall the name. "The office was open, but no one was in."

Oliver leaned closer like he was sharing a secret. "Well, maybe that is because they just took Ramon Knowles out of here in a body bag."

Dimitri feigned surprise. "What happened?"

"The police believe he was killed by a tourist, but I met them, and they certainly did not strike me as killers."

Dimitri pulled the corners of his lips down so he wouldn't laugh. He had suddenly remembered as a child being taught a line from the old American war propaganda: "Loose lips sink ships." This man was like a dream come true.

"Who do you think killed him?"

Oliver shrugged. "Who knows? I think we all should be more careful."

Vadik scoffed and Dimitri shot him a cross look. "Yes, you make a good point. Thanks for the warning." He nodded politely and turned to go, but Vadik nudged his arm.

Mateo was hurrying up the dock. He whistled and leveled a finger at Oliver. "I told you, Mr. Rolle, this portion of the dock is closed. You have to leave, and right now."

The policeman tipped his head to the side and raised his eyebrows at Dimitri and Vadik. He might as well have been holding up a sign that said *I need to talk to you.*

Oliver glanced at Dimitri and Vadik. "What about them?"

"They're leaving too; as I said, this portion of the dock is closed."

"But I have to take a tour out in the morning," Oliver protested.

"The dock should be open by then, but I can't make any guarantees."

"Do you have any idea how closing the dock will impact my business?" Oliver's eyes narrowed.

Mateo snapped, "You have a boat. Pull forward twenty meters and you'll be fine."

Oliver flushed. Then he nodded curtly, untied the bow and stern lines, and cast off. As he powered away, Mateo said, "I heard from the station. They released the tourists."

"They didn't arrest them?"

"No. But they are suspects. The inspector is having them followed."

Dimitri inhaled the salt air and looked out to sea. It was a habit that always helped him think. And right now, he was wondering if these tourists were really just sight-seeing.

*Perhaps they were the other bidders. And they did their bidding with a knife.*

"What are their names?"

"Jack and Alice Stratton."

Dimitri nodded and headed toward the gate to exit the pier. He had a new goal: to find Jack Stratton, crack him and pull information from him like meat from a lobster.

# 16

After the policeman dropped Jack and Alice off at their car, and reminded them curtly not·to leave the island, they drove back to the resort and gave the car to the valet. Taking the walkway around the large hotel and the outdoor pool, they watched the last rays of sun disappear on the horizon. From behind the main cabana, music and delicious smells from the grill wafted toward them. Although he hadn't eaten since breakfast, Jack had a craving stronger than for food. He slipped his arm around Alice's waist and said hopefully, "Want to go back to the room and make this gorgeous night extra special?"

Before she could answer, Alice's stomach rumbled loudly, and they both laughed.

"Yeah, that's an even better idea," Jack said, taking her hand and changing direction toward the outdoor restaurant. As they strolled toward the flickering lanterns, Jack couldn't take his eyes off Alice. Even after scuba diving all morning and spending the rest of the afternoon being interrogated about a murder, she was the most beautiful woman Jack had ever seen. Her complexion was already a light tan and her green eyes sparkled above the glow on her cheeks. The skin on her hand was soft and warm. Jack's eyes wandered from her bare, toned legs all the way up her body.

Jack tried to swallow down his passion as the waiter greeted them and showed them to a table. He gulped down the glass of water and caught himself transfixed by his new bride and couldn't think of anything to say. She seemed to liquefy his body and brain. All he wanted to do was lie naked with Alice and swim in her emerald-green eyes. Didn't she know that she was the only woman in the world to him?

They both ordered drinks, and after Alice took a few sips and had some salty-sweet plantain chips, she was her animated self again, recounting the details of her interrogation, which mirrored his. The inspector interviewing her started out treating her like a witness, but as the interview went on, it was clear that he regarded her as a suspect.

Her green eyes blazed. "And then they thought I stole that pot that I found. I dropped it when you told me Ramon was dead, but I don't think the inspector believed me. He said, 'If you thought it was treasure, why would you drop it?'" She dramatically raised her hands toward the ceiling. "I said a man was dead and that was more important than money." She looked at him sharply. "Are you listening to anything I'm saying?"

Jack grinned roguishly. "I probably shouldn't say what I'm thinking about in public."

Alice's sun-kissed cheeks turned even more crimson.

He swirled a prawn in lime butter before holding it up toward her lips. "Here, lean over and try this. I promise I'll pay very close attention."

Alice rolled her eyes. She took a quick bite, closed her eyes, and moaned. "Oh, that is so good. But this is serious, Jack. They think we killed the guy."

A soft breeze of island air whispered in the palms outside. Alice turned her face to the immense ocean and the bowl of the night sky pierced with stars.

Jack reached across the table, took her hand, and said softly, "Let's take a walk on the beach."

Her eyes sparkled in the dancing light of the lanterns.

Jack gave the waiter their room number to charge the dinner, and the newlyweds strolled out arm in arm. When they reached the edge of the sand, Jack stopped. He slipped off his shoes, then knelt down and removed hers. They walked hand in hand down the beach to where the first foamy waves lapped at their ankles. Alice turned to him and parted her lips as if to say something, then burrowed her head into his shoulder and wrapped her arms tightly around him. For a few minutes they clung to each other, and Jack felt a peace and calm and rightness that he knew was not just the island magic—it was the circle of her arms, her scent, the heat of her body.

"Alice," he whispered.

"What?"

"Can I kiss the bride?"

She gave him a smile that melted his heart, and he leaned in for a kiss that seemed to last forever. When he came up for air, he looked at her and suddenly knew how to handle their intimacy challenge. She was ready, more than ready, he could feel it. She just needed to trust him.

Alice lay her head against his chest. "Right now, all I want you to do is pick me up, carry me back to the hotel room and make love to me but..." She sighed. "I'm worried, Jack." She gazed up at him, concern darkening her eyes. "The police think we killed Ramon and there's nothing we can do to convince them otherwise."

Normally, the choice for Jack would have been easy—but staring into Alice's pleading eyes sent mixed signals through his brain. Every synapse was enflamed with desire for her. But he knew Alice. There was no way she'd relax while they were under a cloud of suspicion. Not unless Jack at least looked into it.

He held her by the shoulders and gave her a roguish grin. "Well … you could just stand there looking gorgeous under the moonlight or do you want to come with me to scope out the dive shop?" Jack walked backward on the sand, beckoning to her. "You know it won't take us that long. We'll just have a little look-see and then we'll come back and have a little fun."

Alice ran toward him and grabbed his hand, pulling him with her. "You want to have fun? Let's catch whoever really killed Ramon and I'll put a permanent smile on your handsome face!"

They slipped on their shoes and walked quickly to the valet station to retrieve their rental car. Jack crossed his arms. "You know that pot you found?"

"The pirate treasure?" Alice frowned. "I thought you didn't believe me."

"One, it's not pirate treasure. I saw another pot inside the dive office that looked a lot like it when we were signing the insurance forms. There was also a couple of shards of pottery in the bottom of the boat that were the same color."

Alice frowned. "You didn't tell me that."

"I didn't put it together until Renard said the pot might be a motive for murder."

"But if the pot isn't really treasure, then nobody would kill over it, right?"

"I thought about that. What if Ramon was running some type of scam on tourists? Maybe he was planting those pots and making them think they found real treasure. He could have ticked off the wrong people."

Alice nodded but raised a puzzled eyebrow. "How do they make money if I find the pot?"

"Inspector Renard told me that if it was old or valuable, you'd have to report it to the police."

"So, after I found the pot, Ramon says that I can't keep it because it's an antiquity?"

"Exactly. Then, me being the lovesick husband, I offer to pay him to look the other way."

Alice's ponytail bounced as she thought about it. "And then when your sweet little wife is heartbroken because she was ripped off—"

"I go to get my money back."

"So you think Ramon was killed by someone he ripped off?"

"It's a theory."

Alice smiled. "No harm in looking in the window."

It was a short drive to the pier. They parked in the same spot they had that morning. The crowd was gone, and it looked like the police had gone home as well. A few people strolled along the pier. Jack assumed they were tourists—loud and inebriated, mostly white, overweight—and a few tired-looking individuals who appeared to be heading home from a very hard and extremely long day of work.

Jack opened his door. "Let's go."

Alice got out of the car and fell into step beside him. They followed the walking ramp down the darkened boat dock until it reached the closed chain-link fence, locked with a thick chain. Barbed wire was coiled across the top.

"It was worth a try." Alice shrugged.

Jack winked, turned and walked back toward the ramp. But instead of going up, he headed over to a dinghy and grabbed the rope. "Hop in."

Alice's eyes went wide. "We're stealing a boat?"

"It's not stealing. They belong to the pier and people use them to row out to their boats moored in the harbor." Jack wasn't entirely certain of his facts, but that's how he thought it worked. Either way, they were only "borrowing" it for a few minutes. "Or you can wait here."

Alice climbed in.

"Hold on tight to my dinghy."

Alice rolled her eyes as Jack pushed away from the dock with an oar. "You sound like you're in junior high school."

"My hormones are raging like it." Jack set the oars in the locks and began to paddle. "I could always row out to the harbor a little ways. We could relax beneath the stars and ... make magic."

Alice made a face and looked around the dirty boat that had a quarter inch of fishy water in the back. "You are such a romantic. Shut up and row."

Jack slipped in next to Oliver's boat, pulling the oars up. After tying off the dinghy, he helped Alice up.

Jack crept over to the shack and peered through the window. Equipment was piled against the walls and windows, but it was too dark to see details. Jack gave the window a shove, but it wouldn't budge. They circled around. Jack tried the door. It was locked, too. Alice grabbed his arm. "We can't go in," she whispered. "It's illegal."

Jack made a soft chicken noise, which made her snort with laughter. They headed over to the edge of the dock, where a little lip of wood ran along the roof shingles, jutting out over the water. A few feet down was another set of windows.

Alice shook her head, but Jack grasped the little ledge in his fingertips and pulled himself up onto the roof. He reached the other window and lay on his stomach to look over. Inside, a plywood panel had been put up to cover the broken glass, but the window slid open easily. He pressed against the plywood. It had only been tacked in place by two nails at the top and came free with just a little squeak from one nail.

But every sound on the water carries. He glanced over at Alice, and she looked ready to shoot him. She held her finger to her lips while pointing at her head with her other hand and making a circle.

*I might be crazy, but I'm going in.*

He set the plywood down on the bench beneath the window and climbed through. He had no trouble seeing in the moonlight. The office was as cluttered as he remembered it, but one thing was immediately different. The computer on the desk was shifted and its case was open.

Jack walked over. A Post-it note said simply, HARD DRIVE DIED. GETTING FIXED.

That was a heck of a coincidence. And Ramon certainly didn't leave that note. From the pile of papers on the desk, he hoped that Ramon was the kind of man who kept paper records, but there were only bills and receipts. Still, he took out his phone and snapped a few pictures. He could go over them later.

Moving on, he headed for the corner, and the pot that looked like the one Alice found was still there, complete with a wilting flower. He pulled back the tarp behind it to reveal more pots. These were cracked and broken, like someone had robbed a clearance sale at a garden center.

Jack snapped a few pictures and noticed a cleared area on the table next to the pots. The entire table was covered with junk except a two-by-two-foot square. That empty spot interested Jack a lot more than the phony relics did. Something about it set off the alarm system in his mind.

He headed for the door and slipped outside. Alice was instantly at his side. Footsteps on the dock made them retreat into the darkness next to the office. The locked gate rattled, then creaked as someone swung it open.

Jack peeked around the corner.

A policeman was walking down the dock, straight toward them. Jack pressed his back to the wall and pulled Alice up against him.

The policeman strolled up to the *Dive Into Paradise* and checked the door. He peered into the window.

Alice stiffened in Jack's arms. He could feel her heart beat against his chest.

The policeman reached into his pocket, took out a pack of cigarettes, and lit one. After letting out a few puffs, the policeman walked back over to the gate. Jack exhaled, but they weren't out of the woods yet. The policeman was still between them and the dinghy.

The policeman's radio crackled to life. "This is Johnson," he answered. They were close enough to hear both sides of the conversation.

"Are you at your post?"

"Of course I am, sir."

"We received a call that someone was trespassing at the *Dive Into Paradise* office."

"What? No!" Johnson raced back to the office door and yanked on the handle. "It's locked, sir."

Jack and Alice crouched in the shadows as the policeman peered into the windows of the dive shop.

"I've been watching for the brother but neither him nor anyone else has been here."

Lights flashed on the pier above and a police cruiser skidded to a stop.

"Another unit has arrived, sir." The policeman hurried over and unlocked the gate.

Jack looked at Alice and pointed at the water. Her eyes widened—he read equal parts fear and excitement. He held onto her hand and lowered her into the sea. She didn't even make a splash. The police were closer now. Jack pointed his toes and slipped over the side as quietly as he could.

After he resurfaced, he pointed at Alice, then at the dock running parallel to theirs twenty yards away.

Alice nodded. She took a deep breath and disappeared beneath the surface.

Jack dove under and kicked hard in the direction of the next dock. Staying underwater as long as possible, he surfaced beside a moored boat. Alice swam up next to him. The police were standing on the other dock talking excitedly, but Jack couldn't make out what they were saying. Alice pointed under the dock, and they started swimming away from the police. Sticking to the darkness beneath the pier, they swam until they saw the beach. A few couples still strolled up and down the sidewalk, but Jack and Alice stayed in the shadows.

"The first policeman that drives by and sees us soaking wet is going to stop us," Alice said. "And our car is back at the pier."

Jack nodded. "That's why I should go get the car."

Alice shook her head and took out her phone. "I told you these waterproof cases were a good idea."

Jack swore as he took out his soaking-wet wallet from his pocket. "I should have picked up one for my wallet." He sighed. "Let's go."

Alice shook her head. "Give it two more minutes."

"Why?"

"The hotel shuttle bus is going to make its last pickup right over there." She pointed at the bathhouse.

"How'd you know that?"

She smiled angelically. "It was listed in our vacation package. I put the bus schedule in my phone."

Jack grinned. "You're amazing."

Alice's eyes widened; she pointed and whispered, "Bus!"

They both hurried out of the water and raced across the sand and grass to the shuttle. The small group of drunken tourists hooted and hollered as they ran up and the newlyweds were laughing right along with them. The driver rolled his eyes as Jack and Alice dripped their way back to a seat.

"We can get the rental car in the morning," Jack whispered as he sat down.

"What did you find?"

Jack told her about the computer with the missing hard drive and showed her the pictures of the broken pots. "Did you hear what the policeman said?"

Alice nodded. "About the brother?"

"Yeah. If anyone knew what Ramon was up to, it would be him."

"How are we going to find him?" Alice asked.

Jack tapped the phone in her hands. "This is where you work your magic."

Alice's eyes lit up along with her phone screen. She connected to the internet and began typing. "I'm on it."

Jack smiled but it quickly faded. Someone had anonymously called the police about the break-in. That meant someone else had been watching the office.

*Who?*

# 17

Alaire parked on the pier and walked over to Gregory and Miles, the two men the Dyab had assigned to watch the *Dive Into Paradise* office.

"How could you have lost them?"

"Dey went down and never came back up." Miles shrugged.

Gregory pointed. "Dey musta jumped in da water from da dock."

"The policeman didn't chase after them?" Alaire scanned the other docks that ran out parallel to each other like tines on a pitchfork.

"Da cop didn't see dem. He was unlockin' da gate for dem uddah cops who'd just arrived."

"Are you certain it was the Americans who came to the office?"

"Yeah. Tall guy an' good-looking wife. Da guy climbed on da roof and went in da window. I call ya and did exacly what ya said."

"How long did it take for the other police to get here?"

"Like five minutes."

"And the police have found nothing?"

"I don' tink so." Gregory looked back at the docks. "But we can' figure out where da Americans went. We didn't see dem swimming."

Alaire was disappointed. If the police had managed to do their job and caught the Americans returning to the scene of the crime, it would have made them appear even more guilty and he had no desire for them to discover Ramon's real killer.

"Tell me, was Andres one of the men who went into the office earlier?" Alaire asked.

"No. Dey were white. I've seen dem before, but I don't know who dey is. Dey were inside a long time. About ten minutes."

"What about the police? They were still there, no?"

"Da two guys spoke with Mateo when dey arrived at da dock. He let dem in da gates." Gregory's voice rose excitedly. "Mateo talked to dem again before dey ga. Dey gave Mateo someting. Small. He slipped it in his pocket."

Alaire scowled. Mateo was on the Dyab's payroll, but Alaire had never trusted him. The man was greedy and stupid. A combination that made him unreliable. Now his treachery had been proven. "Describe the men that Mateo let by."

"White men, but not tourists. One real big guy, with a beard. Da other guy is much shorter."

"Did they take anything from the office?"

"Not that I saw."

"Dey spoke to anuddah man besides Mateo," Miles added.

"Who?"

"Dat white dive guy." Gregory cast a sideways glare at Miles. "Oliver someting. He was in his own boat and got out to talk to dem when dey left da office."

"Did you hear anything that was said?"

"No. I was too far," Gregory said.

"You didn't move forward?"

"Ya tell me just watch."

Alaire resisted the urge to stab him. "Where did they go?"

"Da two guys jump in a silver car and left. Four doors. Oliver stayed on da dock."

Down at the pier, another police car arrived. Even from this distance, because of the tan uniform and short height, Alaire could identify Inspector Renard as he stepped out of the cruiser.

The inspector owed the Dyab his life and didn't even realize it. Alaire had wanted to kill the inspector a year ago, but the Dyab refused. Not killing him made no sense to Alaire. Renard couldn't be bought and was a competent policeman. And now that the rest of the Dyab's enemies had been dealt with, Alaire found himself in the unenviable position of being a warrior in a time of peace. The Dyab believed that killing the inspector now would bring too much attention.

Renard walked down the dock and called all the policemen over. After a few moments, the inspector began ordering everyone around. Renard thrust out his arm, and a police officer would hurry down the dock; he'd jam a finger another way, and a different officer would salute and take off running.

"Both of you stay here," Alaire ordered. "If you see Andres, the Americans, or *anybody*, Miles will follow them and you, Gregory, will call me immediately. Do not lose them. Am I clear?"

"Yes. Perfectly."

Alaire looked at them and smiled. "You see, I must not have been clear before, because you lost them once already. So let me be *perfectly* clear now. If you lose them again, I will cook parts of you and eat them while you are still alive and watching. *Now* am I clear?"

They both looked like they were about to throw up, but they managed to nod. Alaire turned away to watch Renard hurry to his car.

The inspector was an irritant, but what really bothered Alaire was the American. This Jack Stratton wasn't behaving typically. Most men with the specter of murder hanging over their heads would be weeping to a lawyer or drowning their sorrows in a bottle.

Stratton was different. He wasn't taking this lying down. Stratton was fighting back.

Alaire smiled. It had been so long since he had faced a real contender. Alaire took out his phone and dialed as he strode back to his car. The Dyab had ordered Alaire to find that sub. There were already many bidders for its location and they would be extremely generous. But so far, the information died with Ramon.

Bashir answered but Alaire knew the Dyab was listening. He relayed all of the information, including Mateo's betrayal.

"Leave Mateo be. We will deal with him later."

"Are your men still watching Andres's house?"

"Yes."

"I should get the wife. She could know where he is. She may even know the location of the sub."

"No. Andres is Bahamian and Bahamians take care of family. He will come for her."

Alaire resisted the urge to scoff aloud. Fool. Andres was on the run and afraid for his own neck. Bahamians may say they are loyal but when faced with death they also knew how to hide themselves, and there was no way Andres would risk his life by going back to his house—even for his pregnant wife.

"The police are searching for Chooch," Bashir continued. "We do not need that scrutiny right now."

Alaire turned to look back at the sea. "Have you disposed of Chooch's body yet?"

There was a silence that stretched on for almost a minute. "No. It's on ice."

"Perfect. I'll handle everything. Including the Americans."

# 18

Mateo sat on his couch flipping through the channels on the TV. It was a rerun of an American game show but really it served as background noise. He was too busy counting the money stacked in neat piles along the coffee table.

*It's time to leave the Bahamas.*

He'd retire and go to Europe. He had enough money now. Besides, it was too dangerous a game he was playing. The Dyab paid generously, and the Greek biologists gave him almost as much. But his newest source of graft had truly bestowed upon him a king's ransom.

Mateo's eyes glistened as he stared at his piles of loot. He'd made more in the last week than he had in the last year. What they were after, he didn't care. He was paid enough to keep his mouth shut. But he couldn't help but keep his hand open. If the Dyab found out he was taking additional money…

His eyes shot to the front door. He hurried off the couch and locked it. He locked the window too then hurried around the house sealing it up. He stood in the middle of his filthy living room and his hand began to shake.

The scientists didn't worry him much. The shorter one reminded him of a junkyard dog, but Mateo had been beaten before. That would probably be the extent of their wrath.

If it was only a matter of taking side money, the Dyab might not kill him. He could cut off a hand or take an eye to make an example of Mateo and knock him back into submission. But now his treachery and greed would cost him far more. A simple maiming would be much preferred.

It wasn't just a bribe. It was truly a deal for his soul. He knew that making it. The Dyab called himself the Devil, but this man truly was the closest you'd find this side of the black gates. He'd never seen such evil in a man's eyes before.

Oh, how much money he offered though. More than he ever dreamed. How could Mateo refuse?

His heart began thumping in his chest. He should have thought twice, but it was too late. No one had ever double-crossed the Dyab and lived. He needed to go—*now.*

Mateo ran into his bedroom and yanked the closet door open. He threw aside boxes and piles of papers until he reached the suitcase. Tugging it out and causing an avalanche of junk in the process, he tossed it onto the bed. He unzipped the larger suitcase, removed the smaller one inside, then dashed back into the living room. He set the case beside him on the couch and sat down next to it. He leaned forward, ready to scoop up the piles of money.

Someone grabbed the hair on the back of his head and yanked him back into the couch. The sofa shifted as it scraped on the tile floor. His front tooth cracked as something hard was jammed into his mouth.

Mateo gagged. His eyes watered. Instinctively, he grabbed the gun.

The attacker rammed the gun into the roof of Mateo's mouth, forcing his head back even further. Through his tears he stared into the coldest eyes he'd ever seen. It was as if he gazed upon the Devil himself.

And the Devil smiled.

# 19

Jack turned over in bed and stared at the cold, empty spot Alice should be in, then rolled back to remember last night. His plan to ease her into love making seemed to be working, and the beauty of it was its simplicity: all he had to do was wait for the inevitable. The island was working its magic and Alice was coming into her own, blooming before his very eyes. Each night, they had a bit more fun than the night before and kept waking each other up to kiss and touch. They had their whole lives in front of them, and Jack knew there was no destination to hurry to—and a million reasons to enjoy the journey.

But today was a different story. He pulled back the sheet and got up. "Alice?" She wasn't in the living room either. His panic started to rise until the breeze billowed the curtains in front of the sliding doors and he saw her out on the deck that jutted out over the turquoise waters. A smile spread across his face. At least she was enjoying the beauty of their surroundings in spite of all that was going on.

He slipped out the door, expecting her to be sipping a cup of tea and watching the waves, but the click of computer keys dashed that hope. Sitting at a little table, she was hunched over her laptop, her fingers a blur.

"Morning," he whispered as he wrapped his arms around her and kissed her cheek.

She purred and pressed against him, then turned back to the screen. "I found something. Sit down, I'll show you."

Jack didn't let go. "Can it wait a few minutes?" He brushed her hair and kissed her neck.

She purred again. "I let you sleep in. We should get going soon."

Jack kissed her once more and sat down. "What did you find?" He helped himself to some fruit and a muffin that his thoughtful wife must have snagged from the breakfast buffet while he was still sleeping.

"I started with everything that I could find out about Ramon Knowles. His girlfriend dumped him a few months ago, and after the hurricane, he came to live with his brother and started working at *Dive Into Paradise*."

"I thought it was his business."

"No, his brother, Andres, is the owner." Alice clicked a couple of buttons and a web page appeared.

"This is an old page. I found it using the Wayback Machine." She clicked and another website opened up. "This is the new page. They changed it after the hurricane."

In the picture, Ramon was smiling broadly with his arm around the shoulders of another man, in front of the dive shack. A paragraph signed by Andres explained, "The hurricane has not stopped us. All around us is the Paradise that God made for us, and now your chances to *Dive Into Paradise* are doubled because my brother, Ramon, has returned to Freeport after many years away. Together we are partners in the mutual love of exploring the sea."

"Hmm. So that's Andres. Did you find anything on him?"

"Married. No kids. He lives in Bain Town."

"What about Ramon? Where did he live?"

"He had an apartment on Abaco. He and his girlfriend shared it but she went back to her family in the Philippines about three months ago."

"How do you know that?"

"Social media." Alice rolled her eyes. "People write everything down. Look." She clicked over to another page. "Ramon posted an apology letter to his girlfriend on her Facebook page after she caught him cheating on her. It's nuts. It's like standing at an intersection under a billboard that says you're a thief."

"You're the prettiest investigator I've ever seen." Jack nuzzled her cheek. "I can't believe what you manage to dig up."

"Thanks, babe. People make it easy." She shrugged. "If they kept their mouths shut, no one would know their business."

Jack shook his head. "It freaks me out sometimes what you can find out on the internet."

Alice nodded. "It should. Big Brother is watching."

"Good thing I have you on my team."

"When do you want to go pick up the car and check out Bain Town?" she asked excitedly.

Jack grinned. "Well ... that depends. Do you want to ..." He wiggled his eyebrows up and down.

A dreamy look crossed Alice's face, but she shook her head and said, "We don't want to lose momentum on our first case as husband and wife!" Her eyes were sparkling again and her ponytail bounced as she pulled him out of his chair. "Can you be ready in ten minutes?"

"Make it fifteen?" Jack asked, standing up.

"Sure. Why?"

He forced a smile on his face. He needed to go slow with Alice, but his head was fighting with his hormones, and losing the battle. "I want to take a quick shower."

*A very short, very cold shower.*

# 20

Irene stroked her tummy, tears streaming down her face. She prayed silently for the safety of her husband. Every time Andres went out on the sea, she prayed for him. But she hadn't this morning. Andres wasn't supposed to go out on the water. Ramon was taking the tour.

But now Ramon was dead, and her Andres was missing.

A sob escaped her mouth followed by a scream wrenched from deep inside of her. Where was he? Had the Americans killed him, too?

A knock on the door boomed through the tiny house.

She leapt to her feet and froze. *Andres would not knock. Who can it be? Is it da police? Have dey found Andres? Maybe dey found him already and dey gonna tell me Andes is...*

Her hand covered her mouth and fresh tears welled in her red-rimmed eyes.

*Please, Lord. Please...*

Her hands shook as she opened the door.

Sister Elizabeth hurried in, pushing Irene back with one hand and closing the door behind her with the other. The elderly nun's lined face seemed to always be marred with an unspoken pain but today it was especially grim.

"Oh, child." Elizabeth took both of Irene's hands in hers.

Irene's breath caught in her throat. "Andres? No…"

"He's okay. He came to the church."

"Tell him he's gotta come home."

"He can't. He thought they may be watching the house." Elizabeth moved away from the window, pulling Irene with her.

"Who is dey? What is goin' on?"

"Sit down." Elizabeth pointed to the couch as she began drawing the shades.

The room was plunged into darkness, small slivers of light creeping through the corners of the windows.

Elizabeth clicked on the end table lamp, but Irene felt like a cloud had swept over her soul.

Since Irene was a child, she had known the elderly nun. Sister Elizabeth had been born on the island but beside that, Irene knew very little about the woman she saw every Sunday. She ran the orphanage but passed on those duties last year because of her age, with a beautiful ceremony to commemorate her hard work.

Elizabeth's eyes locked with Irene's. "Ramon and Andres tried to make a deal with the Dyab."

The words scattered Irene's thoughts like gulls chased by a dog. *Ramon is stupid but could he have been dat stupid? Would he? No... No. Andres would've talked him out of it. Andres never done anyting dis bad ever...*

"Do you know anything about the business Ramon and Andres had with the Dyab?"

"No! Andres would never do nuttin' with da black market. Dat had to be Ramon. All of it." Irene's hand traveled to her protruding belly. A tear ran down her cheek. "Where is Andres?" Irene seized Elizabeth's hand.

"I don't know. He left. He's hiding. He's trying to get somewhere safe and bring you there. He wants you to come with me. You'll be safe at the church."

Irene's skin went so cold she began to shake. If the Dyab was after them, was there anywhere she could go to protect the baby growing inside her?

"It won't be safe dere. The Devil is gonna come for me."

"Even the Dyab wouldn't dare break the covenant of the sanctuary of the church. Besides, I will go out the front and pretend to talk to you through the front door while you go out the back. Head straight across to Caspian Drive and I will meet you there."

"But what 'bout Andres? You say he left. What's gonna happen to him?"

"He'll be okay. I'll go speak with the Dyab."

Sister Elizabeth's words almost made Irene laugh out loud. Her? An elderly nun confront the Devil himself? But all Irene could manage to do was shake her head.

Sister Elizabeth patted Irene's leg. "The Lord goes with me."

"No!" Irene grabbed the nun's wrist as the old woman rose from the couch.

"Dat's crazy, Sister. It's too dangerous. Ya don't tink we should go to da police?"

"The Dyab may listen to an old fool." Sister Elizabeth smiled. "Besides, my mind is made up. You must think of your child's safety as well."

Fresh tears ran down Irene's cheeks. "But what 'bout yawz?"

The old nun chuckled and shrugged. "I have lived a very long life. Besides, he is not really the Devil. The Dyab is just a man and salvation is available to all men, even those as wicked as him. Now, go and get a few things together."

Irene hurried to the bedroom. She hastily grabbed a change of clothes, silently praying for herself, her child, her husband and the elderly nun who was risking so much for them. But as much as she loved Sister Elizabeth, Irene was convinced that she was wrong.

No one was safe speaking with the Devil.

# 21

They took the hotel shuttle back to the beach and, to their relief, the car was still there and didn't have a ticket. Alice walked toward the car, but Jack grabbed her elbow and led her away.

"What are you doing?" Alice whispered as she fell into step beside him.

"Smile. Keep walking." Jack forced himself to stroll with a natural gait. "We have to leave the car here."

"Why?"

"Look at the car beside ours. It has a ticket. So do all the others."

"That's weird."

"Renard's smart. He must have run the plates from the cars in the parking lot."

"Then he knows we were here last night."

"Yes. And most likely the police are watching the car right now."

"How are we going to get to Andres's house?" Alice asked.

Jack pointed at the motorbike rental shop ahead.

Alice blew a raspberry. "Do you even know how to drive a motorcycle?"

Jack grinned. "Sure. I'm like Evel Knievel."

"Wasn't he the stuntman who crashed all the time?"

"Not all the time."

"Crashing on a motorcycle *once* is too much."

"Trust me." Jack winked.

Twenty minutes later, they were buzzing down the coast with the sea breeze in their faces. Alice was clinging to his back but grinning like a kid on Christmas Day.

Alice used the GPS on her phone and tapped on Jack's shoulder to guide him down the streets toward Andres's bungalow. They got there all too quickly for Jack. He drove up to the little house and decided to park the bike on the grass by the porch. Alice gave him a quick squeeze before she let go and hopped off the bike.

"Okay." She smiled. "I'll admit it. That was really cool."

Jack lifted her chin and kissed her lips. "Told you." As he parked the bike, he quickly assessed the pedestrians who stared as they passed by. He gathered that tourists seldom left the swankier parts of Freeport, but the distrustful eyes of the locals didn't faze him—he and Alice had grown up on the "wrong side" of town, too. Suspicious neighbors were one thing. Who knew what was waiting for them behind Andres's front door? "Why don't you stay here and keep an eye on the bike?"

Alice held up her hand and wiggled the finger with her wedding band. "We're in this together now, buddy. Sickness, health, guns, murder ... Where you go, I go."

Andres's one-story bungalow was small and painted a bright yellow. The front yard was immaculately groomed. Over in one corner near a bird feeder was a bench, beside it a statue of Mary.

Alice followed Jack up the stairs to the porch and waited beside him after he rang the doorbell. He waited a full minute before ringing it again. Pressing his hand to the glass, he peered inside. The little home was as tidy as the lawn. It was small but not cramped. The wall on the left was covered in framed photos, the back wall looked like it led to the kitchen. On the wall to the right hung a crucifix next to a painting of Jesus. All the lights were off, and no one appeared home.

"She's not here." Alice's breath fogged the lower part of the window as she too stared inside. "But if you were missing, I'd be out looking for you too."

Jack turned back around to stare at the small driveway next to the house. His experience as a bounty hunter kicked into high gear. He shook his head. "You would go out looking for me but you're exceptionally…*strong willed.*"

"That sure beats stubborn but I prefer determined."

"But you're an exception. Most people don't take the initiative. They wait. And since that driveway is only big enough for one vehicle and the police found Andres's parked at the docks—"

"His wife is pregnant too. The detective interviewing me laid that fact on pretty thick."

"Renard said the same thing to me too. So, I doubt she's walking around looking for him."

"If I couldn't go looking for you"—Alice crossed her arms and chewed her bottom lip—"I'd wait here."

"You're thinking about it all wrong. Don't think about what you'd do. What would Irene do. Where would she go?"

Alice followed Jack's eyes to the statue of Mary in the corner of the yard.

"Church," they both said in unison as Alice pulled out her phone.

"The nearest Catholic church is Saint Francis on Royal Poinciana Drive. It's a three-minute drive."

"Let's go."

\*\*\*

Jack parked the motorcycle in the little parking lot beside the church. Two cars were parked next to the building but from the dust, it appeared they'd been there some time.

Alice walked up the granite steps behind Jack to the large, double, wooden doors but when Jack tried to pull them open, they didn't budge. He raised a puzzled eyebrow and tried again.

"That's weird," Alice said.

Jack rapped on the door.

Hushed whispers sounded from the other side.

Jack knocked again.

The door on the right creaked open a crack. A young nun, not much older than Alice, peered out. "Hello. I'm so sorry but…we're…closed."

"Closed?" Jack repeated as a crooked grin crossed his face.

"For renovations." The nun exhaled and smiled, seemingly quite pleased with her own explanation.

"We're looking for Irene Knowles," Alice said.

The nun's eyes darted toward the sanctuary, but she shook her head. "No one's here. Just me. Sorry. Maybe come back later. Tommor— Next week! We should be done by next week." She started to close the door.

Jack blocked the closing door with his foot. "I'm Jack Stratton. It's very important—"

"You're da Americans who were out with Ramon!" a woman called from inside.

The young nun winced.

"That's right. And that's why we're here," Jack said. "We just need to speak with you for a moment."

"Go or I will call the police!" The nun pressed against the door but couldn't budge it with Jack holding it.

"Please!" Alice begged, calling through the open door. "This whole thing is crazy. One minute we're scuba diving on our honeymoon, and the next we're suspects in Ramon's murder. But we didn't have anything to do with it. I'm praying you can help us. Please?"

The nun pushed harder but a woman walked up behind her and placed a hand on her shoulder. "Let dem in, Sister Anne."

The nun hesitated for a moment, then stepped aside. A petite, pregnant black woman stood in the doorway. She peered into Alice's green eyes for a moment and exhaled. "Why are you here?"

"We're trying to clear our name. My husband is a detective—in America. Can we speak with Andres?"

A myriad of expressions fluttered across Irene's face like ads on a subway stop as the train hurtled by. Her lip trembled. "I haven't seen him since yesterday. What trouble did Ramon land my Andres in?" She burst into tears.

Alice wrapped her arms around the woman's shoulders and let her cry. She rubbed her back and spoke softly to her until the woman said, "Please, come inside."

The nun closed the doors behind them.

Irene led them into a small room off to the right. Old chairs and a small sofa lined the walls. Jack sat on a chair while Alice sat next to Irene on the couch. Sister Anne didn't follow them. Jack heard her footsteps slowly fade inside the church.

"I'm Irene. Sorry for cryin' …" Her lip trembled again.

"You're fine," Alice quickly added. "I'm sure you're very concerned for your husband."

"I could wring his neck—" Irene launched into a steady stream of Haitian Creole. Jack couldn't understand what she was saying, but he could tell it wasn't good.

"You said something about Ramon getting Andres mixed up in something," Jack said. "What did you mean by that?"

Irene rubbed her forehead. "My husband's bruddah was a wannabe playah. He always husslin' someting or someone. He used to drink and nevah went to church. Andres hadn't seen him for near ten years when he showed up." The bangles on her wrist jangled together with her agitated movements as she unleashed another volley in Creole. "He bring more bad luck dan da hurricane." She hastily crossed herself. "I tell Andres don't fool with him, but ... dey is bruddahs. I tell him dat's all da more reason not to, but Andres wouldn't listen." She turned to Alice. "And we have a baby comin'." She patted her tummy.

"These hustles, what were they?"

"It all talk," Irene said. "But if ya believe dem like Andres did, Ramon would be rich any minute. He talk 'bout making dey own YouTube channel. First it was going to be like *Survivor* but out on the water. Den dey was gonna be the next Jacques Cousteau. Last month it was real estate and before dat it was shipping."

"Were they scamming people?"

"No." Irene shook her head. "My Andres is an honest man. It was Ramon with dem big ideas, but dey were legal. Stupid, but legal."

"Can you think of anyone that would want to kill Ramon?"

She exhaled. "No, but I know dey reach out to Ramon's cousin, Chooch. He got less sense den Ramon." Irene looked around the room and leaned forward like she was sharing a secret. "I warn dem. Both of dem. Chooch is work for the Dyab. Sister Elizabeth tell me dat Ramon reach out to him."

"The Dyab?" Jack repeated.

She looked around the room, as if someone were listening from behind the religious pictures or the potted plants. "The Devil. He rules all da black market on *all* da islands. He earn dat name. He straight evil."

"Can I speak with Sister Elizabeth?" Jack asked.

Irene shook her head. "She say she going to try talk with da Dyab. Plead our case. She hasn't come back yet."

"Where is this Dyab?" Alice asked.

Irene motioned for Alice to lower her voice. "No one knows. I don't know how Sister Elizabeth knows, but she must. She said she's going to go speak with him. I tried to talk her out of it, but she wouldn't listen."

"How did she find all of this out?" Jack asked.

"Andres came here. To da church, but he left right away. He just wanted to get a message to me. He said he'd find a safe place to hide then bring me to him."

"Where do you think Andres is?" Alice asked.

Irene pressed both of the palms of her hands against her eyes. Her shoulders slumped. "I don't know. I'm so worried 'bout him."

Jack didn't want to upset the woman any more than she was but he needed her help. "Can you think of anywhere he would go?"

"Without me? Nowhere. He would never leave me behind. He's comin' back. I know it in here." She touched her chest— "And here"—her hands moved down to cradle her stomach.

Alice asked, "What if Andres needed help? What would he do?"

Irene shook her head, her eyes brimming with tears. "It's just the two of us. Before, I would have said Ramon but Andres has got no family here on…" Irene sat bolt upright and crossed her chest. "To his uncle Victor! Andres has an uncle. He lives on Great Abaco, in Marsh Harbor. Dere's a bar, da Lost Dog.

Victor is da bartender. But, after the hurricane, I don't know if it still standing. But if Andres needed help, he would reach out to him."

"Did you tell the police this?" Jack asked.

"No."

"Don't. Not yet. Let me see if Andres is there first. Please."

She nodded.

Jack handed her a business card. "If Andres comes here, or if you think of something, anything, will you call me?"

Alice squeezed Irene's hand. "Please."

"I will. I promise."

"Irene." Jack took a deep breath and put on the neutral mask he was taught to wear when delivering bad news. "I think Andres is mixed up in something very bad. Whoever killed Ramon may be after Andres too."

Irene started to tremble.

Alice wrapped a protective arm around her shoulders. "Is there anywhere you can go? Maybe you could visit a relative?"

"No." The tiny woman's shoulders slumped. "I've gotta stay here and wait for my Andres. Besides, there's nowhere safe from da Devil."

# 22

Inspector Renard slipped underneath the police tape crossing Officer Mateo's front door. A camera clicked and flashed as a lab technician photographed the scene. Another tech was taping paper bags over Mateo's cold hands. It was standard procedure. They would test for gun residue later.

Officer Susan Rigby stood stoically beside him. He was surprised by the new cadet's composure. The scene was gruesome and he felt his own stomach flip in spite of the hundreds of crime scenes he'd witnessed.

Mateo's body sat on the couch. Blood and brain matter had splattered everywhere—including the coffee table in front of him covered with piles of cash. Without counting it, it was easy to see it was more than Mateo possibly could have saved legally. Renard had long suspected that Mateo was taking bribes. He had personally filed three reports to the Internal Investigation Division but nothing had come of it. Mateo had neither been exonerated nor found guilty. The reports had all been closed without a finding.

Renard carefully circled the crime scene, Officer Rigby following close behind.

"What are your first observations, Officer?"

Rigby snapped to attention and pressed her hands to her sides. She stood as crisply as her uniform was pressed. Even her black hair was coiled into a bun so neat, not a strand was out of place.

"Judging by the wound and the fact that Officer Mateo's service revolver is still in his hand, it would appear to be a suicide, sir."

Renard was careful neither to nod nor shake his head. "Continue."

Rigby cleared her throat. She scanned the room. "There is a suitcase on the bed, an overnight bag next to him and a large sum of money. It would appear that Mateo was getting ready to flee."

"Flee? Interesting choice of words."

"I don't know Mateo's financial situation but that is far more money than someone of his rank would make in years. The source should in the least be investigated but I would think it would have to be...illegally obtained, sir."

"I too find the money very interesting. With that much money at his disposal, why would he not *flee*, to use your own words?"

Rigby's mouth open and closed. Her large, brown eyes narrowed. "Perhaps guilt? Maybe he realized he'd broken his oath to uphold the law."

"Interesting. But Mateo was not the kind of man beset by morals."

"Then why do you think he killed himself?" Rigby's voice had a slight hint of annoyance to it. "Sir?" she quickly added.

"Did he kill himself?" Renard pointed at the gun in Mateo's hand and turned to the lab tech with the camera. "How many suicides involving firearms have you processed?"

"Over a dozen, sir."

"Have you noticed anything unusual regarding Mateo's body?"

The lab tech lowered his camera. He sighed loudly and his tone dripped with annoyance. "If you're going to say that the firearm should have fallen out of his hands, you're wrong. That's a myth. In twenty-five percent of suicides involving handguns, the gun remains in the person's hand."

"Very good." Renard nodded. "But that is not what I was going to point out. Shine your camera light along Mateo's right forearm."

Clearly puzzled, the lab tech did just that. Both techs leaned forward and so did Rigby.

"Bruising!" Rigby said. "There are bruises on his wrist."

The lab tech started photographing the marks. "Someone grabbed him. It's a hand print."

"Judging from the position of the marks"—Renard walked around to behind the couch—"the person stood behind Officer Mateo and held the gun in his mouth."

"He was murdered?" Rigby asked. "But why leave the money?"

"Why indeed." Renard smoothed his mustache. "Perhaps they were sending a message?"

"That Mateo was on the take?"

Renard nodded. "Maybe Mateo had done something to displease them. Criminals rule through fear. They want to show that money is not important to them. Obedience is."

Rigby pointed to the pile. "That's a very expensive way to get a point across."

# 23

"What do you say we try to find Uncle Victor?" Jack said as he and Alice started down the church steps and toward the motorcycle.

"How do we get there? Rent a boat?"

"Kind of." Jack stopped by the bike and took out his phone. He switched to his photos and pulled up the one he had taken of Alice outside the *Dive Into Paradise*. He zoomed in on the back of the boat in front of her and the phone number printed there.

"Who are you calling?"

"The only boat captain I know." He dialed and waited.

"Good morning, Oliver Rolle here."

"Oliver, it's Jack Stratton. We met yesterday."

"You ... and your wife, yes! I hope she's recovered well."

"She's fine. I was wondering if you give tours of the islands."

"Of course. When would you like to go?"

"Today. Now, if possible."

"Now? Is it just the two of you?"

"Just the happy couple." Jack winked at Alice and she made a face. She hated when he didn't clue her in beforehand—which he would have, but he was flying by the seat of his pants.

"Certainly. When can you be here?"

"Actually ... Could you pick us up at the hotel dock? We're staying at the Royal Palms."

Alice raised an eyebrow at his lie but Jack had many good reasons not to meet up at their real resort, which the police were undoubtedly watching.

"I can be there in half an hour," Oliver said.

"Fantastic. We'll meet you there."

"That was a great idea." Alice playfully smacked his shoulder, though there was some force behind it. "But why didn't you tell me *before* you called?"

"I was just ... acting before thinking it through," Jack admitted.

"You know what Aunt Haddie would say about that?"

Jack grinned and put his helmet on. He was all too familiar with what his foster mother, "Aunt Haddie", would say. Ever since he was little, he'd been sat down for many of her lectures about thinking your actions through *beforehand.*

Jack raised his voice and did his best Aunt Haddie impression. "Way to go for taking the initiative."

"Yeah, right. She'd say that many counselors lead to wise decisions. Think before you act."

Jack tapped the side of his helmet and held his hands up like he couldn't hear her.

She smacked him in the arm again, harder than before. "I know you can hear me."

Jack started up the motorcycle and Alice climbed on behind him. He pulled out and headed back east toward Freeport.

At a stoplight, Alice patted his back and held her phone so he could see it. It showed a street map to the Royal Palms. The streets near the dock were outlined in red, indicating traffic.

Jack gave her a thumbs-up and took a left. As he drove down the left-hand side of the tree-lined avenue, he kept having to force himself to remember that the Bahamas was like England and he wasn't driving on the wrong side.

The back road to the hotel must have been breathtaking before the hurricane. It was still beautiful, but there was a number of fresh stumps where thick, old trees had recently stood. Jack stopped at a four-way stop, even though these back roads were deserted, a fact that brought additional attention to the car that was slowing down far behind him.

Alice patted his left shoulder. He drove straight through the intersection, watching the car in his rearview mirror. When the green Camaro reached the four-way stop, it rolled through and followed them.

As he approached the next intersection, Alice tapped his left shoulder. Jack took a right.

"What are you doing?" Alice yelled. "You're heading toward the traffic."

"I know!" Jack checked his mirrors.

The Camaro made the same turn.

He wanted to clue Alice in, especially since she'd just lectured him about it, but he didn't know how she was going to react.

"Don't turn around and look. Okay?"

"Okay," Alice called out.

"We're being followed."

Alice turned around.

"Hey!" Jack snapped.

"Sorry!"

The Camaro sped up, as did Jack. Holding the throttle back, the little motorcycle whined as Jack took another right and raced toward the crowded main street.

"We're going to get stuck in traffic!" Alice yelled.

The light in front of Jack turned red. He kept the throttle back.

"I have a plan."

Alice's grip tightened around his waist. "And what would that be?"

Cars beeped and drivers laid on their horns as Jack flew into the intersection and turned in to the traffic. Jack zipped between cars, weaving to avoid striking their side mirrors. He passed so close to them he could touch them.

"I call this the Death Star Trench Run!" Jack yelled as he threaded the needle between the two lanes of cars.

"Good name for it!"

If one car tried to change lanes or Jack made a mistake, the chase would be over—and not in a good way. In his rearview mirror, he saw the Camaro stuck halfway into the intersection he had just barreled through. Jack grinned. He would have laughed, but he was having a hard time breathing with Alice holding onto him so tightly.

***

Dimitri drove along the road that ran parallel to East Mall. He watched as the Strattons darted between the lanes of traffic to lose the Camaro.

"How did you know he was going to do that?" Vadik asked.

Dimitri shrugged. "He's smart. He realized that he was being followed."

"Who do you think was in the Camaro? They weren't the police."

"Obviously." Dimitri drove with his window down and let his arm hang on the side of the door, the breeze against his skin helping him think. "They could be the people who killed Ramon."

"Why would they follow the Americans?"

The tight muscles along Dimitri's jaw suddenly relaxed. "They don't know where the sub is either."

"What? How can you know that?"

"The men in the Camaro were watching Andres's house. Why?"

Vadik shrugged.

"They are looking for Andres too. And if they're looking for him, they don't know the location of the *Red Star*!"

"We will find him first," Vadik boasted.

Dimitri shook his head. "The American will do it for us."

Vadik scoffed. "We are the true hunters in this pursuit."

"On the sea we are hunters," Dimitri corrected him as he took out his phone. "This Jack Stratton was a bounty hunter. He tracks people. And he is very good at it." Dimitri unlocked the phone and gave it to Vadik. On the screen was an article on Jack catching a man known as *The Giant Killer*. "Do the work and research your enemy. It will pay off." Of course, it also helped to have a bloodhound's instincts. Dimitri couldn't count the number of times he had beaten a competitor to a claim by mere minutes, but now it had never been more important to get there first.

"What are we going to do? Nothing?"

"Of course not. We follow Stratton. When he finds Andres, then you will be free to put your special skills to work."

Vadik's eyes sparked with excitement as a wicked grin spread across his face.

# 24

From the pier, Alaire nodded politely as Oliver steered away from the dock and toward the entrance of the harbor. He'd have to find out later where Oliver was sailing to. Alaire sat down on the large cooler behind him and lit a cigarette. People were very much like cats in their thirst for answers. But it wasn't curiosity that got them and cats killed. It was a lack of self-control.

Alaire could easily have called out to Oliver and asked his destination. People were not afraid to be nosy here—a practice Alaire detested, but he knew he would not seem odd by being so direct. But now wasn't the right time to find out. Nor was it appropriate for him to look into the enormous cooler that doubled as his seat.

But oh, how he wanted to open the box and gaze at the body. Human skin glistened like diamonds when it was properly frozen. Alaire puffed on his cigarette and fondly recalled that day almost ten years ago. It was the arrogant man from Amsterdam. Nothing they were doing would make him talk. So Alaire dragged him out into the snow, still tied firmly to his chair. The Americans thought waterboarding was effective. They should try it at twenty below as the winds howled and froze the liquid as it poured.

And oh, how he talked then. Alaire didn't think he'd ever shut up. But instead of ending his misery, Alaire brought another chair out and watched the man freeze.

*I wonder if Chooch's skin sparkles like black diamonds? Did the cold tighten the muscles and make his eyes open back up?*

Alaire stood. One little peek couldn't hurt.

But the sound of an approaching motor drew his gaze back to the harbor. Raul steered his small fishing boat toward him. Alaire had never used Raul for a job. The man was the father of a low-level courier. Alaire hated using unseasoned men, but for this job he needed someone like Raul—a nobody with no police record and a reason to be loyal—and Raul would say nothing or his son would die. He knew that.

Alaire stared at the older man's leathery face as he tossed a rope for Alaire to lash the boat to the dock. Raul hated working for the Dyab. You could see it in his eyes, in the stiffness of his shoulders. But after Raul lost his house in the hurricane, what choice did he really have?

Once the boat was secure, Alaire pointed to the cooler and together they heaved it onboard. Once they were both in, Alaire motioned Raul closer. He draped his right arm around the old man's shoulders and opened the lid of the cooler just enough to peek in. Raul gagged and tried to step back but Alaire held him in place.

Chooch's skin sparkled. Cold, lifeless eyes stared blankly at the blue sky.

"Do you see that knife?" Alaire pointed to the blade protruding from the center of Charles Knowles' chest. He'd driven it in deep and twisted it, catching the grooves in the fabric of Charles's colorful shirt. "Make sure it stays in the body."

Alaire took one last look at his victim's glittering skin and opaque eyes and forced himself to close the lid.

*Discipline.*

"Take the body to these coordinates." He handed Raul a map. "Can you read a map?"

Raul, cowering, said softly, "I know where it is."

"Dump the body in the water and wait with it for four hours."

Raul, still in shock, looked questioningly at Alaire.

"It needs to defrost. Let some little fish nibble on it, but make sure the knife stays in and wear gloves if you touch it. Understand?"

Raul nodded.

Alaire pointed to the two long wooden poles with barbed ends that fishermen used for getting large fish into the boat. "Secure the body with those before you put it in the water. If it floats away, I will make you take another trip out to sea."

Raul, who had regained some of his composure, stared at Alaire with darkening eyes.

Alaire smiled. The old man still had some fire. "After four hours, you can radio the harbormaster. You were fishing and found the body, nothing more."

Raul said nothing. He lifted his chin. It was a slight gesture but Alaire read defiance in the motion.

"I don't believe I was entirely clear with you a moment ago." Alaire stepped closer. "If you screw this up, I will make you take another trip to sea *with two more coolers.*"

Raul swallowed and swayed with the rocking boat.

"One for your son and one for your wife. After you've finished watching the sharks turn their bodies to chum, you'll go for a swim. Now, have I been clear?"

Raul nodded vigorously.

Alaire stepped onto the dock and watched till the boat disappeared around the curve of the inlet. He took out his phone and called the Dyab. Bashir answered.

"Everything is in place. In four and a half hours the police will have enough to arrest the tourists. Where are they now?"

"The men watching Andres's house lost them."

"Must I do everything myself?"

"We have another issue. Mateo is dead," Bashir said.

"How?" Alaire started walking for his car.

"He was murdered. Whoever killed him tried to make it look like a suicide."

"Have you discovered who the two men were who bribed Mateo on the dock?"

"Russians. They are looking for the sub."

"Maybe they wanted their money back. Do you need me to find out if they killed Mateo?"

"No. We can deal with the Russians. You are to locate Andres."

"Where is his wife?"

Bashir hesitated. "Saint Francis Church."

"We should take her. Force him to come to us."

"We have men watching the church."

Alaire wanted to point out that he had men watching Andres's house and they lost the Strattons but he forced himself to keep his mouth shut.

"I will locate Andres." Alaire stopped beside his car but did not get in. "I have a plan."

"Bring him to the villa unharmed."

"Understood."

Alaire disconnected the call and chuckled. His plan was gelling together. Every piece falling into place. He strode over to the driver side and slipped behind the wheel of the gray Audi.

The leather seats quickly cooled as the air conditioning swept into the car.

He headed out of the parking lot and across town. He had no intention of looking for Andres. Sooner or later, like a rodent scurrying out of its hole, Andres would surface, and Alaire would kill him. Right now, he needed to relax and the club was the quickest place to do it.

But something bothered him. Nothing tangible. It was more of a prickling along his arms whenever he thought of the American's name—Stratton. In spite of his disdain for all things in the United States, something about this maverick police officer placed Alaire on edge.

Alaire glanced out at the harbor one last time before turning toward the city. In four hours, it wouldn't matter. The police would arrest the Strattons and that would be the end of it.

# 25

At the Royal Palms, Jack turned in at the ornate gate and parked in the lot next to the docks. Alice shook her ponytail out from the constricting helmet and looked up at her husband. "Who do you think was following us?"

Jack shook his head. "It certainly wasn't the police."

"How do you know that?" One eyebrow was raised in skepticism, but he heard the tinge of pride in her voice.

"If the police were tailing us, they never would have sped up when I went to lose them. They would have radioed another car."

She kissed him. "You're brilliant, Jack Stratton."

He was going to kiss her back but she was already heading for the dock. Jack locked the bike and hurried to catch up to her.

Oliver's boat was moored at the end. He waved and climbed out, dressed in another of his loud Hawaiian shirts and slacks, with a fisherman's cap set jauntily on his close-shaved head.

"I was surprised you called me." Oliver held out his hand to help Alice in, but Jack beat him to it, smoothly lifting her up and over the side.

His bride cast him a quick frown once she regained her balance. "Thanks, honey."

"Where would you like me to take you today? Would you like a tour around the island or do you have a destination in mind?" Oliver asked.

"We want to go to Marsh Harbor on Great Abaco. There's a bar there called the Lost Dog."

Oliver sucked in his cheeks. "Are you certain you want to go there? Abaco sustained extensive hurricane damage, and even before that ..." He looked away, busily coiling up the stern line. "It's not really a tourist destination."

"I'm positive." Jack smiled and hopped into the boat.

Oliver cast off, and came on board. "Abaco is avoided even by most locals. It is ... a rough place. But I have a friend there. I will text him now. Hopefully it goes through."

"How much do you charge?" Jack asked, eager to give Oliver the motivation he seemed to be lacking.

"Well ..." Oliver took off his cap to scratch his head and Jack could feel him sizing up the thickness of his guests' wallets. "There and back will take all day. Five hundred dollars."

Alice nodded. "Do you take credit cards?"

Oliver shook his head, and said he was very sorry that he would need at least some cash up front. Jack quickly peeled off two hundred dollars and handed it to Oliver, who brightened up a bit.

"There is a bank there—or there was. We can arrange the rest of the payment at that end," Oliver said.

"Will do," Jack said quickly. "We'd really like to make the most of this trip and see as much as we can. Is this boat fast?"

"Very." Oliver walked over to the steering console.

"Good." Jack sat down. "If you get us there quickly, I'll throw in a hundred-dollar tip."

Oliver grinned. "Hang on tight."

\*\*\*

Jack stood at the stern of the boat, watching the dolphins play. In spite of the serious reason for this trip, Jack couldn't help the thrill that stirred in him with the slap of the boat against the waves and the salt spray in his face. He felt just like the dolphins that were leaping and somersaulting beside the boat.

Alice had moved to a spot under the shade of the awning in the front. When Jack came up to join her, she and Oliver were chatting away.

Jack frowned. Oliver was sitting awfully close to Alice on the bench seat.

"Did you know that there's a beach on Eleuthera Island where the sand is pink?" Alice asked Jack as he walked up.

Jack smiled, taking a seat at the rail. "Between that and those dolphins, this place feels surreal." To Oliver he said, "Working down here, you must know all about the islands."

"I love them. I grew up here, after all."

"But you have a very pronounced English accent," Alice noted. "The locals have an accent too, but yours sounds to be from across the pond."

"You're spot on," Oliver said. "I was born and raised here, but my family moved to England when I was nine. My father is a navy man."

"Did you follow in his footsteps?" Alice asked.

"I inherited his love of the sea." Oliver chuckled. "But my love was too strong for me to let someone else tell me where I could go with her. So, no, the navy life was not for me."

"Jack was in the army," Alice said proudly.

"If I had joined the military, with my luck they'd have sent me to the middle of a desert and leave me to die." Oliver laid his hand on Alice's shoulder.

"Speaking of dying—I've got a strict no-touching policy with regards to my wife."

Alice winced.

Oliver removed his hand and moved over on the bench to increase his distance from Alice. "I meant no offense."

"None taken." Jack tried to reign his jealousy back in but there was something about Oliver that bothered him. Still, he needed his help and information, and it was no good alienating his source. "So, when did you return to the Bahamas?"

"A little over a year ago. I was in Asia before that, but I needed to come back. I missed these waters."

"Did you know Ramon well?" Alice asked.

Oliver shrugged. "We talked on occasion. All the tour operators do. I was relatively new in the business, but they seemed to accept me. The police will have a hard time solving that case."

"Is that so? Why do you think that?" Jack said.

Oliver shrugged. "Ramon had his share of vices. He liked the women." He glanced at Alice when he said it, a brief curl appearing at the corner of his mouth. "Perhaps he was killed by a jealous husband? But he also liked gambling. So it could be a bookie, it could be ... a lot of people, I guess. Honestly? He wasn't my cup of tea. I feel sorry for his brother. Andres was trying to help him."

Jack turned to watch the sea racing under the boat. A jealous husband could certainly escalate to the level of murder, and so could a bookie or an enraged brother, but how to explain why someone was following them? There had to be something else.

"Have you heard of the Dyab?"

Oliver scoffed. "The Devil? It's a story that mums frighten little boys with to keep them from growing up to be bad men."

"I heard that he runs the black markets?"

Oliver shook his head. "Everywhere has a black market. The combustible element here is that we are a free trade zone as well. You'd think that would be enough, but every place you go, there is someone selling something—artifacts, property, graft, fraud— it's a madhouse." He laughed sharply. "The real devil here is money. There's too much of it, and yet never enough to go around. But the Dyab?" Oliver shook his head. "No man could control all the black markets. It's too much power to rein in."

Jack nodded. Judging from the way Oliver spoke of the "madhouse," he doubted Oliver was speaking from much experience. "What about Ramon's brother, Andres? What do you know about him?"

"He is a good man." Oliver looked at his GPS and made a course correction.

The boat rocked as a wave caught the side.

Alice slipped sideways but Oliver steadied her by grabbing hold of her arm. Oliver threw a smile at Alice then turned to Jack. "My apologies." He released his grip. "Just keeping my guests safe."

Jack crossed his arms. The charming tour boat operator was ticking him off.

Alice stood up. "I'm going to get some sun. Do you have a minute, sweetie?"

Jack begrudgingly followed her and sat down next to her on the bench seat in the back.

"I was trying to find out if he knows anything," Jack said.

"I know, but I just spent the last half hour getting information out of him."

Jack frowned. "I didn't know that."

"Because you're too busy getting jealous."

"I'm not jealous."

Alice rolled her eyes. "You looked ready to feed him to the sharks and all he did was touch my shoulder."

"What guy goes around touching someone else's woman?"

Alice lowered her voice. "Me Jack. You, my woman. You sound like caveman." She chuckled.

Jack scowled.

She kissed him. "I like my caveman guarding me, but Ollie is just being nice."

"Ollie?"

Alice scratched her armpit and pretended to swing a club. "Looks like my caveman is back. Relax. His friends call him Ollie."

Jack scowled again. Whatever it was about Oliver that bothered him went beyond the fact that he was tall, handsome, and had an English accent. "He's not your friend. Don't get too close to this guy."

"That's going to be a little hard considering we're on this little boat. Besides, I'm just being nice."

"Be nice—from a distance. What did you find out?"

"He said that Ramon was very happy the last couple of days. Like really happy. Ramon said his luck had turned around."

Oliver whistled. Jack and Alice looked to the front of the boat.

"There's Great Abaco." Oliver pointed at the long strip of whitish-pink in the distance. "Are you still certain you want to go there?"

Jack nodded.

Oliver sighed. "Don't say that I didn't warn you. Abaco can be a dangerous place, especially for tourists."

# 26

"Abaco is quite different from the main island," Oliver said as they pulled into the harbor. The difference was striking. Here there were no resort hotels, casinos, or cruise ships. The fishermen paused as the unknown boat headed over to the ramshackle dock. Jack's eyes traveled along the pier. A few scattered groups of men gathered at the railing, puffed on cigarettes and watched them closely from dark eyes.

"My friend can show you around," Oliver said. "He also has a car."

"That sounds like a good idea," Alice said as she moved closer to Jack.

Jack nodded. He agreed with Oliver on this one.

Twenty minutes later, Jack and Alice sat in the backseat of a blue Kia while Oliver rode in front with Lukas, a powerfully built black man with a shaved head, who hadn't said more than hello to Alice and merely nodded to Jack. He looked more put out than anything. He spoke to Oliver in whispered tones as they drove along the narrow main street, where all the businesses and homes were either boarded up or reduced to rubble. Here and there, tents had been erected, and people sat outside these tents, fanning themselves and following the little Kia with their hopeless eyes.

Alice shifted nervously beside Jack. "Is it difficult driving on the left side of the road while you're sitting on the left?" she asked.

Lukas shook his head. "No."

"You get used to it," Oliver explained. "The Bahamas follow British driving customs, but most of the cars are imported from the States."

Lukas pulled the car over to the curb and parked. Jack sat up. This guy was supposed to drive them to the Lost Dog, but there was only a bank next to them and a boarded-up clothing store across the street.

Oliver cleared his throat. "Lukas thought it would be best if he got a partial payment first. The ride is a hundred dollars—American. There are only two banks operating on the island, and this is one of them."

Jack grabbed Alice's wrist and slid out of the car. "Certainly. We'll be right back."

Alice followed Jack inside.

"Boy, that driver sure is Mr. Personality," Alice said.

"Stay close to me."

"I promise I won't leave your side."

He grinned despite his worry and inserted his card into the ATM. "They have a five-hundred-dollar limit. I'm not giving Oliver his full cut until we get back to the main island anyway." He put two hundred in his pocket, gave Alice a hundred, and tucked the other two hundred into his sock.

Alice knew exactly what he was doing. They had both grown up in the hood. You kept a little in your pocket as mug money but you carried most of your cash hidden. If someone stuck a gun in your face, you only lost a small portion.

They headed back to the car. Jack got in first this time so he could sit behind Lukas. He handed him fifty dollars. "You get the rest when we get back to the dock."

Lukas nodded and started the engine.

They rode in silence through the town, past endless blue tarps on the roofs that still existed, tree limbs piled askew, cars overturned, children scrambling through the rubbish heaps.

"I had no idea it was so bad," Alice said. "I'm so sorry."

Lukas nodded. "Some of the other parts of the island are much worse."

"What about Marsh Harbor?" Oliver asked.

"Still standing," Lukas answered tersely.

They drove through a section particularly hard hit. The sun had set and in the faint light, all Jack could see was the remains of collapsed buildings.

"Storm surge," Lukas muttered.

After a few more minutes, some little side streets opened out, and the main strip showed a few signs of struggling commercial life as the little car wound its way up a hill until they reached a large building framed by hanging lights on its roof and railing. It looked like it belonged more in New Orleans than the Bahamas. All manner of cars, trucks, and motorcycles were parked out front. No one looked in their direction as Lukas stopped at the edge of the parking lot. He kept the engine running. "I'll wait here."

Oliver raised an eyebrow. "Aren't you coming in with us?"

Lukas shook his head. He turned around in his seat. "She should wait here, too. The Lost Dog is no place for a lady." That was more words than they'd heard from him so far.

Jack turned to Alice, but he knew there was no way she was staying in the car. She would be safer at his side anyway. Jack nodded. "I agree with you, but my wife and I are a team."

Alice hopped out and slipped her hand in his.

Oliver surprised Jack when he climbed out of the car and said, "I suppose a cocktail wouldn't hurt."

Jack looked at the bar and the enormous bouncer at the door. "In this place, it might."

The three of them walked to the wooden porch and stepped inside. The bar was decorated like Atlantis had a Mardi Gras. Colorful beads swayed in the breeze created by huge palm fans suspended from the ceiling. But the decor seemed to have little impact on the customers. Two dozen sour-faced men eyed them suspiciously. There were only two women present besides Alice, both staring at her.

Alice moved closer to Jack. Having grown up in the projects, Jack was used to being the only white person in a room. He had never felt uncomfortable about that until now. But this was different.

"European?" a man whispered to his friend as they passed his table.

"No." The man's lip curled. "American."

Jack ignored their glares and headed for the bar.

The bartender was an older man with receding salt-and-pepper hair. "What'll it be, an Island Breeze?" he asked mockingly. Laughter tittered through bar.

Jack was tempted to ask for a Hurricane, but he didn't want to try to fight his way out with Alice beside him. "I'm looking for Victor. We're friends of Irene's."

The bartender's eyes didn't move from Jack's. "Three Island Breezes comin' up," he called out loudly and the men at the bar laughed and pounded the worn wood.

Jack watched the bartender making the drinks. He was whistling and making a show of it, but each time he met Jack's gaze there was an intensity there. He took down three glasses, walked to the far end of the bar, and poured the drinks. "Would ya be wanting anyting else? Perhaps a shrimp cocktail or one of dem lil parasols for ya drink?"

"What's a parasol?" one of the drunks asked his friend.

"One of dem tiny umbrella tings."

They both howled with laughter.

Jack, Alice, and Oliver sat down and the bartender held out his hand. "Twenty-five dollars."

"We'll start a tab," Jack said. "You must know Victor," he persisted.

"Shut up and listen," the barkeep whispered. He started wiping the bar down with a dirty rag. He leaned close to Jack but didn't look at him. "Tell Andres not to come here. People are watchin' da bar."

Jack picked up his drink and took a sip. "Have you heard from him?"

"Yesterday. He called and left a message. He said he got no phone so no way to call him back. He said he'd call me back soon as he finds a way. But he can't come here. He's gotta leave da Bahamas. Finish ya drinks quick and go. Dey watchin' ya now too."

Jack grabbed two twenties out of his pocket and covertly stuck his business card in them. "I can get him and his wife out of the Bahamas. When Andres gets in touch with you again, call me."

Victor nodded and headed down the bar to refill drinks. Alice took a sip of her drink and coughed. The drunks at the other end of the bar laughed.

Jack and Alice stood up.

"Well, if she's not going to have it ... cheers!" Oliver picked it up and gulped it down, exhaling loudly when he finished.

Jack nudged Oliver toward the door. "Let's go." He grabbed Alice's hand and took point. As he neared one of the tables, a mountain of a guy stood up and stepped toward Jack. It appeared that he was intentionally trying to bump into Jack, but Jack stepped out of the way just in time.

The big guy scowled and looked confused for a second before dribbling his own beer on his own shirt. "Hey!" he shouted loudly enough that everyone in the bar turned to look. "Ya spilled my drink." The man thrust an accusatory finger toward Jack. "Ya need to buy me a new one *and* pay for my shirt."

Three men who had been sitting with the big guy stood up, their chairs scraping on the wooden floor.

Jack inhaled. He could give the guy the mug money from his pocket, but from the hate-filled glare on the big man's face, Jack knew he wasn't just looking for money. He wanted to fight, and even if Jack gave him everything he had, it wouldn't be enough.

"Well?" The big guy puffed out his chest.

Jack looked around the room. There were too many for him to take them all on, and there was no way he could talk his way out of the situation. He had only one choice.

Jack turned to Alice. "Give me a hundred dollars, please."

Her hand shook as she handed him the money.

A sneer crossed the big guy's mouth. "My shirt is worth twice that."

"I'm not paying for your shirt or buying you a drink." Jack held the five twenties up high. "This is prize money," he yelled. "The first guy that knocks this loudmouth out—wins!" Jack tossed the money onto the table.

It took a moment for his words to sink in, but once they did, a dozen men rushed from all over the bar, knocking over chairs and shoving tables aside to get at the guy. The loudmouth was getting pummeled from every direction, and soon men started fighting each other to reach him.

Jack grabbed Alice's wrist and ran for the door with Oliver hurrying after. They burst out of the bar and down the steps.

Oliver stared, his mouth opening and closing. "Where is he?"

Jack swore.

Lukas's car was nowhere in sight.

The sound of an engine made them turn. The little Kia raced around an outbuilding and toward them. It skidded to a stop in front of the bar. Oliver fumbled with his door as Alice jumped in and Jack climbed in beside her.

"Go! Go! Go!" Jack called out.

Lukas didn't need any encouragement. He gunned it out of the parking lot as Oliver was still shutting his door. Jack glanced back at the building. No one came running out to follow them.

Alice laughed.

Oliver looked at her like she had three heads. His hands were shaking. "That wasn't funny. I thought we were going to get killed in there."

She shrugged. "Actually, it wasn't my first bar fight."

Jack let his head fall back against the seat and chuckled at the memory. When he was a patrolman, he had responded to a 911 call reporting a wild bar fight at the university. It turned out that Alice was at the center of the brawl and emerged unscathed. Three guys weren't so lucky. He laughed again and gave her a quick kiss.

"What do we do now?" Alice asked.

Jack's laughter faded. "Andres reached out to Victor. He'll call him again. All we can do now is wait."

# 27

The Dyab strolled along the rooftop deck of his massive villa, staring at the lights of Nassau twinkling far below as he waited for the call. His power extended farther than he could see in every direction, but there were limitations and dangers, even for him.

He stared up at the moon and wondered if he'd tried to rise too high. He—the boy who had grown up in the slums, the son of a washerwoman with no idea who had fathered him—ruled over all the factions of every island. Everyone gave him a cut. From the peddler to the politician, the Dyab was in control. But his reach ended at the edge of the sea. What started as simple calls to feel out the amount of interest from potential bidders began promisingly enough.

He knew better than to deal with religious fanatics, but for some reason he had to take a bite of the forbidden fruit and find out how much they were willing to pay. And, just as for Eve, there were severe consequences for his ambitions.

A small group of zealots known as the New Dawn entered the bidding. Known for a recent string of bombings, shootings and a chemical attack, the organization had already developed a ruthless reputation. The New Dawn wasn't just interested in the sub, they'd had the audacity to demand it. The highest bid for the location was a million. It was just the location, after all. And there was no guarantee of the cargo. He got greedy. He raised the price so high that he expected the small group to drop out of the bidding—ten million. But they agreed and declared the bidding over.

It was rumored that the New Dawn were behind the deaths of a Russian Oligarch and an Egyptian Sheik who refused to do business with them. The Russian was murdered by derailing the train he was on, resulting in the death of him and eighty-three other riders. The Sheik was injected with motor oil and set ablaze.

And now their man with the money was headed to the island.

But the Dyab, with all his power, and his guts in negotiating, had no idea where the sub was. Someone had killed Ramon. Did he divulge the location before he died or did the secret die with him?

*No. He must have told his brother. Brothers always share secrets.*

The Dyab stared at the floor. His own brother was locked five floors beneath him, trapped in perpetual darkness. He would have confided the location to his brother. Ramon must have shared it with Andres. They were dive partners after all. But Andres had fled. With the Dyab's men watching every dock, airport, and major road, there was no way for him to escape. There were people watching his house and his office, every place he had been known to or was likely to frequent, but so far Andres Knowles was more of a ghost than the Dyab was. Still, he thought Andres had never left Grand Bahama. He was on the island somewhere—hiding.

And now Mateo had been murdered. By whom and why, the Dyab didn't know. It was infuriating. Mateo was a fool and made many enemies, but he was a police officer and all of the Dyab's men knew to leave him alone. Someone else had done this.

The only advantage was that the police would be rattled by the loss of one of their men, but it did not lead him closer to Andres. He needed Alaire to finish this business of framing the Americans and move on to getting the location of the *Red Star*. With the Americans being arrested and charged with two counts of murder tomorrow, the attention would shift to them and off any talk of the Dyab. He wouldn't be happy until that was reality. He preferred the shadows.

He looked down at his phone. He would take this call himself. He did not want Bashir here. The New Dawn were making demands and he found himself in a position that Bashir might consider weak.

And no one could ever think of the Dyab that way.

The phone rang. A man immediately began speaking. "We are on the island. Where is the meet?"

"There are complications. I need a week."

"You have four days."

He bristled and his other hand tightened around the metal railing. Who were they to threaten him? "You are guests on my island. You do not make demands."

The man on the other end started to chuckle.

*Who is this man who dares to laugh in the face of the Devil?*

The Dyab held the phone close to his mouth, ready to tell the man to go to Hell, but what he heard next froze the words in his throat.

"Listen to me very carefully, Sebastian. I know everything about you and your organization. You have four days. Look at your chest."

He glanced down. A red light shimmered and danced on the skin of his bare black chest.

The caller hung up, and the sniper sight winked out.

Glaring out in the darkness, his hand balled into a fist. He'd been betrayed. All who knew his real name were dead. Or so he'd believed. Yet this man discovered his true identity.

*And* located him.

Everything he had thought secure was threatened.

For the first time in a very long time, the Dyab was afraid.

# 28

Lukas parked the Kia in front of a small house with a blue
tarp covering the roof, and Jack handed him another
fifty.

Lukas nodded. He turned to Alice. "We have a guest house
out back. It survived da hurricane. My wife, she—"

The front door of the house opened and a woman peered
out. "Lukas? Why are you comin' home so late, honey?" When
she noticed Jack and Alice in the backseat her eyes went wide,
and she grinned from ear to ear. "Guests! One moment!" She
disappeared inside.

Lukas sighed. "My wife fixed up a guest house in de back.
She wants to start a bed-and-breakfast. You would be our first
guests." Lukas seemed very shy and gentle on his home turf. "It
is only seventy-five dollars a night."

Alice smiled. "That sounds wonderful."

The woman reappeared carrying a bag and armful of towels.
She hurried down the steps and over to the car.

"Welcome." She smiled as Jack and Alice got out. "I am Betty, ya hostess. Ya met my husband, Lukas." She made a motion for him to get out of the car. "He will get ya bags."

"We don't have any bags," Alice said.

"It was an impromptu trip," Jack added.

"It's our honeymoon," Alice said.

Betty looked like she was going to tear up. "And ya spendin' it with us? I am so honored. Den we will give ya da honeymoon suite!"

"There's only one suite," Lukas muttered.

Betty elbowed him and shot a quick glare at her husband. "If ya would follow me, I show ya to ya accommodation."

Jack, Alice, and Oliver started after Betty but she stopped abruptly after a few steps. "Not you, Oliver. You can sleep on da couch."

"What?"

"It's deir honeymoon. Explain to him, Lukas." She wiggled her eyebrows at Alice, and said, "Am I right, child?" Alice blushed and smiled at Jack.

Betty led them around the house to a darkened backyard. Jack could just make out the silhouette of a small hut.

"One second," Betty said, handing Alice the bag and Jack the towels. She stepped off the path and jogged around to the side of the house. After rummaging around in the bushes, she lifted up an orange extension cord and plugged it into the humming generator. Alice gasped as tiny white Christmas lights lit up the walkway and framed an adorable little cottage in a golden glow.

Betty smiled and took back the bag and the towels. "Right dis way."

Across the threshold was a sign: *Welcome! May all who enter leave as friends!*

Betty opened the door but blocked Jack when he started to walk through. Jack was about to explain he preferred to go into a room first to make sure it was safe, but Betty held both her arms out, pantomiming carrying something.

Jack cast a puzzled look back at Alice and she mouthed, *Me.*

"Oh." Not only had they not consummated their marriage yet, but he'd never carried Alice over the threshold. He'd injured his hand just before the wedding and Alice didn't want him to risk accidentally hurting it again. But one look at her face and he realized she wanted him to do it now.

Betty stepped to the side with a squeal and a little clap when Jack swept Alice up in his arms. She molded herself to his body and fit perfectly in his arms as he carried her inside, careful not to bump her head.

"Oh, wow!" Alice said as Jack set her down, blushing and smiling up at him.

Betty placed the bag and the towels on a side table. "Let me know if you need anyting." She grinned. "I doubt you will." She winked and closed the door behind her.

It was only one room, with a bathroom off to the right and a huge bed in the center, but the room felt much larger because the entire back wall was a sliding glass door, and beyond it was the ocean.

Alice strolled over to the glass door and opened it up. Jack moved to her side. A warm sea breeze wrapped around them.

"It's so beautiful," she whispered.

"So are you." He brushed his lips across hers, then moved down her neck with little kisses. Her arms wrapped around his waist and up his back. He held her close, the warmth spreading in his chest.

When her breathing sped up, he hoped she was feeling the same excitement he was. He lifted her and carried her over to the bed, kissing her even more passionately as he laid her down on the bed. Alice closed her eyes and tensed up.

"Look at me, angel," Jack whispered.

Frightened green eyes peered back up at him, but Jack held her gaze till the fear left.

"It's me, sweetheart." He kissed her again.

"I thought we were going to wait until after we caught the guy," Alice said, kissing him back.

After a minute, Jack pulled away and grinned at her. "Why? Don't you trust me to catch him?"

Alice nodded. "You know I do."

She started to close her eyes and Jack brushed her cheek with his hand. "Don't close your eyes. I want you to see how much I love you. I promise, Alice Stratton, I will never hurt you."

A tear ran down her cheek.

Jack brushed it away.

"Look up," Alice whispered. "That's how much I love you."

Jack looked through the giant skylight to the stars above. He gazed back at his wife and dove into her emerald eyes. Then, wrapped in the warm Caribbean breeze, they made love beneath the stars.

# 29

Oliver slipped out of Lukas's house, closing the door quietly behind him. Lukas and Betty had gone to sleep a while ago, Betty so happy that someone was staying in their backyard hut, you'd think that Lukas had made Christmas come early.

But Lukas was on edge, and no matter what Oliver told his old friend to calm his fears, Lukas was still nervous about the American tourists.

A pang of guilt swept over Oliver like the waves lapping at the shore. If Lukas knew how dangerous a game Oliver was involved in, he'd have nothing to do with it. And he hated involving Lukas, but he had no choice.

The street was deserted, and very few lights shone through the darkness. He continued to glance down at his phone as he walked, hoping his cell signal kept the one bar it was clinging to. Phones were working here again, but it was spotty at best now. He reached the bend in the road and looked out across the sea. Maybe, when all this was done, he'd go somewhere. Someplace inland, where he could get away from the constant lies and webs of deception.

If they'd let him go.

Oliver inhaled and turned his phone on. Just as quickly he shut it off, covering the glow from the screen by holding it against his chest.

A light had turned on in the hut where the Strattons were staying. Through the palm trees he could see Jack walk out on the little deck in the back. He was looking out to the endless sea. He suddenly started moving about, raising his hands up and ... dancing?

Why? He and his bride were being hunted by one of the most ruthless men imaginable. What reason did he have to be so joyful?

Jack stopped his happy dance and sat down on the railing. But he was no longer facing the water. He was looking inside the hut.

Oliver shook his head. Try as he might, he could not figure this Jack Stratton out. *He comes outside with paradise all around him, but instead of gazing at the stars or sea he stares back at what? A one-room hut? The only thing in there is his wife, and he just left her.*

*Oh ...* Oliver chuckled. *Newlyweds.*

Another pang of guilt washed over him. He hated deceiving them. They had no idea the true danger they were in, but what choice did he have?

Jack stretched and went back inside. Oliver dialed. The phone rang once. Two short mechanical beeps were followed by a long one and two more short ones.

"Currently on Abaco. Getting closer. Instructions?" Oliver waited. Sometimes someone on the other end spoke. Most often there would only be two acknowledging beeps and the line would go dead.

"You have three days. Then terminate."

Oliver inhaled sharply. As the questions churned in his mind, the line beeped twice and the call ended.

*Only three days?*

He swore. Stratton was doing a far better job than he at tracking down Andres. Oliver's plan had been sound. Help the Strattons find Andres, and then ... he closed his eyes.

*Then what?*

As he started to walk back to Lukas's, the sound of laughter from the newlyweds' hut drifted on the wind. Oliver stomped into Lukas's house so he wouldn't have to listen anymore and brushed the sand off his feet before throwing himself down on the lumpy sofa bed that Betty had made up for him.

Jack had three days to lead him to Andres. After that ... the honeymoon would be over.

# 30

The Dyab raced down the staircase and dashed to the cellar door. The metal door was secured with a keypad that only a few had the combination to. He punched in the code and yanked it open.

Lights flicked on down the stairs and along the corridor. The cellar had been modified into five separate rooms. The Dyab had made his *guests* as comfortable as he could. Each room was furnished like an upscale apartment complete with large scale TVs and spa baths, but there was still no denying what they were—cells. From the reclusive German businessman who really owned the villa, to the tourists whose bank accounts he was slowly draining, all of the rooms were full.

He headed to the end of the hall and opened the door.

The room was an immaculately furnished apartment. It was the largest of the basement dwellings with two sleeping quarters, a living room and a kitchen. Because of the lack of windows, there was an abundance of lights, although only one of the guests needed them.

Sitting on the couch was a nun next to a very thin man. She was reading aloud from a book but closed it shut as he stepped into the room.

Sister Angelica was in her early twenties. Her rich skin was even darker than his, a fact that somehow bothered him. Her brown eyes rounded in fear and she swallowed. She'd been sworn to service and lived here for two years now but still she was terrified of him. She nodded, whispered to Samuel that she would be in her room and hurried through the door on the left.

"Sebastian?" Samuel called, a thin smile crossing his gaunt face. His eyelids flickered, revealing the pits where his eyeballs had once been—before Sebastian had gouged them out. "She was just getting to the good part."

"Hello, brother." The Dyab walked over to the couch and sat down in the spot Sister Angelica had occupied. "We need to speak."

Samuel's face contorted in pain. "Is it the Dyab? Has he found us?"

"I told you, brother. The Dyab can no longer hurt you—ever."

Samuel nodded. "He took my eyes. I can't see, Sebastian."

Sebastian's nails dug into the palms of his hands. The memory of the day filled his mind and once again he felt like that helpless nine-year-old boy. He and Samuel had been catching fish in the marsh when they heard the shots. Samuel had gone to see what the noise was but Sebastian had been too afraid.

A large man had chased Samuel back through the weeds and straight to Sebastian. He caught the two boys and held them at gunpoint. As he pointed the gun at Sebastian's head, it didn't scare him. But the brand on the brute's forearm did. Three Vs on top of a straight then wavy line had been burned into the man's flesh.

The mark of the Devil.

"Please," Sebastian begged.

"Did you see the other man with me?" The man pointed the gun at Samuel.

Samuel nodded.

"You have seen the face of the Devil." The man stepped closer to Samuel. He raised the gun. "I can't let you live."

"Please don't kill my brother. Please!"

The man threw a knife at Sebastian's feet. "There is only one way I can spare his life. He must never be able to identify the Dyab."

As the tears rolled down his face, Sebastian picked up the knife.

After the deed was done, the man left. Samuel lived but his mind was never the same.

"Are you certain, Sebastian? He was a fat man with a mustache. Tall, like Father but with a hooked nose."

"The Dyab is dead," Sebastian explained for the hundredth time. He'd never admitted to Samuel that he killed the Dyab with his own hands. Even though the man had cost his brother his vision, Samuel would not approve of murder. But Sebastian couldn't let the Dyab live. Every day Samuel would describe him and every night Sebastian would go looking for him.

But if you seek out the Devil, it will lead you to hell. So Sebastian joined the black market. To get his revenge, he became what he detested. Everything Sister Elizabeth had warned them about in the orphanage was true. But Sebastian was willing to sell his soul to take the Devil's heart.

But there must always be a Devil. So Sebastian became the Dyab and embraced the power that came with the title. Then he had the man who tasked him with blinding his brother fed to crabs—alive.

"Have you spoken to anyone, brother?" Sebastian asked. "Anyone about me or our past?"

Samuel shook his head. "No one. As I promised. I've done just what you said. I only speak to Sister Elizabeth when she visits. Are you going to speak to her soon? You should. She said you keep avoiding her."

"I was away the last time she came to visit you."

"You are always away when she comes. She loves you. She prays for you—"

"Enough," Sebastian snapped.

Samuel cowered in his seat as if he had slapped him.

"I'm sorry." He placed a gentle hand on Samuel's shoulder. "You need to eat more, brother. You're too thin."

Samuel nodded.

The Dyab moved his hand to the back of the couch. The spot where Angelica had been sitting was losing its warmth. He could still smell her scent. Whatever soap she used smelled like a coconut. For a nun, with no makeup, she was an attractive woman. But he could not touch her. He'd given his word to Sister Elizabeth. In trade for a nun to take care of his brother, he would leave the church alone. He stared at Angelica's closed door. Oh, how he would love a taste of the forbidden fruit but she was very kind to his brother. He wouldn't cause him any more pain.

"What about Sister Angelica? Have you said anything to her?"

"No. I promised." Samuel tucked his chin to his chest.

Sebastian could tell Samuel was lying but the good sister's order was to Saint Anna, the patron saint of the blind. He was certain, even if she knew, she wouldn't say anything.

"I will come visit later," Sebastian said.

Samuel started rocking. Slowly back and forth with his hands on his knees. He was done speaking.

Sebastian closed the door.

Besides him and the nuns, no one ever spoke with his brother. But someone had told the New Dawn about him. The question was, who?

# 31

Renard set his breakfast sandwich down on the passenger
seat of his police car. Staring across the field of grass,
Renard watched his daughter on the swingset in the
playground, accompanied by two other little girls. It appeared
that she was making friends at her new school.

Renard twisted his wedding band on his finger. The divorce
wasn't finalized yet. As a policeman, he was never home. If he
were a sailor, he would mostly be at sea. If he were a lawyer, he
would be in court all the time. Still, it wasn't fair to them to be
involved so little in their lives.

That's why he'd left. His wife needed a husband to be there
for her. And his daughter needed a father. But now Bella seemed
so ...

The two girls playing with Bella ran off. Bella sat by herself
on the swing, but she wasn't swinging. Holding the chains with
both hands, her head was hanging and her shoulders were
slumped.

*What happened?*

He wanted to get out of the car and rush over to her—

"Inspector Renard?" the dispatcher called. "You've been requested to report to the north side docks immediately. Chief Inspector Fletcher will meet you at Pier 137 in half an hour."

Renard swore.

He started up the car, taking one last look at his daughter. Another girl was speaking with her now and Bella was talking animatedly, her ponytails bouncing as her head rocked on her shoulders.

*She'll be okay.*

Renard pulled onto the main road and waited until he was some distance away before turning on his sirens and lights. Normally, because of the tourists, he'd prefer not to draw undue attention, but Renard wanted to get to the docks well before the chief inspector.

Staying on the backroads, he bypassed the clogged center and reached the Grand Bahama Highway in less than five minutes and was at the north side piers in another five. A large crowd had gathered, and it was an agitated group. They started shouting questions as soon as he got out of the car. "Where are dem Americans? Ya got dem in custody? Where is ya investigation now? One of our bruddah's been killed, are ya gonna do anyting 'bout it?"

"I hear you, and we will be responding shortly," Renard repeated several times as he made his way down the dock and toward the group of police gathered around a small fishing boat.

Officer Rigby was busy trying to keep the crowd back while Officer Archibald, a competent man, marched up to Renard and saluted. "Sir, the fisherman over there"—he pointed to an older man with a blue-and-white bandana tied around his head and holding a wide-brimmed hat—"found a body early this morning."

"Name?" Renard asked.

"We haven't identified the body yet, sir."

Renard revised his earlier assessment regarding Archie's competence. "The name of the fisherman."

"Oh, of course, sir." Archie cleared his throat. "Raul Loquillo."

Renard marched over to Raul. "I am Inspector Renard. You discovered the body?"

Raul nodded. "It caught on my line and I pulled him in."

"Where were you fishing?"

"Off Crab Key."

Renard inhaled sharply but did his best not to reveal his surprise. The sea was a dangerous place, but still, two bodies in as many days in the same location went beyond coincidence.

"Did you touch the body in any way?"

"I pulled it into da boat." The man's expression soured. "I tought 'bout tyin' it off and comin' in with it but worried I'd lose it."

Renard nodded. "Please give your contact details to this officer and wait over there."

As Archie led Raul away, Renard turned his attention to the body. It was inside the boat and covered with a worn blue tarp. For some reason, the area of the chest was tented up.

Renard squatted down and carefully pulled the tarp away. The man's face was bloated and sunburned but otherwise usable for identification. The body couldn't have been in the water for long. A knife was protruding from the center of the man's chest. It was the same make as the knife used to kill Ramon Knowles.

Renard stood up and took out his phone. He pulled up the missing person's report for Charles "Chooch" Knowles. Flipping through the report on his phone, he located the picture and compared it to the dead man. In spite of the disfigurement, he was certain this was Charles Knowles.

A man in the crowd pushed forward and pointed into the boat. He cursed loudly.

"Control the scene, Rigby!" Renard ordered.

Rigby moved to push the man back but the larger man drove her back. "I saw dat guy two days ago! Leaving da harbor with Ramon."

Renard stood bolt upright and waved the man over. "Your name?"

"Judge Puckett. I seen dat guy with Ramon."

"When?"

"I did some night fishin' off Grey's Point a couple days ago. Was comin' back round nine in da mornin' when Ramon's boat was headin' out. I saw dat guy"—he thrust an arm towards Charles's body—"talkin' to Ramon. Dey both waved but da two snobs in da back didn't even look my way. Dey were too busy fightin'."

"They were fighting with Ramon?"

Judge shook his head vigorously then spit. "Each uddah. Quite da row. Da tall white guy was yellin' but da little woman was shoutin' back louder."

"Could you hear anything they said?"

"Da lady said she wasn't flirtin' with nobody. I could hear dat 'cause she was really lettin' him have an earful."

Renard held up his phone and showed the picture of Charles Knowles to Judge. "Is this the fourth man you saw on the fishing boat?"

Judge squinted then nodded. "Yeah, dat's him. Why?"

"You are certain that this man left the harbor on the boat with Ramon and the American tourists?"

Judge nodded.

"I need you to verbally confirm that fact."

"Yeah. Dat's da man I seen leaving on da boat with da Americans."

Renard called over to Officer Archibald. "Take this man down to the station. I want his declaration videotaped and witnessed."

"I've gotta be someplace," Judge complained.

"It will have to wait. We appreciate your cooperation."

Judge shrugged and nodded.

Officer Rigby hurried over to Renard's side. "Sir, the chief inspector is here." She pointed to the pier.

"Thank you, officer." Renard straightened his jacket. "Please keep the crowd controlled and away from that boat."

Rigby saluted. In a voice that seemed too loud for her frame, she ordered everyone back. "Quit your gawking. Have some respect. Step back now."

As Renard hurried up the pier, the chief inspector was marching down the plank. Renard snapped to attention, saluted and waited for Fletcher to reach the dock before he spoke.

"Dispatch reported a fisherman found a body off Crab Key where Ramon Knowles was diving."

"That's correct, sir. The victim has been positively identified as Charles Knowles, a missing local and Ramon Knowles' cousin."

"The Strattons said that the cousin was never at the docks."

"They're lying, sir. We have a credible witness who swears that he saw Charles Knowles leaving the harbor on Ramon's dive boat with the Strattons."

Fletcher pinched the bridge of his nose and exhaled loudly. "Just when I was hoping that the worst was behind us after the hurricane. Two tourists accused of murder is going to create a media storm." He leveled his gaze at Renard. "You're certain of your facts? This witness is reliable?"

"I am." Renard squared his shoulders. "Even the murder weapons are the same. The knife that killed Charles was thrust with such force that it is still stuck in his chest. That, the location of the body and the witness statement make me certain that the Americans are guilty."

"Then I will issue an arrest warrant for Jack Stratton for a charge of double murder."

# 32

Alice woke up with a smile dawning across her face. Before she even opened her eyes, she felt the warm tropical breeze blowing in from the open sliders. The man she loved was sleeping only a few inches from her. She rolled up on her elbow. His handsome face looked so peaceful. He'd been so patient. Most men, she would imagine, would have been going out of their mind, but not her Jack. He'd waited for her. Now she was the one who couldn't wait.

She brushed back an errant strand of hair from his brow. He moaned. She let her fingertips brush down the side of his face, his neck, his chest ...

His eyes fluttered open and filled with wonder. "Good morning, beautiful," he whispered. He kissed her. It was so intense her toes curled and her back arched. She wanted to feel him. Become one with him again.

Jack's phone rang. His hand shot out and he held it to his head. "This is Jack."

"Dis is Victor. He called."

"When?"

"Just now. He's afraid, hiding."

"Where?"

"In Freeport. He's gonna call me again at noon tomorrow. I told him I'd leave now."

"So will we. I can help him, Victor."

Victor exhaled. "He is da only male who carries on da family name. My dead bruddah's only remaining son. I'm trusting ya."

"I'll call you when we get back."

Victor hung up.

"That was Victor. Andres is on Grand Bahama," Jack said as Alice slid out of bed, narrowly avoiding his hands reaching for her.

"No, no, no." Alice shook her head as she grabbed her clothes off the floor.

Jack rolled onto his back and folded his hands behind his head. "Didn't you enjoy last night?"

"Too much." Alice blushed. "If you kiss me, I'll never let you out of that bed."

Jack jumped out and started getting dressed. "You mean that?" He flashed a roguish grin. "All the more reason to find Victor quickly so we can *really* start enjoying our honeymoon."

"Don't you worry. When this is all done, I'm going to lock us in a room together for a week."

\*\*\*

As the three of them reached Oliver's boat, the morning sun was a fiery red.

Alice's stomach tightened. "Oh, no. Looks like we're in for it."

"In for what?" Oliver asked, casting off the bow line.

She pointed at the sky. "Red sky at night, sailor's delight. Red sky in the morning, sailors take warning."

Oliver chuckled. "Do you really believe that old wives' tale?"

Jack gave a dismissive shrug of his shoulders. "Sometimes wives tell tales because they're true."

Once they had left the shelter of the harbor, they realized that the old wives were right. The sea was extremely choppy and black clouds hovered on the horizon. Oliver had to slow down because of the swells as the small boat was buffeted. Alice's stomach was starting to do flips.

A loud crash in the back of the boat made the three of them turn around. One of the bungee cords securing the diving equipment had let go and three air tanks and several pieces of gear skittered across the deck of the boat.

"Alice, can you take the wheel?" Oliver asked over the pounding surf.

Alice took the helm while Jack and Oliver collected the equipment and tried to lash it down. The captain's chair was too high for her, so she remained standing and planted her feet. The muscles in Alice's forearms stiffened as she gripped the steering wheel. Like trying to stay in lanes on a highway, Alice tried to keep between the swells as she struggled to steer the boat toward the harbor in the distance. After a few moments, she became so confident reading the water, she grabbed the throttle and began slowly speeding up or slowing down depending on the sea. She glanced over her shoulder at Jack. He finished lashing down the gear and he and Oliver held onto the railing as they made their way to the front of the boat.

"You didn't spare any expense with your gear," Jack said to Oliver, taking a seat beside Alice. "That stuff is top of the line."

"I got a great deal on it," Oliver said as he sat opposite Jack. "But business has been slow since the hurricane."

"I bet it'll pick up," Alice said, surprised Oliver hadn't tried to take over steering.

"Not with weather like this." Oliver shrugged. "But I took out three tours last week."

"Three!" Alice smiled. "That's awesome."

"How many typically go on a tour?" Jack asked.

"Anywhere from two to six. Not too many go solo, but I read that solo vacationing is starting to trend."

For the rest of the uneventful trip, they made small talk until they entered the harbor. Once they rounded the jetty, Alice guided the boat smoothly between the buoys and Oliver directed her toward his spot.

Jack stood up. "There are police at the dock."

Oliver shrugged. "Maybe they're still processing Ramon's boat?"

Jack shot Alice a quick look and shook his head. Her heart sped up. She knew that look on Jack's face—the one that made her feel like she was about to jump out of a plane. It meant, get ready for anything.

Oliver smiled. "Come up parallel to the dock, and then turn hard so we are facing back out. It makes leaving easier. I'll tell you when."

"Would you like to do this part?" Alice asked.

"You try it, Alice," Jack said. "I'm sure you can do it."

She picked up on his tone. He wasn't just being encouraging. He wanted her at the helm for some reason.

"See?" Oliver said. "We both believe in you."

Alice nodded and cut the wheel.

There were almost a dozen police on the dock. And standing by Inspector Renard was a man that appeared to have more seniority.

"Stay in the boat," Jack said. He untied the bowline and hopped out as the boat bumped against the dock.

Renard marched forward. "Detective Stratton." Like a military unit, all of the policemen, including the one who appeared to be his supervisor, also stepped forward. "You are under arrest."

"On what charge?" Jack asked.

"Two counts of murder."

"Two?"

"A fisherman confirmed that there were four of you who left the harbor in that boat. The other body has been discovered. Now drop the rope, turn around, and place your hands on top of your head."

Jack turned around but he didn't let go of the rope. He stared at Alice and that adorable, infuriating, crooked grin made his dimple pop. He mouthed, *GO!*

Alice jammed the throttle forward. Water shot high into the air as the engine roared to life. The rope in the back whizzed as it uncoiled.

Jack ran three steps and dove.

For a moment it looked like Jack was parasailing without a sail. The rope pulled taut and he flew through the air like a kite before plunging into the water.

"Halt!" Renard bellowed. "Stop that boat!"

The policemen on the dock stood there for a moment in disbelief before they started shouting and running around. Some of the police ran down the dock, chasing the boat on foot, while others ran in the opposite direction.

"Oliver!" Alice shouted. "Keep the rope away from the engine until I can stop!" The last thing she wanted was to escape the police only for Jack to be entangled in the boat's propellers.

"You should stop now!" Oliver yelled as he ran to the back of the boat. "The police ordered you to."

"I will," Alice said as she sped up. Glancing over her shoulder, she held her breath until Jack's head came out of the water.

He was clinging to the rope and staring at the policemen running along the dock beside them. With one hand he waved Alice forward. She jammed the throttle forward and the boat shot across the harbor.

"Bloody hell! You're not stopping!" Oliver yelled. "Pull the throttle back!"

Alice had no intention of stopping until they were clear of the end of the dock. Once she was a good way out into the harbor and certain no one could reach them, she pulled back the throttle. The boat slowed to a drift.

Oliver hauled in the rope and helped Jack over the side of the boat.

Jack stood up and brushed back his sopping mop of dark hair.

Alice ran to his side.

"Why the heck did you go so far?" Jack wiped his face.

"You waved me forward."

"I was waving at you to stop." Jack winced as he rubbed his wrist.

"Sorry." Alice shrugged. "I thought you wanted me to get where they couldn't shoot at us."

"They're Royal Bahamian Police," Jack said. "They're not going to—"

A bullet shattered the fiberglass siding to her right. Oliver hit the deck and Jack pushed Alice down. He raced to the front of the boat, grabbed the throttle and shoved it forward. The engine roared and water cascaded high into the air.

Another bullet hit the control panel.

"They can't shoot at us!" Oliver said. "That's against procedure!"

"Tell that to them!" Alice yelled as she crawled toward Jack. He was crouched down and peering over the steering wheel as they headed for the safety of the choppy seas outside the harbor. Alice crouched beside him and in spite of the fact that he was dripping wet, she hugged him. "What now?"

Jack stuck his hand in his pants pocket and pulled out his phone in the waterproof case. He kissed her. "First off"—he held up the phone—"these cases were genius."

Alice wiggled her eyebrows and kissed him back. She of course had no idea how useful they would be when she purchased them, but so far, they were better than travelers' insurance.

"We need to go someplace, hide, and wait for Victor's call," Jack whispered to Alice.

She nudged Jack's arm and motioned to Oliver, who was still hiding in the back of the boat.

Oliver held his hands up. "I don't want any trouble."

"Listen, we didn't kill that guy. Either of them." Jack pointed at the steering wheel and Alice took over driving.

With no idea where they were going, she kept the island within sight.

"Someone is framing us," Jack continued to explain to Oliver. "I don't know who or why, but you've got to believe me. When we see a spot, we can drop you off."

"You're taking my boat?"

"Look at it as a long-term rental. I'll pay you a thousand dollars a day."

Alice was surprised that Oliver seemed to be contemplating the offer. He thought for several moments, looking back and forth between Jack and Alice as the boat rocked on the waves. "I believe you. But either way now, I'm screwed." Oliver swore. "The police have to think I'm involved. I was with you when you escaped. You told them there was another boat out there when

Ramon was killed. The police probably think it was mine now." Oliver shook his head. "I'm as jammed up as you."

"We'll let you out and you can explain it to them."

"You think they're going to believe me when they didn't believe an American detective?"

"He's got a point, Jack," Alice said.

"It's Oliver's choice. Either we drop him off somewhere or he comes with us. What do you want to do, Oliver?"

Oliver exhaled and his heavy brows came together. "I can't believe I'm saying this, but it looks like we're in this together. I need to prove my innocence as much as you."

"The only one who knows what Ramon was mixed up in is his brother," Jack said. "We need to find someplace and wait until Andres contacts his uncle Victor or Irene and they reach out to us."

Oliver walked over to the console. "I know a place where we can hide."

# 33

The Dyab stormed across his grand living room, throwing open the twelve-foot doors to his office and marching through. Bashir scurried after him. A warm breeze blew in from the ocean and fluttered the papers on his desk. At the memory of the sniper's red dot on his chest, the Dyab stepped away from the open doors leading out to the balcony, kicked one shut with his foot, and leveled a finger at Bashir. "Close that door, too."

As if he sensed the danger, Bashir stayed close to the wall and shut the balcony door, darting across the opening like a rabbit in a field.

"Are you certain?" the Dyab seethed.

"The police are certain. The Strattons escaped."

"How?"

Bashir stepped to the side, back toward the office entrance, but the Dyab pinned him in place with a glare. Bashir swallowed. "I am still gathering the details, but one of our men was there. He is outside, and I'm sure he can fill in—"

The Dyab waved his hand and his two huge enforcers flanked both sides of the door, raising their machine guns to chest level as they went.

"Bring him in."

Bashir waited for the Dyab to move behind the screen before he opened the door and motioned in.

A young man, just out of his teens, walked through the door on shaking legs. He paled when his blindfold was removed. His eyes traveled around the room until they landed on the tri-paneled, ornate screen. Crafted from African blackwood, one of the hardest woods on the planet, the tinted screen panes not only shielded his face but they were bulletproof as well. The panel itself did little to instill fear. Until the Dyab had his symbol crafted in bone on the top. The legend quickly spread that it was made from the bones of his enemies and the legends were true.

"Tell me what happened at the docks."

"The cops blew it. They let da guy get out of da boat but da lady was still at da wheel. The inspector tells da American to put his hands up and turn around but da guy didn't drop this rope he was holdin'. I tought it was weird but the lady gunned it and da guy held on and ..." James's eyes widened. "He flew through the air like Batman. He held on and she drove out into da harbor."

"When did you shoot?"

James started tapping his foot. "When dey stopped. The cops were running around on da docks like rats. Word was you wanted the Americans caught and I thought—"

"I want them *caught*. Not *dead*. The police chased you?"

His legs were shaking so hard, his knees knocked together. "I lost dem after da beach parking lot."

The Dyab looked down at his desk. He could just shoot the boy and send a message to his men, but ... "Did you know Chooch?"

"We were friends."

The Dyab smiled. "Go to the police and turn yourself in." The man's eyes widened, while the Dyab's narrowed. "You will be well compensated. Tell the police that Chooch told you he was going out with the Americans two days ago. That was all he said—he and Ramon were taking two American honeymooners out on Ramon's boat—and now two friends of yours are dead. When you saw the Americans escaping, you became so angry you shot at them. Understand?"

He nodded.

"Take him straight to the police," the Dyab ordered.

The enforcer nodded, replaced the blindfold and led the man out of the room.

In forty-five minutes, James would be back in Freeport and doing the Dyab's bidding. Still, this was only damage control. He needed to tip the balance back in his favor.

The Dyab marched over to his desk, removed the crystal stopper of the decanter of rum and poured himself a drink. "These Americans are proving to be a real problem. Put the word out that whoever locates them gets fifty thousand US dollars."

Bashir acknowledged the order with a nod.

The Dyab turned toward the closed balcony. He downed half the glass in a gulp. He wanted to feel the sea breeze on his face, but he couldn't enjoy even this simple pleasure now. He was trapped inside his own house, a panther longing to breathe the jungle air. "There is now a reward of two hundred fifty thousand dollars for Andres. I want him found today."

Bashir nodded, but his rounding mouth and slight gasp betrayed his surprise. "There are two other things you should be aware of, sir. Oliver Rolle is with the Americans."

The Dyab raised an eyebrow. "Did he go along with them willingly?"

"That we do not know. But he is with them."

"And?"

"Sister Elizabeth is on her way."

The Dyab frowned. "Tell her I'm not here. She wishes to visit with Samuel anyway."

"Actually, she specifically requested to speak with you. She said she had to ask you a personal favor."

The Dyab walked behind his desk and sat down. "Leave now."

Bashir nodded and backed out of the office, closing the large doors behind him softly.

The man the world knew as the Dyab sat staring at the metal palm fronds of the ceiling fan slowly spinning. He couldn't be bothered with the silly nun and whatever it was she desired. She probably wanted to pray once more for his soul.

He had more important matters to attend to. If Oliver was still with the Strattons, and the Dyab played his cards right, he could solve all of his problems with one move. A smile slowly dawned on his face. He downed the rest of the rum, setting the glass down with a loud click. He leapt to his feet, his chair sliding back and bumping into the bookcase.

He marched over to the balcony and threw open the doors. The sea breeze rushed to embrace him like an old friend. Strutting forward, the Dyab stopped at the railing and slowly unbuttoned his shirt. He glanced down at the ebony sheen of his chest. No red dots appeared, but he was certain they were watching.

He flashed a broad smile, raised his arms out wide and laughed into the wind. He would show everyone what happens to those who take on the Devil.

# 34

J ack and Alice sat in the back of the little toolshed Oliver had
brought them to. He'd said the friend who owned it was
traveling so there was no need to explain their presence. Still,
Jack wondered why Oliver had the combination to the lock. As
soon as Oliver dropped them off, he said he had an errand to
run and he'd be back as soon as he could.

The shed was no bigger than Jack imagined the prison cell
would be if he didn't get them out of this mess. It was filled with
miscellaneous parts from boats, cars, and one old hybrid
motorcycle with keys in the ignition.

"What are you thinking about?" Alice asked.

Jack wiggled his eyebrows and she blushed.

"You really need to work on your timing," Alice said. Her
smile faded. "I think we are in real trouble. We've gotta make it
home to Lady."

Jack knew Alice would've taken their one-hundred-twenty-
pound King Shepherd with them if she could've, honeymoon or
not.

"I'm sure Lady is fine with Mrs. Stevens. She is probably giving her homemade treats every hour on the hour."

"You're right about that. Mrs. Stevens is the world's best dog sitter."

Jack took her hand and twirled her wedding ring a few times around her finger. "I'm debating about going to a friend of mine at the State Department. They may be able to get us out of the Bahamas, but we'll still be charged. And then we'd have to rely on someone else trying to prove we're innocent."

Alice made a face.

"Exactly." Jack grinned. "If I'm going to go to jail, I'd rather go down swinging."

"If *we* go to jail." Alice moved over to sit beside him. "Sickness and health, blah, blah, blah... Remember?" She bumped his shoulders. "You're not thinking about trying to fly solo on this, are you?"

Jack sighed. His mind was consumed with keeping Alice safe, even if that meant calling in a Yakuza assassin to do so. "I really don't want to, but I can't even think about you in prison. If we don't find Andres soon, I'm calling Kiku to get you out of here. She can make you disappear."

"You mean, she can make *us* disappear?"

Jack shook his head. "If we both go on the run, the manhunt will be crazy. If I turn myself in—"

Alice flicked his ear.

"Ow!" Jack swore. "That actually hurt."

"Good." She grabbed his chin. Her green eyes were tearing up. "I need you like I need air. We are in this mess together."

"Kinda soon to be calling our marriage a mess, wifey," Jack teased.

Alice kissed his ear.

Jack's phone buzzed in his pocket. They both jumped up as he pulled it out.

"Hey, buddy!" his father said. "How goes the honeymoon?"

Alice chuckled and Jack rolled his eyes.

"Actually, Dad—" His phone buzzed again and the caller ID showed an unknown number. "Call you back," Jack blurted out as he switched calls.

Alice snuggled back up beside him, angling her head so she could hear.

"Stratton?" Victor asked.

"Yes. Have you heard anything?"

"He just called again from a payphone. He's very upset. Ya need to promise me dat you ga get him to da American Embassy."

"I will. I need to get myself and my wife there as well."

"Dat's why I tell you dis. Ya ga ... skin in da game. Andres hidin' in an equipment shack at da Mayfield Beach and Tennis Club, back of da lake. Can ya find it? It near East Palm Beach. I told him ya ga come."

"Hold on, Victor." He turned to Alice and said, "Got that?"

Alice nodded.

"We'll find it. Did he say anything else?"

"He scared. Da Dyab put a bounty on his head. A quarter a million US dollars."

Alice gave a low whistle. Jack's stomach plunged. Whatever Andres was involved in, someone took it very seriously.

"Dere is also a reward for you and ya wife of fifty thousand dollars. I ga now." The call disconnected.

Alice was scowling. "Why's the reward for us so little?"

"Because you are," Jack joked.

"That's not funny." Alice gave him a light punch in the gut, but it was harder than her usual teasing. Her karate training was paying off.

"We have to get out of here." Jack stood up, straddled the old motorcycle, and turned the key. The engine sputtered and didn't turn over. He tried three times more and it finally coughed to life. "Looks like we have a ride," he said.

Alice opened the shed doors.

Jack rolled the bike outside.

The storm had blown past and the sun was shining. Jack stared from the little puddles on the ground to the blue sky above. He closed his eyes and prayed that the storm he and Alice were in passed as quickly.

"I sure hope this thing doesn't blow up while I'm on it." Alice climbed on behind him.

"What happened to *we?*" Jack grinned.

"My butt is more delicate than yours," she shot back.

Jack pulled away from the shed and down the sandy road. The bike's engine started to even out, but with the bald tires and bad shocks, it was a bumpy ride.

"You don't want to wait for Oliver?" Alice asked.

Jack reached the main road and sped up. "I don't trust him," Jack admitted. "And it's going to be hard enough convincing Andres to trust us without three of us showing up."

Alice nodded and took out her phone, glad she and Jack both had theirs. She'd learned a lot doing private investigation work and what to do to your phone to not be tracked. "It's a twenty-minute drive. Do you think this thing will make it?"

The bike was shimmying a little, but the engine sounded a little stronger. Jack believed the bike could survive the ride. What he didn't know was what they'd find once they got there.

# 35

Jack slowed the little motorcycle down as the light in front of him turned red. The engine sputtered. Jack planted his feet and gave it a little gas. It choked and coughed. He started rocking the bike back and forth.

"What are you doing?" Alice asked, tightening her grip on his waist.

"There might be water in the gas tank. The bike must have been sitting for a while."

Jack's heart sped up as a police cruiser pulled up behind him. The engine sputtered and died.

Jack flipped up his visor. "Cops behind us. Don't turn around." This time Alice complied. He tried starting the engine. It cranked and chugged but didn't turn over.

The light turned green. A car beeped its horn. The cruiser hit its lights.

Jack swore. Flipping his visor back down, he started walking the bike over to the side of the road. "Wave the police on. Look ditzy and pretty."

Alice started motioning for the policeman to go around them, but the cruiser pulled in behind the motorcycle. Alice's voice took on a slight sing-song lilt, "He's getting out."

The police cruiser door swung open.

Jack tried again, but the engine only sputtered.

The middle-aged policeman with a bit of a paunch slid out of the cruiser and ambled over.

"Act like a tourist," Jack whispered as he slid off the motorcycle. "Hi, Officer," Jack called out. "Thanks for stopping, but I got this. A little water in the gas."

The policeman nodded, smiled, and ignored Jack as he strolled up. "Boy, what's that? An '82?"

Jack shrugged and looked at the pieced-together motorcycle. "It's more of an '82, '83, '87 ..."

The cop laughed. "Johnny Cash, 'One Piece at a Time'! I love that song." He walked over and stared down at the engine. He stood there for a minute and reached out. "Excuse me, miss." He leaned forward as Alice, who was still sitting on the bike, leaned back. The policeman removed the gas cap and held it up for Jack to see. "The air vent is blocked." He rapped it against the handle bars, screwed it back on and said to Alice, "Give it a try."

Alice made a face. "I only know how to hang on."

"You need to learn to be more than just ballast." The policeman gave her a fatherly look. "I taught my daughters to ride. All five of them." He peered at the dashboard. "It's already in neutral and the engine is warm, so you don't need the choke. Pull the clutch in. It's the handle on the left."

Alice pulled the handle in.

"Hit the start button."

She did and the engine sputtered to life.

"That's awesome." Jack smiled. "Thank you so much." He reached for the handlebars.

"Hold on there a second." The policeman frowned. "Your tag is expired. I'm sorry, but I'm going to have to write it up. I need your license."

Jack nodded and reached for his pocket. He feigned surprise as he patted himself down and then gritted his teeth. "Oh, no! I left it at that restaurant."

Alice rolled her eyes. "All of our money's in there!"

"Both of you hold on." The policeman shook his head. "It's not the end of the world. Take a deep breath and we'll figure this all out."

"But it has all of our credit cards too!" Alice whined.

The policeman gave her a sympathetic smile. "Both of you just wait right here."

The engine started to sputter as the policeman walked away.

"Give it a little throttle," Jack said. "The one on the right."

Alice gave it some gas. "What are we going to do, Jack?"

"Hey, what restaurant was it?" the policeman called back.

"The Fair Wind!" Jack called back, remembering the name of the little diner they passed a few miles back.

The policeman's eyes widened. His hand shifted to his gun.

Jack swore. Now as he pictured the restaurant's parking lot, he didn't remember seeing any cars in the parking lot. Maybe it was closed. Either way, the cop was no longer buying their story. Jack jumped on the bike behind Alice.

"You're in the wrong spot!" Alice shouted but Jack didn't have time to get her off the bike and back on behind him.

"Put your feet on the front pegs!" Jack shouted before pinning back the throttle and flying across the intersection.

Police sirens sounded behind them. Cars pulled out of the way. The little engine revved as high as it could, but the bike topped out at sixty. There was no way he was going to outrun the cruiser rapidly gaining on him.

"Hang on!" Jack called out.

"To what!?!" Alice screamed. With Jack's hands on the grips, the only place she had to hold onto was the center of the handlebars.

Jack jammed on the brakes, cut the wheel, and did a U-turn onto the sidewalk. The cruiser skidded to a stop, but the policeman looked completely confused as to what to do next as Jack rocketed past him. Pedestrians leapt out of the way as Alice waved with one hand, shouting, "Sorry!"

Jack turned down the first side street he came to. On the left, there was an alley with two cement poles blocking the way from vehicular traffic. But the space between the poles was wide enough for the motorcycle to fit—hopefully.

Jack turned down the alley, chancing a glance over his shoulder back at the street. The cruiser was nowhere in sight. He slowed down on the uneven pavement of the alley, dodging trash cans and boxes lining the walls.

"Let's switch places," Alice called out, but Jack kept going.

"No," he yelled, "if a cop sees us from behind it will look like one rider on the bike and not two." At least he hoped it would.

At the end of the alley, Jack turned back onto the road. He heard sirens two streets over but they were moving in the other direction. Slowing down, he stopped at the red light, next to a delivery truck.

"Find directions to the Mayfield Tennis Club using backroads," he said.

Alice wiggled the phone in her hands. "Already on—GO!" Alice screamed, looking to the right.

Jack didn't have time to look, but he trusted Alice implicitly. He cranked the throttle back and shot over the curb just as a Mustang careened toward them.

From the determined look on the driver's face, there was no doubt what his intentions were. He was trying to crush Jack and Alice into the side of the truck.

Alice screamed.

Jack pulled the handlebars hard to the left, keeping the throttle pinned back.

The Mustang's bumper passed inches away from the rear tire. Metal and glass crunched behind them as the car smashed into the side of the truck.

The motorcycle skidded into the intersection as pieces of glass pinged off Jack's back.

A horn blared as a van slammed on its brakes, skidding straight at them. Jack jammed on his brakes and cut the wheel.

The motorcycle stalled.

As Jack tried to restart the engine, he chanced a look back at the car that almost killed them. The driver was gunning the car in reverse but the Mustang's front bumper was caught on the side of the truck.

The man in the passenger seat was yelling something as he tried to deflate the airbag that had deployed in his face. He turned to glare at Jack and raised a gun.

The motorcycle's engine coughed twice and started. Jack cranked the throttle.

The Mustang's tires spun, sending smoke billowing into the air. Metal shrieked and the front bumper of the car tore free.

Jack drove between two parked cars and back onto the sidewalk. Pedestrians scrambled out of the way as Jack turned in between two large buildings. A grassy courtyard divided the buildings with a walkway in between, but it was crowded with people. Jack cut the wheel and headed across the grass, but riding across the slick turf was like driving on ice as the bike slid at the slightest adjustment. He was grateful Alice was in front of him so she'd be shielded from the gunshots, but depending on the caliber of the bullet, his body might not provide enough protection for her.

"Are you okay?" he yelled.

"Yeah!" she shouted. "But I should have gotten a picture of their license plate."

Jack reached the next street and checked his rearview mirror. A different muscle car was racing up behind them—a Camaro.

"Hold on!" Jack took a right and sped up.

The road widened into three lanes.

The Camaro slid into the curve and started gaining rapidly on the small motorcycle. Jack cut to the left of a line of busses riding in the middle lane. The Camaro cut to the right. The Camaro's engine roared as the driver punched the gas and quickly pulled parallel to them on the opposite side of the busses.

"Drive straight!" Alice yelled, taking off her helmet.

Jack hesitated. If he kept going straight, once they passed the last bus, they would be directly next to the Camaro. All the driver would have to do was cut the wheel to take them out.

"Trust me!" Alice shouted.

Jack kept the throttle back and the bike on its course. They passed the front of the last bus at the same time as the Camaro.

There were two men in this car, too. The driver smiled.

The bike rocked as Alice's weight shifted. She threw her helmet as hard as she could. It spun through the air and smashed into the driver's face. Blood splattered the Camaro's windshield. The driver jerked the wheel to the right and the Camaro slammed into the back of a parked truck without hitting its brakes.

The sound of rending metal filled the air along with the muffled explosions of airbags deploying.

Jack took a left and slowed down. "Great shot!" He patted Alice's back.

Sirens blared as the police descended on the scene from all directions.

"Take this left." Alice pointed.

Jack turned onto a tree-lined street and gunned it. From the volume of the approaching sirens, the police were pulling out all the stops.

Alice leaned back against him. "What now?"

"The cops are going to try to box us in. We need to get out of here before they do."

Alice yelled back, "What are our chances?"

Jack put his lips against her ear and said, "With you at my side? How can we fail!"

# 36

Renard shouted into the police radio, "Block off Sunrise Highway at Coral Road and Santa Maria. Block off The Mall and Beachway!" He held onto the roof handle as the cruiser cut around a truck.

Officer Rigby took one of her hands off the steering wheel and pointed down the street. "Suspects sighted, sir!" Her voice rose excitedly, as did the speed of the car.

Renard glanced at the speedometer. Because of the tourist traffic, there was an official limit of seventy-five miles an hour for police chases. "Observe the regulations, Officer Rigby," he reminded her.

Rigby slowed down but they were still gaining on the motorcycle, which was headed straight to the roadblock on Santa Maria.

Renard smiled as he checked his side mirror and saw two other police cruisers behind them. His adrenaline was kicking in, but so were his fears. This Jack Stratton was proving to be a major embarrassment. The story of his escape from the dock was already circling around the police station, and Chief Inspector Fletcher had requested a personal meeting with Renard. Lately their interactions had been less than friendly.

Renard grit his teeth. Jack Stratton wouldn't escape this time. They had him cornered.

"He's slowing down," Rigby said.

"Prepare to stop," Renard said, then repeated the order into the microphone.

He watched as Stratton gunned the throttle, cut to the left, and shot across the yard between two homes.

Rigby turned after him.

"Do not attempt to follow!" Renard held up his radio. "We will simply tighten the net until he has nowhere to go." He ordered the other units into position.

Rigby took a hard left, but they only caught a glimpse of the motorcycle as it cut across the street and continued to drive between the houses. The road they were on reached a T intersection and Rigby headed right.

"What's in that direction, Officer?" Renard asked as he attempted to read the map on the console while the cruiser swerved around traffic.

"St. George's High School," Rigby said. "My son goes there. They're out on break."

"This is unit 42." The radio crackled. "Suspect vehicle in sight. Heading east on Sunrise."

"Unit 7, block off Sunset Highway. Unit 14, move to Britannia Circle." Renard was feeling more like a football coach than a police officer as his eyes finally focused on the map.

"This is unit 42. Suspect is driving across the school field. Permission to follow?"

Renard gritted his teeth. "Denied. Stay on the road. We have him boxed in."

Rigby reached a straightaway and sped up.

Renard depressed the microphone button. "Unit 42 report."

Both Rigby and Renard stared at the silent radio.

"Unit 42? Confirm," Renard called again.

"This is unit 42. We lost visual."

Renard and Rigby exchanged a puzzled glance.

"How could you lose sight of him?"

"The suspect went *into* the school, sir."

"All units." Renard exhaled, a smile stretching across his face. "Suspects now on foot. Converge on—"

"This is unit 42. That's incorrect, sir. Suspects entered the school still riding the motorcycle."

Rigby chuckled and Renard scowled. "Block off the entrance, Unit 42."

"Which one, sir?"

Renard glared at Rigby. "You know the school. What entrances are there?"

Rigby shrugged. "Dozens. At least the main one and one on both the East and West sides. And the classrooms have doors that open to the outside, too."

"Speed up."

"I'm at the limit, sir."

"Damn the limit. Get us to that school!" Renard's grip tightened on the ceiling handle. "All units report locations."

One by one the responding police cruisers radioed in their locations and Renard's fears started to ease. With over a dozen responding units, there was no way Stratton could get away this time. He had nowhere to go. They'd herd him toward the beach and he'd be trapped by the sea.

"This is unit 42. Still no visual. What? Wait. He's behind us!"

"Turn around!" Renard wanted to climb through the radio.

"Suspect is cutting across the field. He's heading out through a small gate in the fence. We cannot follow."

"I order you to continue pursuit!" Renard bellowed.

"We're continuing pursuit but... the cruiser can't fit through the gate, sir."

Renard jammed his finger down on the console screen and turned to Rigby. "Is that a farming field Stratton is heading to?"

She shook her head. "It used to be. There's a new tourist business there now. Paramotoring."

Renard's eyes widened.

*Would he? Could he? No!*

"Attention all units! Converge on the field north of Lucaya Beach."

# 37

J ack and Alice raced across the field toward the small group of people standing next to the shed that Kevin used as his base of operations. Jack braked and gave the old motorcycle a pat—she'd gotten them as far as she could.

Kevin stepped forward, a confused look on his face that changed into a smile when he recognized them. "Jack? Have you returned for a repeat ..." The smile disappeared and the two couples waiting for a lesson took a few steps back as sirens filled the air and police cruisers approached from all directions.

"Not exactly." Jack hurried over to the power glider and began putting on the harness. "I hate to do this to you, Kevin, but I really need to borrow one of the tandems. I'll pay for it later."

Kevin grimaced and one beefy hand balled into a fist, which the two couples took as a cue to run for the safety of the shed. "Are you crazy? I can't let you take my equipment!"

"Hold onto this." Alice handed Kevin a credit card. "There's five thousand on it and we'll pay you double."

"I promise we're good for it," Jack said. "And you gotta believe me. This"—he pointed back at the approaching cruisers—"is all a big misunderstanding."

Kevin rolled his eyes as he pushed the card back to her. "I knew you were trouble, Jack Stratton. I can't help you but I won't stop you. Besides, insurance will cover it." He turned and ran to join his clients cowering by the shed.

Jack started helping Alice with her harness as two police cruisers raced down the dirt road, huge clouds of dust flying into the air behind them. Four more were barreling across the field.

Jack hooked Alice's harness to his. "Alice, I know you really hate heights, but—"

She cut him off, shouting over the roar of the fan. "What do I have to do?"

"Start running with me and then hang on. Ready?"

"Not really!" she yelled, but they were already breaking into a quick jog together. The glider behind them caught the wind, and Jack pulled down on the toggles. The jolt in his stomach as they lifted off was two-thirds exhilaration, one-third fear. Alice screamed and pressed her body against Jack's as their feet were jerked away from the ground.

Jack pulled down on the cables and the glider rose a little, but not as quickly as Jack would have liked.

A police cruiser skidded to a stop fifty yards in front of them. Two policemen climbed up onto the roof.

With so little windspeed, Jack didn't dare turn and risk stalling. But one of the cops was tall ...

The policemen jumped.

Alice screamed as his hands bumped her feet. The taller cop caught hold of Jack's ankle and the glider pitched toward the field. Jack cranked the throttle and shook his leg but the policeman wouldn't let go. They were heading back to earth. The engine whined. It wasn't strong enough to get aloft with the weight of the three of them.

Jack lifted up his right foot, ready to kick blindly at the policeman's hand. They were only a few yards away above the field and once the policeman's feet touched the turf, he would pull them back down to the ground.

Jack peered between his feet.

The policeman's grip tightened on Jack's leg. He looked up at Jack and grinned.

Alice leaned forward and threw up.

It smacked the cop right in his wide-open smile. Gagging, he let go and bounced off the field as the power glider shot upward.

"Sorry!" Alice called out.

Jack laughed.

The glider lifted higher and Jack breathed a sigh of relief as he saw the police cruisers surrounding the field. There would have been no escape if they'd stayed on the motorcycle. Now they had a chance.

The air was swirling with dust from the cruisers, but Jack recognized the short, rotund figure of Inspector Renard standing with his door open, speaking into a microphone.

Turning the glider south, Jack took them higher. A hole appeared in the glider canopy, quickly followed by another. Jack swore as he twisted the handles and rocketed back toward the ground.

"Not down again!" Alice shrieked.

"Someone's shooting at us!" Jack shouted. "It's not the cops."

The muzzle flashes were coming from a truck parked alongside the road. Two men stood next to the truck. Further up the street, another car skidded to a stop. The driver got out, but he had a rifle.

"Hold on."

"Please no. Please no," Alice groaned as Jack steered for the treetops at the end of the field.

Jack flew even lower, aiming for just above the trees, hoping to use them for cover as more holes appeared in the canopy.

"Trees! Trees!" Alice shouted as leaves and branches rustled just a few yards beneath their feet.

"Sorry!" Jack shouted, but there really was no good choice between getting shot or Alice's fear of heights.

A loud, metallic clang pinged over the roar of the motor.

"Are you okay?" Jack yelled.

Alice answered by throwing up again.

A glance backward showed Jack that the cars that had been shooting at them were now racing off in the opposite direction, with several police cruisers chasing after them.

Jack eased the glider up but still stayed low. They might have lost some of the cruisers following them, but the police had radios and plenty of backup.

Steering south, Jack headed toward the coast. All he had to do was follow it a couple of miles until they reached East Palm Beach and the tennis club.

He risked giving Alice's shoulder a quick squeeze. "Hang in there, babe."

"I don't have much choice!" Alice called back. "I'm fine. Thanks for saving us."

"It's a good thing those guys shot at us."

"How's that?"

"They must be the guys who killed Ramon. Maybe the police will believe us now."

***

Renard grabbed the microphone and took a deep breath. His men were all shouting into their radios. The Strattons had miraculously escaped, skimming over the treetops while shots were being fired from two different unknown cars at the far side of the field.

"Units 42 and 9, pursue suspect truck southbound on Pinta. Units 7 and 14, pursue vehicle fleeing west on Beachway. All other units follow me." Renard hung up the microphone and glared at Rigby, who was pouring a bottle of water on Hansen's head to wash the vomit from his face.

"Come on, Hansen. You're not shot! Wipe your face off and follow me. Rigby, drive!"

Rigby dropped the water bottle and rushed over to the car as Hansen used his shirt to wipe his face.

Renard picked the microphone back up and called dispatch. "This is Inspector Renard requesting an immediate helicopter unit." Once Stratton got to the edge of the field, it would be very difficult to follow in a vehicle through the warren of inlets and canals beyond East Palm Beach.

"Please repeat that, sir?" the dispatcher asked.

Renard inhaled and spoke very slowly. "This is Inspector Renard. I am requesting a helicopter unit."

"I'll need authorization, sir."

"I'm authorizing it!" Renard snapped.

"I'll have to contact the chief inspector, sir."

"Go ahead. Now. And once you get it, inform the helicopter that the suspects are in ... It's a ... a glider with a giant fan."

Rigby cleared her throat. "A paramotor, sir."

"A paramotor," Renard repeated and hung up the microphone. "What are you waiting for?" He glared at Rigby. "Drive."

"Where, sir?"

"East Palm Beach," Renard muttered, leaning out his window and glaring in the direction the Strattons had gone.

Rigby stomped on the gas and the cruiser bounced across the field.

The radio crackled to life. "This is unit 16 ... Inspector Renard, sir. You're not going to believe this."

Renard picked up the microphone with one hand and smoothed his mustache with the other. Regarding the Strattons, right now nothing would surprise him.

"We lost them, sir."

"How in the bloody world could you lose them? Look up!"

"They're nowhere in sight."

*Where can they have gone?*

"Orders, sir?"

Renard closed his eyes for a moment to gather his composure before speaking. "They either crashed or landed. Have all available units respond to the area."

He glared upward and saw not even a cloud in the sky, let alone the Americans who were causing so much trouble. Still, he felt calmer as he looked around. He was on his home turf; he knew these islands and these streets like he knew his daughter's face. Stratton might have gotten away for now, but there was no way he would ever escape the Bahamas.

# 38

Dimitri searched the sky as Vadik drove the car slowly down the beach road, as police vehicles zipped around them with their sirens on.

"Who do you think was shooting at them?" Vadik asked.

Dimitri cupped his hand against his brow and squinted at the tree line. "Not the police, obviously."

"Then who?"

"Think. Whoever killed Ramon is trying to get the Strattons blamed for his murder. It looks like they are now trying to give them to the police too."

"So it is the other bidder. The one who killed Ramon."

"*Da.*"

"But who is that?"

"If the situation were reversed, and you found something that was valuable but you didn't know what to do with it, where would you go? If you were home, that is."

Vadik shrugged. "Not to the police."

Dimitri continued to scan just above the treetops. He always tried to get his men to reach conclusions themselves. It built them up and drove the point home at the same time.

Vadik's eyes widened. "I would go to the underground."

Dimitri nodded. "Here, that would be the Dyab."

Vadik's brow wrinkled as he slowed down and stopped at a red light. "So you think the Dyab is the other bidder?"

Dimitri nodded. "Or acting as an intermediary."

Vadik put on his left turn signal.

"Go straight."

"But the police said the paramotor crashed over that way."

"Stratton did not crash."

"How do you know?"

"The police think he crashed because they can't see him. He was flying just over the treetops."

"But we can see over the trees." Vadik kept the left directional on.

"Now he is flying lower than the trees."

"Down a street?" Vadik laughed and rolled his eyes. "That's impossible because of the telephone lines."

Dimitri thrust his arm out, pointing straight down the road. "No. He's taking the canal. Go! Go!"

The light changed and Vadik sped through the intersection.

Dimitri frowned at the cloudless sky. "Pull over. Shut off the engine."

Vadik did as he was told and Dimitri opened his door to listen, trying to ignore the hum of traffic from the street. Over the ambient noise, he heard a different kind of motor—the kind he was listening for. It was drawing closer. Where the trees thinned out and the canal emptied into the marshy section of the coast, the paramotor briefly flew into view. Stratton was flying just above the surface of the water.

Vadik pointed and his mouth fell open. He swore both in Russian and Greek.

"He's heading for the beach." Dimitri pointed at the sky. More paramotors and parasails dotted the skyline in the distance. "Don't lose them."

"I won't." Vadik started the car and sped toward the coast.

Every fiber of Dimitri's body tingled, his senses sharp. He was on full alert with Jack and Alice in his crosshairs.

# 39

The Dyab sat in his office waiting impatiently. He sipped a glass of rum and glanced at the empty decanter. He'd always been able to hold his liquor but he really should slow down. There were too many loose bits flying that he struggled to make sense off. Someone was making a move against him. That much was clear.

After just putting down one uprising, he thought it would be years before there was another. But Ramon and Mateo were dead. Someone had fed information to the New Dawn. He would find out who.

There was a faint knock on the door and silence.

The Dyab smiled. He waited.

Another knock, only slightly louder.

"Come in," he called.

The door creaked open.

Sister Angelica peered across the threshold but didn't come in. She didn't move. Like a doe in the forest, she stood there frozen, looking like she would flee at any moment.

Like the timid deer, there was beauty in her vulnerability. Her brown eyes widened. Her slender throat swallowed.

How long had it been since he'd been with a woman?

"You wanted to see me, sir?"

The Dyab motioned to the chair across from his desk.

With quick, fleeting steps, Angelica hurried over and sat.

"I need to know about you," the Dyab began, pausing to take a sip of his rum.

"Me, sir?" She didn't meet his gaze. "Is everything alright with how I am caring for Samuel?"

"Fine. Fine." The Dyab rose. "But I want to know about you, Angelica." He slowly circled the desk until he was next to her chair. "You tell stories to my brother." He reached down and lifted her chin. It trembled as she looked into his eyes. "Tell me your story, Angelica." Her skin was soft, warm.

"I don't really have a story, sir. I'm a nun."

The Dyab let go of her chin and chuckled. "You weren't always a nun, were you?"

"No, sir." She looked down at her lap.

"Uh, uh." Once more the Dyab lifted her chin. "Didn't Sister Elizabeth teach you that it's impolite not to look someone in the eyes when they're speaking with you?"

Angelica met his gaze. Her eyes watered. A large tear clung to her thick eyelashes. He imaged just how beautiful they would be with makeup.

"Did you grow up in the orphanage?"

"No, but I went there when I was fifteen. My parents died in an accident."

"And you had no family?"

She shook her head.

The Dyab walked around to the back of the chair. He placed both hands on her shoulders.

Her muscles tightened. Her body quivered. Her knuckles turned white as she gripped the arms of the chair.

"Why did you choose your order?" The Dyab began to massage her muscles with firm but gentle pressure.

"My grandmother. Could you... She was blind."

The Dyab leaned down so his mouth was so close to her neck he was certain she could feel his breath on her skin. "And this oath you swore to your order?" The fine, delicate hairs on her neck rose. "Tell me about it."

"All nuns take three vows. Poverty, chastity and obedience." A tear ran down her cheek.

The Dyab lifted it off with a slender finger. "And are you keeping yours?" He chuckled.

"Of course, sir."

"Are you? Your apartment is furnished extravagantly, but I suppose you could say it is my wealth—not yours. And there is no arguing that you are the perfect servant to my brother. He goes on and on about you whenever we visit. But I do wonder about the chastity part. Are you committing a carnal sin with Samuel?"

Angelica leapt from the chair. She spun around to face him, her hand poised to slap him, her brown eyes blazing.

The Dyab laughed. He raised his own hand and shook his finger back and forth. "Striking me would result in my killing you. A mortal sin for us both."

Angelica's hand shook but she didn't lower it. "I have never... I have kept my vows before God."

"Of course you have. Relax." He held out his finger until it touched her hand then slowly pushed her arm down. "I just needed to be sure."

The fire in her eyes cooled. "Your brother... wants me to get him ready for Sister Elizabeth's visit. May I be excused?"

The Dyab smiled. She was smart. He thought she was lying but the excuse was plausible. "Go."

She turned to hurry out the door but he seized her arm. She stared at him, fear once again pinching her face.

"If you need anything, Angelica." His thumb caressed her skin. "Ask and it will be given."

He let her go and she bolted out of the office, leaving the door open behind her.

Even in her light blue habit that was as stylish as a flour sack, Angelica had a feminine grace as she raced down the hall. When Sister Elizabeth arrived, he'd have to ask her to start the search for a replacement for the young nun. He had other plans for her.

# 40

Jack pulled hard on the cables, managing to slip by the sailboat moored just yards away on the left. They were flying inches off the water. This low, the trees and houses lining the canal shielded them from view. Paramotoring over water, especially so low, was a dangerous gamble, but he had to take it. If they were to hit the water, they could get caught in their harness as the contraption pulled them under, or the glider could fall on top of them and trap them. Either way, they'd drown.

"I need to see the map again," Jack shouted. Andres was hiding behind the tennis club. They were getting close, but arriving without being seen was another problem.

Alice's hand shook as she held her phone up. They approached a yacht on the right, and a group of sunbathers waved from the deck.

"Wave!" Jack called out to Alice.

"What?"

"We want people to think we're happy tourists."

Alice waved back. "The canal runs all the way to the ocean. We should follow it and cut back toward the club."

As they passed the last of the trees, Alice pointed up ahead. All along the coast, paragliders floated along the breeze. Pulling the handles back, Jack's hope rose with the glider. They soared into the air, joining the traffic of brightly colored crafts flying up and down the shore.

Jack saw that Alice had gone very pale. "We're on our way, babe. Hang in there."

Jack pulled on the left handle and let the wind fill the wing and pull them out over the blue waters. Beneath them, people swam and played along the shore. Up ahead, a dock jutted out over the water, and to his right Jack saw the buildings and grounds of the tennis club.

Alice pointed and said something, but Jack didn't hear her over a deep cough from the engine. He glanced back over his shoulder. A puff of dark smoke marred the sky behind them. Jack swore under his breath.

"When this is done," Alice was saying, "I'm going for a swim."

The fan blade behind him started to vibrate and slow down. The glider shuddered and began to quickly descend.

"I said when we're done. Not now!" Alice's voice rose.

Jack glanced at the dock as they sailed over it. People were pointing at them and energetically waving their arms.

Heat flashed against Jack's back.

"Fire!" Alice shrieked. "The engine's on fire!"

Jack could tell without looking around. His entire back was warm and getting hotter fast.

Pulling down both handles, he steered for the beach as he tried to get as close to the water as quickly as possible.

The flames jetting out of the engine licked upward and touched the fabric on the wing, igniting it in seconds. Wind fueled the fire and the paramotor plunged toward the sea.

Alice screamed.

Jack fought to pull up. If they hit at this angle, Alice would bear the brunt of the impact. She'd hit the water first and then Jack and the motor would slam into her back. The muscles in his forearms strained as he started a tug-of-war against the metal cables to battle gravity. The plastic handle snapped but Jack hung onto the metal cable and pulled harder with his good hand. The burning wing caught one last gust of air and for a moment, he and Alice hung suspended just over the surface of the waves— until a brightly colored fireball ignited over their heads and they plummeted from the sky and landed in the sea. Warm water enveloped him as the engine strapped to his back hissed and bubbled.

Jack's exhilaration at surviving the impact died as the heavy motor quickly dragged them down, both of them still strapped securely by their harnesses.

Alice twisted and wiggled in front of him. Her harness straps floated in the water as she swam free from the wreckage. Jack unclicked his own straps, but the one around his chest wouldn't depress. The plastic felt deformed beneath his fingers and was hot. The release must have been pressed against the burning engine.

The paramotor strapped to his back was swiftly becoming an anchor pulling Jack down beneath the surface. There was nothing for him to push against for leverage and no matter how hard he yanked on the strap, he couldn't break free.

Alice was suddenly beside him, her green eyes wide. She planted her feet against the fan and tugged at the strap frantically. Between the two of them, he was confident they could open it, but with each try, his grip was getting weaker. His lungs burned and the corners of his vision darkened.

There was so much that he wanted to say. So much he wanted to tell her.

*Pin the murders on me. Say I did it. If they think it was me, you can live free.*

Bubbles drifted out of his mouth and the pressure eased in his chest. Alice was pulling at the strap but Jack's hands slipped off. His arms floated up, his hand brushing her cheek. Oh, how he wanted to make love to her one last time.

Last night, when Alice had finally let down her guard and met his desire with her own, he felt like he'd flown to heaven and back, and heard the angels singing their approval. He'd returned to earth a different man, as if every cell was filled with light and joy. As he held her in his arms, knowing that they were together, body and soul, he'd never thought their first time making love would also be their last.

Jack felt the sand beneath his body as he landed face down on the ocean floor. The fallen paramotor that'd given him the freedom to soar like an eagle now moored him in a watery grave.

# 41

*lease, God! Please!* Alice silently prayed as she fought to save her husband, turning his face to the side. Bubbles were rising out of his mouth and his eyes were closed.

The huge metal blade on the engine would be sharp enough to cut the strap pinning Jack to the motor! She grabbed the harness and pressed it toward the blade. The strap came within inches of the edge, but there wasn't enough slack to get it to touch.

Rough hands pulled her aside as two huge men swam next to her. A knife flashed and one of the men sliced the strap tethering Jack to the motor. The other man grabbed Jack by his shirt and pushed off the sea floor, rocketing the two up to the surface.

Alice and the other man swam after them. The moment Alice's head rose from the sea, she was shouting Jack's name.

A bear of a man was floating on his back, holding Jack against his chest as he coughed and spat up water. "Calm down," the man said to Alice.

*What is that accent… Russian?*

Alice treaded water beside them. "It's okay. You're okay," she tried to reassure Jack.

Jack gave her a thumbs-up as he coughed and spat out more water.

"Thank you." Alice smiled at the rescuers. "Thank you so much."

The man holding Jack whispered something to him that Alice couldn't hear and pointed at the vehicle racing along the beach. Jack brushed back his hair and looked around. Emergency vehicles were already pulling up on the sand.

The man holding Jack waved at the Jet Skier who was racing over to help. The Jet Skier stopped next to them and slipped into the water. With all four of them helping, Jack managed to pull himself onto the Jet Ski.

"Up you go, little lady," the large, bearded rescuer said. His accent was clearly Russian.

Alice looked to Jack, confused. He was too weak to drive. Surely it would be better if the owner of the Jet Ski or one of the other men brought Jack to the beach and …

The flashing police lights on the beach reminded her that they couldn't go to the beach. Alice looked suspiciously at the bearlike man who'd just saved Jack's life.

*Does he know the police are after us?*

The large man smiled like he knew what she was thinking. "Get on behind him. Head down the coast. We will go speak with the police."

Jack coughed. "We have to go."

"I can drive him," the Jet Ski owner said.

"They both should go," the smaller man said, grabbing hold of the Jet Skier's life preserver. "You can swim with us." His smile was unsettling.

Alice quickly clambered up behind Jack.

Jack pulled back the throttle and the Jet Ski started moving. He nodded at the large man, who returned the gesture.

As they sped away from their rescuers, Jack didn't aim straight for the beach; instead he steered parallel to the shore. Alice could see the puzzled gestures of the onlookers on the beach. Some even started jogging along the sand after them.

Alice realized what Jack was doing. With the police there, they'd be arrested before their feet touched the sand. She waved her arms and pointed back at the three men treading water. The people onshore stopped as Alice waved some more and gestured again to the men in the water. With any luck, they might think they were the ones who crashed. The crowd turned their attention back to the three men now swimming toward shore.

Jack's face was pale and his lips had a purplish tinge to them that was worrisome. But his jaw was set in that stubborn, determined line that meant it was useless to try to argue with him. Even though he almost died just now, he was a man on a mission and nothing was going to stop him.

Not even his wife.

She wrapped her arms around his waist and laid her head against his back. Miraculously, he was still alive, but was Jack in any shape to keep this fight going? And did she have the strength to take the lead if she had to?

# 42

By the time Dimitri and Vadik emerged from the surf, the owner of the Jet Ski had swam ahead and now stood in the middle of a group of policemen, gesturing wildly.

"Ask them!" He pointed at the Russians as they walked out of the water. "They saw the guy steal ..." His voice trailed off as the Russians came closer and Dimitri loomed over him.

Dimitri scanned the faces of the men in uniform, but Mateo was not among them. The sergeant had not returned his most recent calls, and this was a matter of some concern. Dimitri needed every source of information he could muster. What he did not need was to become a person of interest to the police.

A commotion made everyone look toward the parking lot as half a dozen police vehicles screeched to a stop and even more uniformed men and women got out and rushed toward the beach.

Dimitri crossed his arms. This was both a blessing and a curse. The longer the police spent talking to him, the more time the Strattons had to escape—but he would also need to find them again. He glanced at Vadik and lifted his chin. They both started walking away.

"You!" a short policeman in a tan uniform called out and pointed at Vadik. "Stop where you are!"

The police officers in front of Dimitri all snapped to attention at the sight of the short man with the thin mustache.

Dimitri motioned for Vadik to stop and he did. The officer who had been speaking with Dimitri stepped forward, slipping somewhat in the sand, and saluted the man in tan. "Inspector Renard, sir."

"Are you in charge?" asked the inspector.

"Yes, sir. Owens, sir."

"I'm aware who you are. Report."

"We received an emergency call regarding a glider in distress."

"Was it motorized?"

"Yes."

"Have you been listening to the radio, Owens? We're searching for a paramotor. That's a motorized glider."

Owens's eyebrows rose slightly. "But the one you were chasing crashed, sir. This one was flying."

Dimitri chuckled and Renard turned his ire toward him. "Who are these men?"

"We're just collecting the facts now, sir. These men all went out to rescue the couple on the glid—paramotor." Owens pointed at the owner of the Jet Ski. "He had a Jet Ski but—"

"They took it!" the Jet Skier cut in. "It was a rental. I went out to help but this man and woman stole it!"

"Which way did they go?"

The Jet Skier and several people in the crowd pointed down the beach.

Renard motioned a female officer forward. "Take down every detail and get all available units headed down the coast."

The woman nodded, taking the owner of the Jet Ski by the elbow and leading him away.

Renard turned back to Dimitri and Vadik, his expression softening somewhat. "You swam out to the couple?"

Dimitri nodded. "We were on the dock and saw the paramotor on fire. We just did what anyone would do."

Renard looked up and down the beach. "Everyone else appears to have only watched. You are to be commended." He straightened up. "I am Inspector Renard. And you are?"

Dimitri and Vadik gave him the names listed on their fake passports. One of the policemen standing behind Renard wrote everything down.

"Can you please describe this couple?" Renard asked.

"Tall man. Dark hair. Petite girl," Dimitri said.

"Very attractive," Vadik added.

"You swam out, then what happened?"

Dimitri shrugged. "They were treading water," he lied. "They said they were fine and the man on the Jet Ski pulled up. The couple climbed on and rode off. I thought they would be waiting for us on the beach."

"They didn't even thank us," Vadik added.

Renard was nodding and appeared to be about to wrap it up when Vadik crossed his arms and lifted his chin. "Do you know Sergeant Mateo? He's a friend."

Dimitri wanted to drag Vadik back to the water and drown him in the surf. He rolled his eyes and chuckled dismissively, giving Vadik's shoulder a push. "A police officer lets him out of a ticket for jaywalking and now they're friends." Dimitri laughed harder.

Renard smiled but not with his eyes. There was a newfound suspicion there. "We appreciate your cooperation."

"Thank you." Dimitri nodded. "Are we free to go?"

"Of course." Renard smiled. "I just need to see your passports. For my report."

"They're in our car." Dimitri gestured toward the parking lot.

As they walked to the vehicle, Renard peppered them with seemingly innocuous questions. Why are you in the Bahamas? How long have you been here? When do you plan on leaving? But Dimitri knew that Renard was fishing for information, and that was thanks to Vadik.

Dimitri reached into the glove compartment and removed the fake passports. The inspector held them up and photographed them. The police radio on his waist emitted a steady stream of chatter, and the inspector seemed to be listening carefully, though his eyes never strayed from the two men.

Dimitri scanned the area, impatient to get this business over with, when he noticed something over Renard's shoulder that surprised him so much, his eyes went wide and he startled. Jack Stratton and his wife were riding a tandem bicycle down the street in the opposite direction they had fled on the Jet Ski. Except for the fact that their hair and clothes were wet, they looked like a typical couple out enjoying the beautiful Bahamian weather.

Inspector Renard started to turn to see what Dimitri found so interesting behind him.

"I'm curious, Inspector." Dimitri reached out and touched Renard's upper arm, bringing his attention and gaze back on him. "Did this couple do something wrong?"

Renard cleared his throat and Dimitri removed his hand. "They're wanted for questioning. Thank you again for your time." As the inspector moved away, he picked up his police radio and began speaking into it.

"Get in the car," Dimitri growled at Vadik.

Vadik headed for the driver's seat. "I told you we shouldn't go after the Strattons. Now we're on that police report."

"Shut up and drive."

Vadik started the car but didn't put it into gear. He turned in his seat and glared at Dimitri. "There is no way the Strattons will get away from the police. They headed straight down the coast. All the police have to do is go along the beach until they pick them up."

"Head toward the shops," Dimitri said, his anger burning away any thought of explaining his actions.

Vadik roughly put the car into gear and exited the parking lot. They didn't drive far before Dimitri saw the Strattons getting off the bike in front of a store.

Dimitri pointed at the curb. "Pull over there."

Vadik looked like he was about to argue when his mouth flopped open. "Oh, pancake!"

"Your English stinks and you underestimated the Strattons," Dimitri chuckled.

Vadik's face scrunched up. "How did you find them so fast?"

Dimitri tapped the side of his head but said nothing. Better for Vadik to think he had some superpower instead of admitting the Strattons rode right by and he saw them. Dimitri pointed at the electric scooters for rent. "Take one of those. I'll drive and we will follow the Strattons until they lead us to the *Red Star.*"

# 43

J ack watched Alice hurry up and down the aisles of the small store. Every couple of seconds she'd cast a worried look his way. If he appeared half as bad as he felt, he must look like death warmed over. His stomach was churning so much he debated making another trip to the restroom to throw up, but that would only cause Alice even more concern. Every minute, she'd pop around a rack of clothes or hurry around a corner to make sure he was still vertical. Each time, he'd give a little wave or thumbs-up and she'd get back to work.

*She'll make a wonderful mom.*

The thought hit him out of the blue. He knew he should have thought about children *before* getting married, but he hadn't really been able to. Sitting there now, he could picture a little boy and girl clinging to Alice's side.

Alice came rushing toward him. "Are you okay?"

"I'm fine."

"You didn't wave when I looked. That's our signal."

"I was thinking. I'm fine."

Alice's green eyes studied him. She'd wanted to take him to a hospital but he shot that idea down. He might as well have gone directly to jail with a bullseye painted on his back.

"I'm fine," he repeated as he forced a smile on his face. "Best honeymoon ever."

She frowned and set a shirt and pair of shorts down on the bench next to him. "I'm almost done. Stay there." She hurried off.

Jack closed his eyes. Even thinking about kids would have to wait until they were out of this mess. And now he had to pay for a power glider. He had no idea what that thing would end up costing him.

Alice came back with a straw hat and a pair of large sunglasses that Jack would never wear normally. "You always said hiding in plain sight is the best disguise, right?"

He had to admit, he had said that, and it was better than anything his muddled mind could come up with right now. Alice gathered everything together and brought it to the register. She was back five minutes later and leading him over to the dressing rooms.

"I look like a moron," he muttered as he walked out of the dressing room. He looked ridiculous in the floral shirt and blue shorts, even without the straw hat and sunglasses. He was about to say something else, but Alice walked out the door and he lost the ability to speak.

The floral dress flowed across her curves and revealed a little more skin than Alice typically felt comfortable exposing. She'd tied her hair up into a bun and the smooth line of her neck seemed to call out to Jack to kiss it.

He strode over, pulled her close, and did just that.

"Easy," Alice whispered. "You're in no condition to get all hot and bothered."

Jack didn't let go. "I've made a miraculous recovery. Can you help me with something in my dressing room?" He wiggled his eyebrows.

Alice looked at him like he'd lost his mind. "You figure we have lots of spare time before Andres runs?"

Jack frowned. She was right, but he didn't want to admit it. He kissed her cheek and headed for the door. Jack climbed on the front seat of the bicycle and Alice got on the back.

"Do we have any idea where to look once we get there?" Alice asked.

"Right before the engine caught on fire, I thought I noticed a few buildings near a small lake toward the far back of the club. It looked like a good spot to check out."

Each push of the pedals felt like he was kicking boulders, and Jack found himself already breathing heavily.

"Don't overexert yourself!" Alice called out as she stood up on the pedals. "Sit back and relax. I got this."

Jack nodded but kept pedaling. The way he figured it, Alice wasn't strong enough to get them both there on her own, and neither was he. But working together, they had a chance.

# 44

Inspector Renard stood at attention in front of Chief Inspector Fletcher's desk. His mentor was talking on the phone with the mayor. The call had dragged on for over ten minutes and Fletcher had done nothing but apologize and try to assure the mayor that the situation was under control.

"Thank you, Mr. Mayor. I will." Fletcher placed the phone back in its cradle and rubbed his eyes. "You lost them…again?"

Renard nodded. "We tightened the net, but the Strattons still eluded us."

"You could see them if you looked up, for goodness' sake!" Fletcher's voice rose to the closest thing to a shout Renard could ever recall hearing. His normally unflappable mentor was legendary for keeping his temper, but it looked as if Jack Stratton was cracking even his patience.

"I've called in all reserves, sir. We'll find them."

Fletcher placed his hands flat on the desk. "It's not your finding them that concerns me, it's *catching* them. The Americans have evaded you by boat, motorcycle, paramotor and now via Jet Ski. Lucky for you there is no train on the island."

Renard hung his head. "I apologize, sir, and take full responsibility for the lack of results of my team."

Fletcher sighed and looked at his hands. He picked up a pen and began fidgeting with it. "Renard, the mayor has recommended that I put someone else in charge of this case."

Renard bristled. "Sir, I assure you. We will capture the American fugitives. If we fail to do so, you will have my resignation on your desk immediately."

Fletcher shook his head as he clicked the pen. "Why would you place your career at risk? Let someone else take the lead, man."

"Please, sir. I will apprehend Jack Stratton. Allow me to show you. If not, you can have my resignation now."

Fletcher set the pen down. "You always have a flair for the dramatic."

"I'm serious, sir."

"I'm bloody well aware." Fletcher crossed his arms. "Know this, if slippery Stratton gets away again, there'll be nothing I can do to save your skin. The mayor will want your head and probably mine as well."

Renard saluted. "Thank you, sir." He spun on his heel and marched out of his office.

The Strattons were making him look like a fool. Now his career was on the line. Everything he worked for. Everything he sacrificed—including his family. He wouldn't lose. He couldn't. He needed to find Jack.

"Inspector Renard." The secretary held out an envelope as he passed by. "This came for you."

He grabbed the bubble mailer, nodded politely but didn't break stride as he hurried out to his car. Every available policeman was on the lookout for the Strattons and he needed to coordinate the chaos.

Renard opened his door, tossed the package on the front seat and sat down. He started the engine but when he turned in his seat to back up, he noticed the return address on the package.

It was sent from Sargent Mateo.

Renard ripped open the package and slid the contents out. A single piece of white paper accompanied a pocket journal.

He unfolded the paper and read.

*Renard,*
*You are the only honest man I know. You'll know what to do with this.*
*Mateo*

He flipped the journal open. With each page he read, his heart sped up. There were dates, times, names and money amounts listed. Renard recognized many of the names. They were the names of missing or murdered men and woman whose cases were still unsolved.

Another page made the breath catch in his throat. Again, the page was divided into columns of names, dates and money amounts but the names on this page Renard knew. Politicians, civic and business leaders there in black and white.

Renard knew Mateo was dirty but these crimes went far beyond fixed parking tickets and petty graft. He flipped to the first page. There was a solitarily symbol on it but the marking made Renard's mouth go dry and his eyes dart around the parking lot. Three red Vs were stacked one on top of the other. The Vs sat above a thick line resting on a wavy one. That symbol had made people in the Bahamas fear for six hundred years. It represented the horns, the nose and the smiling mouth of the Devil hovering over the islands.

The sign of the Dyab.

***

Renard spent all night going through Mateo's notebook, carefully taking pictures of each page. If the journal was to be believed, the Dyab's net of corruption had been cast over all the islands. Police, politicians, judges, even the rich and famous were all listed as being in cahoots with the Devil. If half of what the journal detailed was true, it would be the largest corruption scandal the Bahamas had ever seen.

And there was only one man that Renard trusted to give the journal to—Chief Inspector Fletcher. His mentor would know what to do with it. Of course, Fletcher's name wasn't listed in the journal. Renard had never met a more honorable man, but he still had to check.

# 45

Like almost everywhere on the island, the tennis club was lush and well groomed. The courts were private, but the hiking trail around the lake and the dockside restaurant were open to all. Standing in front of the information sign, Jack and Alice blended in with the three other tourist couples doing the same thing.

"The lake is there." Alice pointed. "Are you sure you saw outbuildings there? There aren't any showing on the map."

"The memory is *burned* into my mind," Jack said.

Alice chuckled and rolled her eyes. "Not funny."

"You laughed," Jack said, walking back to the bike.

"That doesn't make it funny. It was terrifying."

"That's why you laughed." Jack gave her a wink before they started pedaling. "If you learn to laugh at something that scares you, you won't be afraid of it as much."

"If that's the case, I should be laughing all the time. This whole thing is scaring me out of my mind."

"It's your choice. You can let fear control you or you can control the fear."

"You sound like Aunt Haddie. She says that all the time."

Jack laughed. "And there's no one tougher than Aunt Haddie."

"Amen to that."

Jack and Alice rode along the path that gently curved and wound its way through the park. They passed by several groups of tourists enjoying the weather, waving back as they went. At the fourth road on the right, Jack turned and slowed. Here the trees and undergrowth were quite sparse and they noticed a cluster of three outbuildings in the distance. They looked to be quite utilitarian, undoubtedly needed to house mowers and other groundskeeping equipment.

Jack pulled over. "If Andres is here, he's probably scared out of his mind. We have no idea if he has a gun."

Alice's lips pressed together and she crossed her arms.

"I'm not even thinking about leaving you behind," Jack assured her.

"Good."

"You wouldn't stay even if I asked, but anyway, this is how we're going to do it." Jack picked up a stick and crouched down. He drew the layout of the three buildings in the sand and explained how they'd approach them.

Alice nodded and listened attentively. When he was done, he erased the drawing with his foot and stretched. "The last thing we want is Andres shooting us or taking off. You promise to follow my lead?" Jack stared into her green eyes.

"I'll do my best."

"That's not the same."

Alice shrugged. "I know, but I don't want to lie. You know how I get."

"That's what I'm afraid of." Jack laughed.

Alice's nose crinkled up. "Wait a second. Are you doing that laugh in the face of danger thing right now because of me?"

Jack thought for a minute and nodded. "Yeah."

"I scare you?"

"Maybe in a loose cannon kinda way." Jack winked.

"I see the near drowning didn't affect your sense of humor."

"Nope. You ready?"

Alice nodded.

Jack moved to the side of the road and watched the buildings. They were all built from concrete block with corrugated metal roofs. The first two buildings were identical in size and faced each other. They had a front door in the center with a garage door on either side. The third building was smaller, really a toolshed, with only one door. None of the buildings had windows, and gravel surrounded all the buildings.

Jack turned to Alice and they exchanged the signal they had agreed on before moving to the closest building. Pressing his back against the cement, he listened. Although the building had no windows, grated air vents circled the building under the roof. Jack cringed as he thought of the heat inside. He thought he knew what being hot was until he served in Iraq, and with so little ventilation, buildings like these were ovens in the summer.

Because of the garage doors, he assumed the larger sheds were for vehicles and equipment. Sticking to the shadows, they moved slowly and kept the crunching sound of the gravel to a minimum. Even the slightest noise seemed booming while approaching someone holed up who could be armed.

Jack reached the end of the larger buildings and stopped. Alice halted behind him. He listened once more to his heart pounding in his chest, his dark thoughts almost making him forget that the sun was shining, and a warm breeze was playing in his hair.

*I'm going to need a honeymoon after this honeymoon.*

Hearing nothing, he signaled to Alice, and they crossed the fifteen yards to the smaller shed. This building too was silent but the moss on the cement threshold in front of the door had been scraped off. Someone had recently opened the door. Drifting down from the air vents beneath the roof was the distinct smell of stale urine. Jack held up his fists and Alice stopped.

Jack led her a few yards away and whispered, "I think he's in there."

"Why?"

"I smelled him."

Alice made a face but didn't ask him to elaborate.

"I want you to come with me. You need to stand to the left of the door. Don't stand in front of it."

She nodded. "I know. Because if he has a gun he might shoot through the door." When he didn't contradict her, she exhaled. "Wow, this just got real."

Jack took her hand. "You spoke with Andres on the phone when you booked the dive tour. He might remember your voice. Tell him we met with Irene and Victor—use their names. Tell him we can help, but he needs to talk with us."

Alice nodded. When they reached the side of the building, they both froze. Someone was moving inside; their footsteps echoed off the metal roof.

"Andres?" Alice called out. The footsteps scurried away. "Andres, it's Alice Stratton. We spoke on the phone. I booked that tour—when your brother... My husband is here with me now. We need your help—and you need our help too, Andres."

Jack moved around her and closer to the door.

"The police think we did it, but you know we didn't have anything to do with it," Jack said. He tried the doorknob. It turned a fraction of an inch and stopped. Inside the shed, the sound of metal scraping on concrete told Jack that Andres might not have a gun, but a pipe or shovel could kill you just as well.

"Andres!" Jack called out. "We spoke to Irene and your uncle Victor. They told us how to find you. We want to help."

"Why?" Andre's question was little more than a shaky whisper.

"Because we're getting blamed for killing Ramon. Irene said you and Ramon got mixed up in something. We need you to go to the police. Whatever it was, we know you didn't kill Ramon."

Jack waited. He couldn't be sure, but the more he strained to hear, the more he thought he could make out Andres's ragged breathing on the other side of the door.

"Irene needs you," Jack pressed. "You know whoever killed Ramon will come after her."

The door to the shed was ripped open. Jack stepped back, moving instinctively in front of Alice as Andres ran out of the shed. His eyes were wild and his unkempt hair shot out in all directions. He clutched a shovel in his hands and lowered it like a spear at Jack's chest.

"You can't let dem hurt her. It's me dey want."

"You need to go to the police. The police can protect you."

Andres shook his head. "No. Dey own some of da police."

"Then come with us to another island," Jack said. "We'll go to Andros."

Again, Andres shook his head. "No. All dese islands belong to da Dyab. Ya don't know!" The shovel shook in Andres's hands. "Ya aren't from here. He controls da police. Da politicians. Can't ya see? Nowhere is safe."

Alice moved up beside Jack. "What about the American embassy? What if we took you there?"

Andres's eyes grew even larger as a dawning hope seemed to push aside his fear.

Alice said, "We can take you. They would give you asylum. Jack knows people there."

Jack nodded. "You know they can help you."

Andres's lower lip trembled, and tears welled up in his eyes. He looked like a broken man as he turned to Alice. "Please. If ya telling da truth, ya have to go get my wife."

Jack shook his head. "We'll get you to the embassy and then they will help us get your wife."

Andres sank to his knees as tears rolled down his cheeks. "No." His hand was a blur as he pulled a boxcutter from his pants and held it to his own throat.

Jack noticed fresh cuts to his neck. He must have been already debating if suicide might be preferable to falling into the grasp of the Dyab.

Jack motioned Alice to take a step back as he moved away, too. "You know if you kill yourself, Irene is as good as dead," Jack said.

Andres shook his head. "No. She knows nuttin' 'bout dis mess."

"The Dyab doesn't know that. He will kill her." Jack crouched down so he was looking Andres in the eyes. "You know that. Your best bet for saving Irene is to come to the embassy with us."

Andres shook his head. "No! Get Irene, den I'll go to da embassy and tell dem erryting."

Alice stepped beside Jack and squatted down so she was on the same level as Andres. She held out her water bottle. "Jack will not let your wife and baby die. I promise."

Andres looked up at Jack, hope and desperation at war on his face. Jack had seen the look a hundred times as a police officer. They'd taught him in police work never to promise something that he couldn't deliver right then. The harsh realities of life had shown Jack why they taught that.

But Alice had given her promise and now Andres looked to Jack for hope. Jack nodded and tried to give him a confident smile. It worked. He saw it when Andres started breathing again and drank from the offered water bottle like a man lost in the desert.

Inside, Jack fought down his own rising fear. How could he save anyone if the Devil was after them?

"Why are they after you?" Jack asked.

Andres leaned on the shovel and stared at the ground. "I tell ya erryting—after ya get my wife."

Jack shook his head. "Since we're going to be helping each other out, let me be one hundred percent honest with you, Andres. Unless you tell me why we're risking our lives to help you, I'm going to take that shovel away from you and drag you to the police right now."

"Jack ..." Alice whispered, laying a hand on his arm. "Easy."

"No. I'm gonna tell dem nuttin'," Andres said.

"You will tell them, because by that time, the police will be your only chance. But you can avoid all that and tell me what you and Ramon were trying to sell to the black market."

Sweat and tears rolled down Andres's face and neck, glistening on his brown skin like rivers running into a delta. He gazed back and forth between Jack and Alice. "We found someting when we was diving. A submarine."

"Where is it?" Alice asked.

Andres shook his head. "No. I won't tell ya where da submarine is. Not 'til you get my Irene."

"Why does the black market care so much about a submarine? What—"

Alice grabbed Jack's arm—hard. "I heard something," she whispered, pointing back toward the road.

"Inside." Jack pushed Andres toward the open door of the shed. Andres didn't need any encouragement. He darted through the doorway like a frightened chipmunk. "Watch him," Jack said to Alice. He pushed her into the shed and the metal door clanged shut on her blazing green eyes. He would have to face her wrath later, but right now he needed to deal with whoever was coming.

He moved slowly around the corner of the shed and waited, his heart rate speeding up. He'd hoped it would be a ground crew or some kind of park ranger—he could just pretend to be a lost tourist—but whoever was approaching was moving slowly, cautiously. And they also stopped to listen.

No car sounded in the distance, and from the amount of noise, it was only one person. Jack strained to hear exactly where the person was and discern which path he was taking. Gravel crunched behind the large building on the right.

Jack carefully made his way around the back of the smaller shed. He moved along the wall to the far corner.

Footsteps gave away the location of the other person as they crossed the gap between the buildings. The footsteps stopped on the side of the shed directly opposite him.

Jack could hear breathing. If the man had heard the closing shed door, that would be his focus.

Jack slowly rounded the corner to the short side of the shed. The man's foot and shoulder came into view.

Jack crouched low.

The man sprang around the corner and swung out with his left hand.

Jack stepped back, easily dodging the blow and countering with a hard right that connected with the man's jaw. The blow made his head snap back and he staggered sideways.

Jack followed with a left to the gut, a solid blow that dropped the man to his knees. The man clutched his stomach and said something in Russian.

Jack had no idea what he'd said, but he recognized a swear even if it was in a foreign language. More importantly, he recognized the man.

"Wait! You saved my life!"

Metal flashed in the man's hand as the man swung a knife in an arc toward Jack's stomach.

Jack dodged the slash of the short, curved knife and lunged forward, seizing the man's wrist. He felt the iron muscles in the man's arm, but they were no match against Jack's superior height and leverage. As Jack twisted the man's hand to the breaking point, the man let go of the blade. Still on his knees, he grabbed Jack's shirt and yanked him off balance with a Judo throw that flipped Jack.

He landed hard on the gravel, flat on his back. Jack's muscles were slow to respond as he struggled to break the hold and get up. Between almost drowning and riding the bike here, he had almost no energy left. The wiry Russian got on top of Jack and pinned Jack's right hand down. The man's other hand encircled Jack's throat. He used the weight of his upper body to slowly crush Jack's throat.

The man's face was so close that Jack could see every freckle and smell the sea and salt on the man's clothes.

Jack summoned all his strength and hit out with a left cross, cutting the man's lip, but the man flashed a bloody grin and squeezed harder. Jack swung again and struck the guy in the face, but there was little power behind it.

The Russian bore down, the smile replaced by intense focus. Jack was about to lose consciousness when a sound like a metal gong filled the air. The Russian's eyes rolled up in his head, he loosened his grip on Jack's throat, and he slumped to the side with a wheeze.

Alice stood there with Andres's shovel in her hands and ready to take another whack, but Jack held up his hand.

"Don't," he said hoarsely, pushing the unconscious man off him and staggering to his feet. "Is there any rope in the shed?"

Andres suddenly appeared carrying a long extension cord. "Will dis do?"

Jack nodded. He tied the man's arms behind his back and between the three of them, they managed to roll him over.

The Russian had another knife in his boot and a .38 caliber pistol tucked into his belt.

"Do you recognize him?" Jack asked.

Andres nodded.

"Is he with the black market?"

"No. We tought dey was Greek biologists, but he's a Russian."

Jack hadn't actually been sure the guy was Russian, but this confirmed it.

"Why are the Russians after you?"

"Ramon contacted dem, too. Dey been looking for da sub."

"Who else did Ramon contact?" Jack asked.

"Just da Dyab and da Russians. That's it. He wanted to start a bidding war."

"He started a war all right," Alice muttered.

"For now, let's stick him in the toolshed," Jack said, grabbing one of the Russian's boots. "Help me. The big guy that was with him can't be far behind."

Together they got him inside the door before the sound of an approaching car confirmed Jack's fears. He held the .38 he took off the Russian and said to Alice, "Wait here."

"But I can help you!" Alice proudly lifted the shovel. Jack scowled. "Fine," Alice muttered, as Andres helped her drag the Russian deeper into the shed.

Jack raced over to the large building on the right and began sneaking along the rear wall. He slowed when he saw an electric scooter leaning against the base of a palm tree near the service road and a silver Mercedes parked near it. As Jack watched, the driver got out to examine the scooter leaning against the tree. His graying hair was on the long side, a bit curly, but his beard and mustache, also shot with silver, were neatly trimmed. It was the other guy who had rescued Jack in the ocean, the real big one.

Jack's grip tightened on the pistol; he was grateful he didn't have to fight this Russian bear hand-to-hand.

"Freeze!" Jack shouted as he stepped into view, aiming the gun at the man's broad chest. "Hands over your head. Turn and face the car."

To Jack's surprise, the man complied.

"You have no legal authority here," the man said.

"But I do have a gun," Jack replied as he walked forward. "Put your hands flat out on the roof of the car and spread your legs."

The man did as Jack instructed but said over his shoulder, "I have a pistol in my belt and a knife on a clip."

Jack stepped forward, grabbed the gun, and jammed it into his own belt. He was about to reach for the knife when his own internal warning sirens went off. Something made Jack pause. The muscles in the Russian's arms were relaxed—not tense. Like a snake, the man was waiting for Jack to get closer before he struck.

Footsteps sounded from the building behind him, and Alice ran into view, the shovel clutched in her hands. Jack stepped back and motioned her over. "Drop the shovel," he said quietly. "Hold this." He handed her the pistol he'd just taken off the Russian, making sure the safety was off. Jack said to the Russian, "She's not that familiar with firearms and I'm worried she might get nervous and shoot you. So don't make any sudden moves, okay?"

The Russian raised a skeptical eyebrow.

Alice scowled. "If you move, I will shoot you."

"She's telling you the truth. She's extremely protective." Jack winked at Alice then took the knife from the Russian's belt. Once he patted him down, he stepped away. "Turn around, keep your hands up."

When the man faced them, Alice glared. "Why would you save us then try to kill us?"

"So they could follow us here," Jack said, watching the Russian's reaction to his words.

"I take it that you are the reason my friend has not come back?" He stared at Jack.

"Yes and no." Jack smiled. "She actually took your friend down."

Alice grinned.

The Russian chuckled. "I believe you." His expression hardened. "Did you locate Andres? Is he here?"

"You don't seem too concerned about your friend's well-being."

The Russian shrugged. "You said she took him down, not killed him. He's been through much worse. I need to speak with Andres, though, as soon as possible."

"That's not an option."

"HELP!" Andres screamed, his cry echoing off the buildings.

As Jack and Alice turned toward the sounds, the Russian dove across the hood of the car and sprinted toward the woods.

"Stop!" Jack shouted.

Alice aimed. "Do I shoot him?"

"No!" Jack started to run after him, but a shriek from Andres made him change direction, and Alice raced behind him. As they neared the shed, Jack spotted the wiry Russian who'd tried to stab Jack earlier darting though the woods, his hands still tied behind his back.

Winded, Jack slowed to a stop beside Andres, who lay on the ground clutching his leg.

"Are you hurt?" Jack asked.

"He bite me!" Andres winced and pulled up his pants leg. There was a large bruise forming on his lower calf, but the teeth hadn't broken the skin.

Alice started to run after the fleeing Russians, but Jack caught her shoulder. "Stop! Don't even think about going after them!"

"If we let them go now, they're going to come after us later," Alice said, glaring off into the woods.

Jack helped Andres to his feet. "Once we get Andres and his wife to the embassy, we'll have nothing to fear from the Russians."

Alice didn't say anything, but he knew what she was thinking—they still had the Devil to deal with.

# 46

Jack pulled the Russians' Mercedes over to the curb, down the street from the church but still in sight of it. Several cars were parked along the street but there were none in the front parking lot.

Alice, sitting in the passenger seat, leaned over to Jack and whispered, "I don't see anyone watching the church."

"Neither do I but they're here someplace." Jack took out his phone and frowned. He had no signal.

Alice glanced at hers. "I've got nothing either. We head toward the coast until we get reception. Then we can have Irene meet us out back."

Andres sat up in the backseat. He eyed the handle on the rear door. "No. We need to get my wife now."

Jack turned in his seat. "Settle down. We'll go get her now."

Alice's eyebrows arched. "What's your plan?"

"Keep it simple. Snatch and grab. You drive. Park out back, I go for Irene. Then we head straight out the back."

Alice cast a worried look his way. "Yeah, simple. Like stealing a hamburger from a pack of hungry wolves."

Jack switched places with Alice. As she drove to the church, he rechecked the .38 and tucked it in his belt underneath his shirt.

Alice pulled into the parking lot and circled around to the back of the building. She parked so the passenger door opened right up to the back door of the church.

Jack pressed the other gun into Alice's hand, gave her a quick kiss on the cheek and hurriedly got out of the car. He slipped through the rear door and into a small foyer. A bulletin board hung on the wall, bathrooms were on the right, a closed door on the left; in front of him was a hallway leading to a dark wood door at the end, which Jack was guessing led to the main sanctuary.

He was right. Besides an old man praying about halfway down, the church was empty.

A door on the far side opened and the young nun that Jack had met earlier stuck her head out. Her eyes widened. She held up her hand, her index finger shaking like a reed in the wind, then abruptly disappeared from sight.

Jack slipped into the very first pew and sat down. The last thing he wanted was to draw attention.

The old man in the back rose and shuffled down the aisle. His back was bent and he moved slowly but Jack kept an eye on his hands. It was habit. In Iraq, insurgents used women, children, and old men as unknowing kamikazes. Maybe the Dyab was up to the same thing.

The old man stopped and smiled, causing his eyes to almost disappear in his lined face. He tipped his gray head, folded his hands in his lap, and sat down beside Jack.

*Why me?*

Jack cast a nervous glance at the double doors at the main entrance then the door the young nun had gone through. When

Irene came in, he would now either have to step around the old man or go down to the end of the long pew. Either way, it would slow him down.

"I don't normally sit up front like this." The old man's voice was just above a whisper but boomed in the silent old church. "I like the back row. But do you know what some people call it? The Devil's row."

Jack tensed. He knew the expression from Aunt Haddie, who always encouraged Chandler and him to sit up at the front during church, but was this some veiled warning?

The old man chuckled. "My mother used to say that." His icy blue eyes studied Jack's face for a moment.

Jack shifted uncomfortably in his seat. Irene would be there any minute and he need to grab her and go.

The old man rose. "Thank you."

"Why are you thanking me?" Jack asked.

The old man held a weather-beaten fishing hat in his hands that he now placed on his head. He shuffled out of the pew and put his hand on Jack's shoulder. "I didn't know why God wanted me to come here today." He smiled. "It was to pray for you."

"Thanks." Jack gave him a stiff nod.

The old man leaned closer. "My mother was wrong. Any place in church is a nice spot. Congratulations by the way." He turned and shuffled for the doors.

The hairs on the back of Jack's neck rose. "For what?"

"Getting married." The old man headed for the doors.

Jack stood up. "How do you know that?"

"You keep playing with your shiny new band." The old man chuckled, but his smile quickly faded. "I prayed for you both." Once more his blue eyes locked with Jack's. "The Lord told me that you're going to need it." There was something behind the old man's look that made Jack's heart start beating faster in his chest. He'd seen the look before but couldn't place it.

The old man had walked out the front doors of the church.

Jack recalled where he'd seen that expression before—on his sergeant's face, just before Jack's first firefight in Iraq. It was his sergeant's fourth tour of duty. Some said the man could smell a firefight coming the way a Sherpa knew it was going to snow.

The door on the side of the church swung open. The young nun walked through followed closely by Irene. Irene took one look at Jack and exhaled like she'd been holding her breath.

Jack waved her over and started hustling her out. "Andres is out back. We need to move."

"Is he safe?"

"Yes."

Jack turned to the nun. "Besides the old man that was here, has anyone else come by today?" Jack asked.

Irene raised a puzzled brow. "What old man?"

"The one who just left ..."

Jack glanced over his shoulder. The double doors swung wide as two men strode through. They took one look at Jack and started reaching for weapons.

"RUN!" Jack pushed Irene and the nun toward the back door. He ripped the .38 out of his belt and cranked off two shots at each of the men. The gun was wildly inaccurate. Jack's first two shots were so off, he almost struck the man on the right when he was aiming for the guy on the left. He adjusted for the misaligned sight and his fourth shot struck the man on the left's shoulder.

The man on the right raised his Uzi.

Jack dashed for the exit.

The molding on the door frame shattered and wood splinters rained down in chunks as Jack ducked low and pushed the two women down the hallway.

The doorway beside the exit opened and a nun peered out.

"Get back!" Jack yelled. To Jack's surprise, the nun stepped into the hallway and attempted to block Jack's way.

"He's helping, Sister Marina," the younger nun assured the woman as they ran by.

Jack and Irene rushed outside; the back door was open.

Andres shouted, "Irene, get in!" and waved her toward the car.

The young nun halted in the doorway of the church.

"Come on!" Jack shouted.

She shook her head. "I will distract them. Go with God." She slammed the door shut and started screaming, "Help! Help! He took her upstairs! Someone go after them!"

"Let's go, babe!" Alice shouted.

Irene practically dove into the backseat as Jack jumped into the passenger seat.

Alice stomped on the gas and gravel pinged off the bottom of the car. The car shimmied sideways as Alice fought to keep the car heading straight. Jack eyed the church doors, which remained closed.

Irene cried as she hugged Andres.

A bullet hole appeared in Jack's window. "Get down!" he shouted, turning to aim out the window. He fired two bullets but when he pulled the trigger again, it just clicked.

More bullets pinged off the car as Alice shot across the street and drove over the front yard of the church's rectory. She cut the wheel to avoid a stone fountain and the rear end of the car started to fishtail.

Andres and Irene, crouched in the backseat, slid against the door.

Jack grabbed the dashboard. "Steer into the skid!" he yelled. Alice started to cut the wheel to the left and he grabbed hold of it. "Other way!"

"Got it!" Alice cut the wheel the other way and pumped the brakes to avoid a stone bench. "How do I get out of here?"

Jack scanned the yard. It was ringed in by a fence on the right, and by bushes around the rest of the property. There was no way he could tell if something was behind the shrubs, and right now, they didn't have much of a choice. He pointed straight ahead. "Head for those bushes!"

"Hang on!" Alice gunned the car straight ahead.

Jack grabbed the other gun that Alice had tucked next to her in the seat.

Branches crashed over the hood of the car. For a moment, Jack felt like he was floating. It took him a second to realize that they had just driven through the bushes and off a three-foot wall. Everybody in the car screamed as the front end of the sedan hit the road and sparks flew up from the bumper. Alice struggled with the wheel as she fought to straighten out the car.

A roaring engine behind them made Jack turn around just as a large pickup truck sped through the gap Alice had created in the bushes. The pickup bounced as it drove off the wall and one of the four men clinging to the back fell out.

But the pickup didn't slow to get the man. It sped up.

Alice pinned the gas pedal to the floor.

The rear window shattered, pieces of glass pinging through the car.

Jack aimed and pulled the trigger. The bullet stovepiped, sticking straight up and jamming the gun. Water dripped on his hand. Jack swore as more bullets slammed into the car.

Alice tore through an intersection.

Jack had to give Alice credit. She didn't even flinch when two large holes were blown into the dashboard above the radio. She gritted her teeth and sped around a double-parked car.

Sirens sounded in the distance.

"Should I head for the police?" Alice asked.

"We can't go to da cops!" Andres shouted. He had draped his body over his wife's in an effort to protect her.

"Keep driving." Ripping the glove compartment open, Jack grabbed the only weapons he knew of in the car—the D batteries. He powered down his window and looked back.

There were two men in the cab and three in the back. The gunman in the back was now more concerned with hanging on than with shooting but Jack clearly saw the gun in his hand.

But his target was the windshield, not the man. He threw lefty and the battery sailed harmlessly over the truck.

"Get your head in!" Alice yelled.

"In a minute." Jack pulled himself halfway out of the car so he could use his right arm to throw.

He gunned the second battery and it pinged off the hood of the truck. The man in the back fired. Andres and Irene cried out. Jack threw the last battery as hard as he could. The battery struck the center of the windshield and punched through it. The truck swerved to the left and clipped a car parked on the side of the road. It skidded sideways, then flipped onto its side. Sparks flew as the truck slid along the asphalt before grinding to a stop.

Alice kept driving as Jack slid back down into his seat and peered in the back. Andres was sitting up but holding a bloody hand over his stomach. He grabbed Jack's shoulder with his other hand. "We found a waterproof box. Silver, da size of a thick briefcase. Ramon took it to ... storage."

Irene was sobbing uncontrollably as she pressed her hand against Andres's side.

"What facility?" Jack asked.

Andres shook his head. "I don't know. He used a false name. He ..." Andres licked his lips. "He had a key ..." He circled a bloody left finger around his right wrist.

"Hang on!" Alice screamed.

As their sedan reached another intersection a police car skidded to a stop and tried to block them off.

Alice slammed on the brakes and cut the wheel. They fishtailed and slammed sideways into the police cruiser, ending up with the two cars side by side. Through Jack's open window, he looked directly across at the disoriented policeman.

"GO! GO!" Jack shouted.

"I'm trying!" The car stalled. Alice shut it off and tried to start it again.

The policeman shook his head and stared at Jack with dazed eyes.

The other sirens were getting closer.

The policeman's eyes widened as the trauma from the accident lifted.

Jack scrambled halfway out his window and stuck his torso into the police cruiser. Ripping the gun from the policeman's holster, he said, "Don't move. I won't hurt you."

The sedan's engine sputtered to life. Alice grabbed Jack's belt and yanked him back into the car just as two other police cruisers pulled into the intersection. Alice hit the gas.

"Take care of Irene!" Andres yelled as he shoved the door open and tumbled out of the car.

"Andres!" Irene shrieked.

Alice lifted her foot off the gas but Jack grabbed her knee and pushed her leg to the floor.

"We can't leave him!" Alice said.

"He needs a hospital." Jack grabbed Irene's arm and kept her from jumping out of the car too. "And the Dyab needs him alive. This is best, believe me."

Irene slumped back into the seat and covered her face as she sobbed into her hands. As the sedan sped down the street, Jack looked behind them. To his surprise, the police didn't give chase. Instead, they all rushed over to Andres lying on the ground.

"Head for the docks," Jack said. Alice cast him a puzzled glance and he answered her unasked question. "We need to get Irene to safety and I have to go get that storage key."

"But we don't know where it is."

Jack shook his head. "Actually, I do."

# 47

The Dyab stood at the end of his long marble bar sipping a rum. The cavernous great room was empty except for the four guards stationed in the corners. He had thought of bringing back Alaire to act as his personal bodyguard with this new threat but he needed the Frenchman to find the location of that sub. The clock was ticking.

The rum warmed his throat as he took another sip and eyed the men in the corners of the room suspiciously. He never trusted anyone and now his distrust had proved to be well founded. Someone not only knew his identity but they provided that information to the New Dawn as well.

As far as Sebastian was aware, only two people had that information. One was Samuel, safely locked in the cellar of this house. The other had coincidentally just asked for a face-to-face meeting. But she would never betray him. It was absurd to think so.

It had to be someone else.

He had considered the possibility that Bashir was the traitor but the thought was equally ridiculous. The man had no drive beyond having his perverse carnal pleasures fulfilled and since the Dyab turned a blind eye to his proclivities, Bashir was a loyal dog. Besides, Bashir knew nothing of his past.

The Dyab stared at the marble and placed his hands flat against its surface. He let the cold wick the warmth from his fingertips, the palms of his hands, until the base of his wrists chilled.

The door at the far end of the room opened and Bashir peeked in. He locked eyes with the Dyab, then stepped aside.

Sister Elizabeth quietly slipped into the room. The same pained expression crossed her face. He'd seen it every day when he was at the orphanage. She was much younger then but she still appeared aggrieved whenever she saw him.

"Tell me why, Sister," the Dyab said as he poured himself another rum. "Why do you look at me that way?"

Sister Elizabeth hurried over to him. She reached for him but when he recoiled, her hand hovered just above his arm. "What way...?"

The pause at the end of the sentence was the place where she would have said his name had no one else been in the room. She had a unique way of saying it. Like she was calling out to him, each syllable rose higher as she said it.

"Pain. Disgust." He took a long sip of the rum.

"No. Never. It's only..." She took a rosary out of her pocket, her fingers rubbing the beads.

"Tell me something. Why did you join the order?" The Dyab pictured himself as a child. The nun would tell him many stories but he couldn't recall anything said about that.

"I had a husband. And a son. My boy drowned. My husband did too when he swam out to save him. I stayed on the beach. I was too afraid to go into the water."

"So I remind you of a dead child?"

She shook her head. "A drowning one. Whenever I look at you, I see a little boy who this wretched world is pulling under. But it's not too late for you..."

He could tell his name caught on her lips. He finished the rum and poured another. "Save your preaching for my brother. He buys it but he's crazy. And you know why."

"It wasn't your fault."

"It was and no amount of penance will wash his blood from my hands. What do you want?"

Sister Elizabeth's fingers shook as she rubbed the rosary. The beads clicked together. "I came to beg for mercy for Andres and Irene Knowles."

The Dyab froze with the rum glass halfway to his lips. "What did you say?"

"They are parishioners—"

The glass tumbled from the Dyab's hand and shattered on the marble. A shard bounced up and sliced into the base of his hand but his shock at her words numbed the pain.

"You stand between the Knowles and me?"

She shook her head. "They are part of the flock. Irene is pregnant. Andres had no idea what his brother was doing."

"You know where he is!" The Dyab seized the nun's arms. She felt thin and brittle beneath her robes. "Tell me!" He shook her.

The old woman's face twisted in fear. Her mouth opened but no words came out.

The Dyab's hands tightened on her arms and his eyes widened in understanding. "You! You know my real name. It was you who went to the New Dawn. You betrayed me! You led them here."

"No. No, child." Tears ran down her cheeks. "I love you. I pray for your soul every morning and every—"

The Dyab shoved her back. He was sick of her prayers. Sick of her words worming their way into his mind.

Sister Elizabeth fell backward. Her head struck the edge of the marble bar with a sickening thud, and she collapsed to the floor.

The Dyab's breath caught in his throat.

One of the men guarding the doors began crossing himself.

Bashir stood rooted in place. He stared from the nun to the Dyab and back again.

Sister Elizabeth lay motionless on the floor.

The Dyab crossed over to her and knelt down. She wasn't breathing. Blood began pooling beneath her head.

"Search her for wires," he ordered.

No one moved.

The Dyab's lip curled.

The enforcer that had not stopped crossing himself yanked open the door. Before he took two steps into the hallway, the Dyab shot three bullets into his back.

"Search her!" he yelled, his gun sweeping the room as the enforcer fell to the floor with a loud thump.

Bashir and one of the enforcers hurried over and patted her down. Besides a small purse and a rosary, she had nothing.

"Sweep the villa," the Dyab ordered as he walked over, grabbed a fresh glass and poured another drink. Did the nun betray him? Now he wasn't certain of the fact. He saw the hurt in her eyes. The pleading. And something else…love.

"Leave me!" he bellowed and the men scattered like leaves in the wind.

The Dyab stared down at the woman who had treated him like a son. Even if there had been a sliver of a chance before, there would be no redemption for him now. Hell awaited him. But he wasn't going to go alone. He'd make sure took whoever made him kill Sister Elizabeth right along with him.

# 48

With Irene sobbing in the backseat, Alice raced down the side streets toward the docks. Sirens filled the air as police cruisers rushed to the intersection behind them, but the street they were on remained empty.

"Dey gonna kill him," Irene sobbed.

Jack reached back and placed a hand on her shoulder. "Irene. Look at me." He gave her arm a gentle squeeze. Tears flowed down the woman's face, but her brown eyes locked with his.

"Andres get hurt. Bad." Jack tried not to show the depth of his concern but as a soldier he'd seen many different types of wounds, and he knew from the dark-red blood how bad it was. Andres had been hit in the stomach; unless he received immediate attention, he would die. If Andres hadn't jumped out of the car, Jack would have had no choice but to surrender. "The police will take him to the hospital. They'll have to operate."

"Dey gonna kill him!" Irene sobbed.

"Not until they get the location of the sub. That gives us a little bit of time to find it."

"But I don't know da location! Andres never told me."

"Andres and Ramon found proof. Alice and I are going to get it. Hopefully, that's enough for the police to at least look into this and to get the U.S. State Department involved. I need you to stay strong. We're going to ditch the car when we get to the docks, and you can't walk down the street crying."

Irene sniffled and wiped away her tears.

Alice glanced in the rearview mirror. "Irene, you need to take your jacket off."

Jack glanced at Irene's bloodstained jacket and hands. He unscrewed the cap of the water bottle and passed it back to her. While Irene cleaned herself up, Jack scanned for a place to ditch the car. "Down that street." He pointed.

"Where are we going?" Alice asked.

"To the docks. We need a boat."

Alice drove down the street and pulled into an open parking space. Irene had cleaned most of the blood off, but her skirt and blouse were stained. Jack motioned to Alice, and she moved over so she was on Irene's left side.

"We blend in. Smile, talk, and act like we're just walking to the store to buy some bread."

Feeling open and exposed as they made their way down the main drag filled with tourists, Jack forced himself to walk slowly. He was grateful Alice chatted away. She even pointed at various stores and stopped periodically to look into the windows.

In front of an ice cream parlor, Jack tensed up. Two uniformed policemen strolled out of the crowd and headed down the sidewalk directly for them.

Alice lightly elbowed Jack in the ribs. "You don't need any more sweets, honey!" She laughed. "Let's go down to the beach."

Jack stared at her, incredulous. She was as calm as a still pool, with two policemen only a few feet away. But Alice's acting worked. The policemen continued down the crosswalk past them.

Alice took Irene by the elbow and Jack by the hand. "I hope the water is iridescent blue today. You know, like in the travel ads?"

Jack wanted to kiss her right then but simply nodded and kept his pace slow and natural. The crowds thinned as they reached the dock. He felt like he was walking across a minefield when they crossed the street and the ground changed from asphalt to wood.

As they neared the water, there was no sign of the police, but Jack recognized Oliver's boat and frowned.

Oliver was circling the harbor, too preoccupied with talking on the phone to notice them.

Alice squeezed Jack's arm. "Thank you, God!" she whispered loudly. "That's an answer to our prayers. We got our boat."

Jack breathing sped up and his adrenaline kicked in. "Follow my lead, Alice."

Alice cast a sidelong glance but nodded.

Oliver caught sight of them and almost dropped his phone. Oliver revved the throttle and drove the boat to an open space on the dock.

The three of them hurried down the ramp.

"Are you alright?" Oliver called out as he jumped out of the boat and grabbed the bow line.

"We're fine," Jack said as he helped Irene over the side.

Oliver stared at Irene's bloodstained clothes. "Has she been shot, too?"

"No, but we need to get out of here." Jack slumped onto the seat and worked up a convincing lie. "Give me a second. I have to go back up to the car. I didn't know you'd be here, so I hid it in the trunk."

"Hid what?" Oliver's eyes widened.

"Andres gave us the hard drive from the office computer. He said everything we need to know is on it."

"I'll get it," Oliver volunteered.

Jack tilted his head toward Alice. "Car keys?"

Alice nodded, but he noticed the puzzlement in her eyes as she handed Oliver the keys. "It's a silver Mercedes. We parked near the dumpsters at the top of the dock."

Oliver leapt over the side of the boat and started running toward the dock ramp. Jack waited a moment before he jumped up. "Get to the wheel." He hopped over the side and untied the line.

"Are we leaving him? He helped us," Alice said, hurrying to the front of the boat.

"Oliver's no good." Jack glanced over his shoulder.

Oliver had reached the top of the dock and was looking toward the dumpsters. He turned back to stare at them. Jack gave a friendly wave, but he'd gotten confirmation of his theory when he saw that Oliver had a phone pressed to his ear.

Jack tossed the bow line into the boat, flipped off Oliver, and jumped in. "Get us out of here!"

Alice cut the wheel, pushed the throttle forward, and headed for the open harbor as Oliver sprinted down the dock. He was screaming something at them, but Jack couldn't make it out and he didn't care.

"Can you please explain why we left him like that, so I don't feel like a complete jerk?" Alice asked.

"Two things." Jack moved up to stand beside her. "He said he's been taking tours out, but his equipment is brand new. All of it, and the safety tags are still in place so it's never been used. Two, we never told him what happened to Andres, but he asked if Irene had been shot *too*."

"Why that lousy ..." Alice let fly a stream of swears as she pushed the throttle forward. "Is he with the black market?" Alice gasped. "Did he kill Ramon?"

At the mention of her brother-in-law, Irene looked up.

Jack shook his head. "I don't know who he's working for, but right now he's my prime suspect."

"What are we going to do?" The desperation in Alice's voice pulled on his heart. But now that the pieces were falling together, it was like opening a baffle on a chimney, and the determined fire that always seemed to burn inside Jack flamed even hotter.

He draped a protective arm around her shoulders. "We need to go to the place where we went diving with Ramon. You have the coordinates on your phone, right?"

Alice nodded. "I saved them." A faint smile tugged at her lips. "I wonder if my pirate treasure is still there? I dropped the vase when we found Ramon."

*If that vase was real pirate treasure, then Oliver Rolle is a good guy and Santa Claus is real.* He wasn't about to tell her that.

"I thought Oliver finding us was an answer to our prayers." Alice frowned.

"It was." Jack smiled crookedly. "Now we have a fast boat."

Alice laughed. "What are you hoping to find out there?"

"Proof."

Jack said a quiet prayer as they headed for the open sea.

# 49

laire strolled through the doors of the hospital. The emergency room was crowded with locals who came because they used it as a clinic and with tourists who had succumbed to too much sun, too much drink, or a combination of both, giving them the false bravado that precedes accidents.

Like a ripple traveling across a pond, his presence caused a stir. Patients and employees alike stopped their conversations to turn and stare.

Alaire kept his icy blue eyes on the information desk, but he felt the attention, and he loved it. They feared him. They sensed he was a dangerous man. Even the grizzled, old emergency room nurse took a step back as he put his hands on the counter and pinned her with his stare.

"A shooting victim was just brought in. Where is he?"

The nurse swallowed, her fat jowls and the folds of her neck shaking slightly. How easy it would be to wring her turkey-like neck.

As if she could read his thoughts, her hand instinctively rose to protect her throat. "I can't tell you dat."

"He's my brother." Alaire peeled three bills off the roll from his pocket and placed them on the counter. "Andres Knowles."

The nurse covered the cash with the flat of her hand and slid it off the counter. "He's still in surgery. E3." She tipped her head toward two double wooden doors on the left. "Nan, I need you to cover da desk. I'm going on break." Without another word she hurried away, but not before casting a nervous glance back over her shoulder.

Alaire was already on the move. He strolled past the nurses' station and toward the wooden double doors where a sign was prominently displayed: HOSPITAL EMPLOYEES ONLY.

Alaire pushed open the doors and passed through. No one stopped him. He walked down the hall with long strides until he saw what he was looking for: a cop posted in front of one of the doors. The policeman glanced in his direction. He'd forgotten the cop's name but not where he'd seen him before, or his weaknesses: he moonlighted doing security at the Pelican Club and liked white women and white powder, two vices that made it very easy to control him.

The policeman's shoulders stiffened. Panic and uncertainty crossed his face. His two personae were colliding. Right now, he was on duty, sworn to protect the man inside. But when your blackmailer comes a-calling...

Alaire motioned him over.

The policeman hesitated.

Alaire waited. This idiot didn't realize that he'd lost this game months ago, when he did his first line of cocaine with a prostitute sitting in his lap. It was all recorded on camera. Alaire doubted he had to remind him of his indiscretion; from the flush rising up the policeman's neck, shame was doing that job for Alaire.

The policeman ambled over—Alaire read the name tag, Dalbert—and glanced nervously around before whispering, "Andres is in a critical condition, but I heard the nurses saying that his vital signs are strong. The inspector was here but the doctors said Andres would be unable to give a statement until he was out of surgery and the anesthesia wore off."

"Notify me when he wakes." He handed Dalbert a slip of paper with his phone number.

"My shift ends in six hours."

"Get it extended."

Dalbert paled. "I ... I don't make my schedule."

"Call it in. It will be approved."

Dalbert lowered his eyes and nodded. The doors at the other end of the hallway opened and Alaire quickly turned so he could see and not be seen. What he saw was several uniformed policemen, and one of higher rank whom Alaire recognized all too well—Chief Inspector Fletcher.

Dalbert glanced back and forth between his two masters with a look of horror on his face like a jaywalker caught in the middle of the road, wondering which of the trucks barreling toward him was going to crush him.

Alaire turned and headed back the way he'd come, keeping a careful eye on the group of policemen by watching them in the mirrors that hung just below the ceiling. The group paid him no attention—except for Chief Inspector Fletcher.

The ER once again quieted as Alaire passed through. As Alaire reached the double doors leading out of the hospital, it was clear Fletcher was following him. Curiosity seemed to have gotten the better of the chief inspector.

Alaire headed toward his car. He glanced over his shoulder.

Fletcher exited the hospital and scanned the parking area. Fletcher's neck was stretched, and his body leaned slightly forward as he searched for Alaire.

He reminded Alaire of the birds he called *grues*—what did they call them here? Cranes.

Alaire reached his car and slid into the driver's seat. The parking lot was gated, and a uniformed security guard manned the booth. Alaire wondered if he was armed.

The chief inspector was crossing the road now, headed straight toward him.

Alaire started the car and unlocked the door.

Fletcher yanked the passenger door opened and got in. "I told you we were handling this."

Alaire raised a dubious eyebrow. "Told?"

Fletcher sat up straighter. "You *requested* that we bring Andres in alive. My men were close to apprehending him."

"No, they were not," Alaire said simply. "Andres was with the Americans and would have gotten away if we had not intervened."

"Your men engaged in a gun battle down a main thoroughfare. It's all over the news. This can't be brushed under the carpet."

"The solution to that problem is in the trunk. But before we get to that, the police officer guarding Andres—Dalbert—is going to put in a request for overtime and continue his shift through this evening. Approve it."

Fletcher opened his mouth as if to protest but closed it again. "Of course."

"A new Dyab is rising." Alaire let his words sink in.

Fletcher gasped. "You?"

Alaire chuckled. "Inspector Renard is now in possession of a book. It contains a detailed summary of the current Dyab's business and some of his allies."

Fletcher paled. His legs began to shake so hard the heels of his shoes clacked off the floor of the car.

"Relax, Chief Inspector. Your name was purposely omitted from the journal. The names in the book are only a drop in the bucket. But in war, there must be sacrifices. As you said, all things can't be brushed under the rug."

"What's in the trunk?" Fletcher cleared his throat.

"Let me show you." Alaire got out of the car. He had circled all the way around to the trunk before the chief inspector opened his door.

Alaire waited.

Fletcher came to stand beside him.

Alaire opened the trunk.

A man, bound and gagged, in his twenties stared at them with large, terrified eyes. He didn't struggle or try to speak.

Alaire slammed the trunk closed then handed the car keys to Fletcher. "You're a hero. You've caught the man who shot Andres."

Fletcher stared down at the keys in his shaking hand. "I thought you recovered the gun."

"That would do little to quell the media or the politicians clamoring for safer streets." Alaire laid a hand on Fletcher's trembling shoulder. "A small sacrifice is needed to satisfy the cries of the people."

"But he saw you. He saw me!"

Alaire nodded. "Personally, I recommend that you make it look like the shooter was killed during his *arrest*."

Fletcher gagged.

"The moment Andres is awake, or you find any information on the Americans, I am to be notified," Alaire said as he handed Fletcher an envelope that was fatter than usual. "Go take care of what's in the trunk."

The envelope crinkled loudly as Fletcher crushed it in his hand, but he wisely chose to keep his mouth shut.

As Alaire walked away, Fletcher got back into the car. The chief inspector had no choice but to get his hands dirty.

But Alaire had just crossed a line. War was imminent. The new Dyab was making his move. And when two devils fought, there'd be hell to pay.

# 50

Seagulls circled high overhead as the boat gently bobbed on the sea. An especially brave individual broke from the flock, swooped down, and landed on the bow. He stood staring at Jack and squawked loudly.

Irene shooed it away. "Andres told me, a seagull landing on your boat before a dive is bad luck." Her eyes were brimming with tears, though she tried to hide it.

"Good thing I don't believe in luck!" Jack reached down, grabbed a handful of potato chips out of a bag, and tossed them high over the side of the boat. The gulls squawked in delight and swooped away after the crumbs.

A faint glimmer of hope crossed Irene's face. "Do you really tink you can help us?"

Alice gave her swim flippers a final tug and waddled over to sit beside Jack. "If anyone can, it's Jack." Her emerald eyes sparkled with pride.

Jack kissed the top of Alice's head.

Alice gave him that look that made him feel invincible. Right now, he needed it. He was running on fumes, and to call this a long shot would be the understatement of the year. He'd have more of a chance looking for a needle in a haystack. But Jack knew he couldn't ask for a better partner—in life or in this crazy mess they were in right now.

"We'll find it," Jack said confidently as he and Alice made their way to the stern.

He was about to help Alice onto the dive platform, but Irene stopped him. "Wait, Jack." She took his right hand and Alice's left so they formed a circle. "Since you don't believe in luck, let me pray for you. *Father, you know da mysteries of da deep. Watch over dese two as dey search for whatever it is dey're looking for. Show dem da way, and be with ...*" She choked back a sob. "*Be with my Andres till we can be togeddah again. In Jesus's name, Amen.*"

Alice squeezed her hand, then gave Jack a thumbs-up. He slipped into the sea and the silence engulfed him. He always loved diving and despite what was at stake, he felt calm, even peaceful. Beneath the waves, he felt like an astronaut in a water world, filled with discoveries and wonders around every corner.

With Alice swimming just behind him, he followed the anchor rope down to the ocean floor, the glow from the light attached to the rope shining like a beacon. They swam slowly over the sandy bottom, not too close, and careful not to stir up sediment, or the light wouldn't do them any good at all.

They'd set up three other buoys to mark off the search square. For the hundredth time he prayed that Alice's GPS coordinates had placed them at least hand grenade close. Swimming side by side, he and Alice started toward the next buoy.

Jack didn't know exactly what he was looking for, but Ramon had dropped something over the side of the boat near the end of the dive session, right before he was killed. Replaying the moment again in his memory, Jack could see the shadow of the other boat approaching and something bright falling over the side of Ramon's boat, bubbles streaming around it as it fell.

Maybe Ramon had sought to hide whatever he dropped into the ocean beneath the waves and figured that once the other boat left, he could dive down and retrieve it. And his plan might have worked if he'd lived long enough.

Up and down, they plied their way along the makeshift search grid. The sea floor was mostly flat, but there were still so many places where something could remain hidden forever. Plants, coral, and rocks could conceal anything, and Jack had no idea exactly what they were looking for. His biggest fear was that it was small and lay buried under the sand, completely invisible. Jack's hopes faded as they crossed the halfway point in the grid.

Alice's whole body suddenly shook, and she darted downward. A cloud of sand swirled around her. For a moment, she disappeared like a statue in a shaken snow globe, but as the dust settled, she triumphantly held up—her broken pot.

Bubbles rose from Jack's regulator as he swore under his breath. That stupid fake pirate treasure! He scowled beneath his scuba mask. Alice shook her head. Even underwater he could tell she was annoyed that he didn't believe her pirate tale.

She pointed at the pot and gave a thumbs-up.

Jack wanted to scream. He pulled up the little white slate Alice had insisted they both carry.

NOT WHAT WE— he started to write but Alice held up her slate, cutting him off.

WE'RE CLOSE!

Jack frowned, then he realized Alice didn't care about the pot, just the fact that it showed them they were searching in the right place! He gave her a thumbs-up and scribbled SORRY on the slate. Alice drew a smiley face.

With renewed confidence, Jack started swimming again. They had to be close. Alice had surfaced with that pot and dropped it right when they found Ramon's body. Whatever Ramon tossed over the side should be in the same area where the boat was drifting at anchor.

Jack's hope started to wane as a patch of seaweed and trash spread out before them. The seaweed gently swayed over the sand, obscuring everything underneath it. Frustrated, Jack swatted at it with his right hand, only succeeding in kicking up a cloud of sand.

He was so angry he screamed, and bubbles roared out of his regulator. As he glared at the ocean floor, a bright-pink scrunchy caught the light. This sparkly piece of trash infuriated him even more until he noticed that something glittered on the end.

The seaweed had settled again and covered the scrunchy from view. Jack focused on the spot where it had been and reached down. Sand rose and seaweed clung to his hand, but his fingers tightened around the scrunchy.

He pulled it up and took a closer look. His eyes widened. This was exactly what he'd been looking for.

# 51

"Do you recognize this" Jack asked. In his hand was a sparkly pink scrunchy with a small white plastic ball attached like a charm. The number 24 was visible on the ball. Dangling down from the scrunchy was a brass key.

Irene nodded. "Dat's for da lockers at Pirate's Cove. A big water park. I take my nieces there sometimes."

"That's at the end of the pier," Alice said.

"It's walking distance from the dive shop." Jack smiled. "It makes sense that he'd hide it nearby."

Alice wrapped her arms around Jack's waist and squeezed. "You are a genius. We need to get what's in that locker."

"So, dis will prove dat you and Andres are innocent?" Irene asked.

"It'll help," Jack said.

"I should go to be with Andres."

"It's way too dangerous," Jack said, taking the key back. "I promised Andres that I would get you to the embassy."

Alice pointed to the horizon. "We may have a problem, Jack." In the distance, two boats riding side by side were headed straight toward them. The sun gleamed off the police light bars on top of their canopies.

Jack started the engine. "Pull up the anchor!" he shouted, but Alice was already hauling the rope.

First one boat turned on its emergency lights, then the other.

Jack gunned the engine. The sea was calm, and the dive boat quickly flattened out. Like his expensive, unused dive equipment, Oliver hadn't spared any expense on the motor, but the police boats were gaining on them.

Alice hurried over to his side. "They're catching up to us, Captain Jack." She grinned, but the tightness around her eyes gave away her concern. "Do you have tricks up your sleeve?"

Jack searched the sea up ahead. There were several boats headed toward the harbor, but at this speed, there was no way they'd reach land before the police caught them.

"Drive," Jack said, grabbing hold of the side rail.

"Aye-aye, Cap'n!" Alice got behind the wheel.

Jack hurried back to the anchor. He took out his knife and sliced the anchor off. He grabbed a dock fender hanging along the side of the boat and cut it off too. The little rubber bumpers were designed to protect the boat when docking, but Jack hoped they'd work for his plan.

"What are you doing?" Irene asked.

Jack tied a bumper to each end of the rope, then a third in the middle for good measure. "Have you ever seen videos of a police chase?"

The boats were closing in on them now. They were less than a hundred yards away and directly behind.

"Yes." Irene held onto the railing as the boat shook over a patch of rough sea.

"The police throw out spike strips ..." Jack started swinging the rope faster and faster around his head. He heaved it and as the rope shot over to the left, he picked up the other end and threw it as hard as he could to the right.

"But dey're boats." Irene's brow wrinkled. "Dey don't have any tires to pop."

Jack stared at the rope bobbing on top of the water. The two police craft were speeding straight toward it. At the last second, the boat on Jack's left cut its engine and steered hard to avoid the rope. The boat on the right surged forward and ran right over it. For a moment, Jack thought his plan had failed, until the police boat's engine whined and died.

"Yes!" Jack grinned and turned to Irene. "Did you see that? Spike strips for the sea!" But his joy was short-lived when he saw that the boat that had swerved had joined the chase again. He started cutting off another section of rope, but Alice yelled, "They won't fall for that again, honey."

Jack kept tying a bumper to the rope. "It's the only plan I have. I have to slow them down or they'll catch us before we even reach shore."

"Attention!" a man's voice boomed over a loudspeaker. "By order of the Grand Bahama Police you are commanded to stop your watercraft and surrender immediately."

"I take it I'm not stopping?" Alice called to Jack.

"Full throttle!" Jack yelled.

"If dey catch us, erryting we done will be for nuttin'." Irene stood up. "You're Andres's only hope."

Jack started to swing the rope. "We can't give up."

He couldn't quite interpret the look Irene gave him as she watched him, one hand shading her eyes from the sun. "No, you can't. Tank you for erryting you've done." She held both hands over her belly and tumbled backward off the side of the boat.

Jack dropped the rope and lunged after her, but was too late.

Alice screamed. She started to throttle back and cut the wheel.

"No! Keep going!" Jack ran forward.

"We can't leave her."

"We have to. She's right. And she's safer not being with us!"

Alice ground her teeth and kept the throttle jammed forward.

Behind them, Irene was shouting and waving her arms, screaming for help. Jack thought the police boat might keep up the chase but when it reached Irene it cut its engine. To his delight, Irene started floating on her back. Officers were shouting at her to swim to the police boat and shouting at each other. The pandemonium behind them grew, and so did the distance between Jack and the police.

"She's stalling so we can get away!" Alice cheered.

"Head for the harbor but we're not going straight in. The police will have radioed ahead."

Alice nodded and pointed at the setting sun. "One good thing. We'll be less visible after dark."

Jack wrapped a protective arm around her shoulders. With the police, the black market, the Russians, and whoever else might be after them, Jack wanted to disappear altogether and just keep going. But if they had any chance of clearing their name, he had to go to Pirate's Cove and retrieve what Ramon was killed for.

# 52

Ignoring the looks of astonishment and suspicion from those on the shore, Jack held tight to Alice and rammed the boat onto the beach. He dropped down to the sand and turned to give Alice a hand, but she landed deftly beside him. The two of them jogged down the coast and headed toward the water park, which looked to be about six blocks away—not too bad, but as they reached the boardwalk, sirens filled the air.

"Drop back and walk twenty yards behind me," Jack said. Alice nodded and immediately stopped to pretend to tie her shoelace.

The police were looking for a couple. Jack hoped that if they separated, they could make it to the water park without drawing attention. How they would make it out of the park was another story ...

Jack forced himself to concentrate on the first goal— reaching the locker. He fell into step behind a group of tall tourists who happily chatted away in German as they made their way down the pier. Jack stayed close and hoped it appeared like he belonged with their group.

Glancing quickly over his shoulder, he was happy to see Alice chatting away with an older couple, matching their slow gait. If he didn't know better, he'd think she was their attentive granddaughter.

A police cruiser sped by, then two more. Jack watched in the reflection of the store windows as he kept walking. One of the cars slammed on its brakes. He shifted his weight to the balls of his feet, ready to sprint away, when the driver of the stopped cruiser started screaming at a jaywalker, who took off his headphones and scurried back to the safety of the sidewalk.

Without giving Jack or Alice a second glance, the police officer sped off.

Jack stuck with the crowds, which increased in size and decibels as he approached the water park. He stopped before getting to the ticket counter and Alice hurried over. Handing her some cash, he spoke quickly. "We don't know if anyone knows about the lockers. They could be watching the water park, so come in after me. Stay at least fifty yards out."

Alice tilted her head toward the entrance. "Metal detectors. What do we do about ..." She glanced down at his waist, where she knew there was a gun hidden behind his belt.

Jack glanced around, then walked over to a trash can beside a bench. He grabbed a crumpled paper bag from a local restaurant. Turning his back to the crowd, he put his foot up on the bench, pulled the gun out of his waistband, and dumped it inside the bag.

Alice slid close to him. She gave Jack's arm a quick squeeze. "We got this." She bravely smiled up at him.

Jack grinned back. He wished he shared her optimism. They were far outnumbered and now unarmed. He laid the bag just inside the trash can and repeated his instructions. "Come in after me. Stay at least fifty yards out." He left off telling her to run if something happened to him. It was pointless. She'd never leave his side, and while he didn't want her in danger, he was grateful for her support.

The ticket booth had been fashioned in the form of a crow's nest. A cheery, redheaded teenage girl with a pirate hat and a name tag that read Tricia greeted him. "Welcome aboard, Matey!"

Jack paid for his ticket and received a sparkly blue wristband in return. "Where are the lockers?" he asked.

Tricia pointed to the right. "On da starboard side, Matey! You can deposit your booty dere!"

"Thanks." Jack nodded and tried not to cringe. He couldn't imagine having to talk like a pirate every day, but maybe the teenager liked it.

The water park was busy, and groups of kids raced back and forth, followed by their weary looking parents.

Jack stopped in front of a brightly painted sign detailing the location of all the rides as he waited for Alice to get her ticket and wristband. Once she was inside the park, he was on the move. Scanning the faces as he made his way toward the wall of lockers, Jack's heart had the same deep rhythm it fell into when he approached a pulled over vehicle; no idea what would come next, but ready for action. Had he just pulled over an absent-minded grandmother who ran a stop sign or had the little old lady snapped, killed her abusive husband and was now holding a .357 low and pointed at Jack from behind the car door?

What was waiting for him in that locker?

Jack reached the cubbies for the metal lockers. He continued down a row until he located number 24. He slipped the sparkly pink scrunchy out of his pocket and stuck the brass key in the lock.

The key clicked in and, with some effort, turned.

He slowly opened the door.

The locker was empty.

*What? How?*

Jack felt like someone had hit him in the stomach with a bat. Gritting his teeth, he glared up at the sky, a stream of profanities ready to erupt from his mouth, when he noticed the large sign on the opposite wall.

LOCKERS CLEANED OUT EVERY NIGHT. SEE LOST AND FOUND FOR MISSING ITEMS.

"Ramon, you idiot," Jack growled under his breath. He spun on his heels and hurried back to the sign with the painted map of the park.

Alice cast him a puzzled glance as he walked past her.

Jack motioned for her to hang back, trying to hide his rising panic. He scanned the park map on the sign, but there was no mention of a lost and found. He headed back to the ticket booth.

Tricia, the girl who sold him the ticket, was there talking with another teenage employee.

"Excuse me." Jack grabbed hold of the fake wood railing and knocked on the glass a little too hard. Both teenagers jumped but they quickly started giggling. "Sorry. Where's the lost and found?"

"It's in da Captain's Quarters," Tricia said, keeping up the pirate accent. "I can direct your course and ensure your passage dere."

"Thanks." Jack let go of the railing and forced himself to smile and not seem like his life depended on finding whatever was in that locker.

Tricia left the crow's nest and let her coworker take over. Jack picked up the pace behind her as she walked quickly to the middle of the park, chatting away as she went. He was grateful Tricia was the focus of her own conversation as he wasn't paying any attention to what she was saying. She opened a side door labeled EMPLOYEES ONLY.

The two of them walked just inside a little hallway and Tricia stopped in front of an open door.

The room was the size of a large closet lined with shelves. It was filled floor to ceiling with clear crates brimming with towels, sunscreen, sandals and sunglasses.

"What did ya lose?" Tricia asked.

Jack scanned the shelves, but nothing stood out.

"Ah ... It was a ..." Jack wracked his mind for something to say but drew a blank about what to say. The truth was, he had no idea what Ramon hid inside the locker. He held his hands up in frustration. The pink scrunchy dangled from his fingers. The little ball with the number 24 slowly bounced on the end.

"You are locker twenty-four!" Tricia dropped her pirate speak and her voice went high. "No way!"

Footsteps echoed down the hallway as two young adult boys appeared in the doorway at the end of the hall.

"It's a guy." The boy on the left elbowed the one on the right. "I told ya it was a guy."

"What's in it?" the other boy asked.

"We've got a pool going," Tricia said. "Some people thought it was jewelry. I did, anyway." She smiled and started to walk down the hall toward the boys. "We kept it in here because we all curious 'bout what it is."

"You're lucky ya came," the taller boy said as he stepped out of the way. "Da manager was gonna give it to da police at da week's end tomorrow."

"Just in case it's like drugs or somethin'," the other boy said.

"It's not." Jack quickly shook his head. His heart was pounding as fast as his mind was racing. He still had no idea what they were talking about, but he didn't want to raise their suspicions any more either.

The boys stepped out of the way and Jack exhaled.

Sitting on the break room table, next to a Coke and a half-eaten candy bar, was a metal box a little larger than a thick briefcase. Besides the combination lock, there were no markings on it.

Tricia reached down and lifted a bright yellow diving bag off a chair. "Dis was in da locker too."

Jack nodded. "Thank you. Thank you all very much." He took the bag from Tricia and picked up the metal box. It was surprisingly light.

"Wait!" the taller boy shouted.

Jack froze.

"What's in it?" all three teenagers asked at once.

Jack exhaled. A crooked grin flashed across his face. "Tricia hit the nail on the head. My wife's jewelry. I'll have to stop by later with a reward for you three."

All of them exchanged excited glances.

"Thank you again." Jack started down the hallway. "I'll also put in a good word with your manager."

"My name's Pete!" the taller boy shouted.

"And I'm Roy," his friend called out.

"Got it!" Jack shoved open the door and drank in the warm air. He felt like he just read the winning lottery number off the TV, and it matched the one in his hands.

Alice stood next to an ice cream cart. When she noticed Jack carrying the bag, her hands covered her mouth, and she closed her eyes.

Jack gave her a quick thumbs-up but when he turned toward the exit, his excitement came crashing down.

Two policemen were standing next to the ticket booth. Another half-dozen uniformed cops were closing the entrance and talking to park security.

Jack started walking directly away from them. The park was large and the fence surrounding it wasn't that high. He and Alice could make for the far corner—

Jack felt something jammed hard against his ribs as a man in a white shirt and gray slacks stepped beside him.

"You Americans certainly have a knack for making trouble," the man said in a French accent, "but you, Detective Stratton, take it to the extreme."

Another man, tan and leathered like a sailor, came up on Jack's left. He had a scar that ran from the side of his shaved head at a diagonal that ended in a chunk missing from his right nostril. His lips curled into a snarl and the gap in his nose widened.

"Relax," Jack said, coming to a stop. "I'm always open to making a deal." He glanced over the Frenchman's shoulder, quickly checking for Alice, but she was nowhere in sight.

"Keep walking, Detective." The Frenchman pressed the gun into Jack's ribs and Scarface took the bag from Jack's hand.

The Frenchman pushed Jack toward the back of the park. "If you yell, you and a lot of innocent people and police will be killed. You are a law enforcement officer. Do you really want their blood on your hands?"

Jack clamped his mouth shut and kept walking toward the rear of the park. With Alice watching out for him, he had a chance, even if he went with them for now.

Scarface motioned to a third man that had emerged from the crowd; a short, stocky guy with bad teeth. "Go find the wife."

"She's right over there." Jack pointed at the last place he'd seen Alice.

The stocky man scoffed and headed in the opposite direction.

"Just trying to help," he called after him.

"Shut up and walk," the Frenchman ordered.

"Now you're hurting my feelings." Jack smirked. The truth was, he was trying to tick the Frenchman off. If he got angry, he'd try to shove the gun hard into Jack's side and that would be the best time for Jack to make his move.

The Frenchman's eyes narrowed. With a hand gesture he ordered Scarface to switch places with him. The Frenchman stepped three steps back.

Jack's smile faded. With two guns pointed at him, they could gun Jack down before he could do anything.

The Frenchman kept a brisk pace but not too fast. He seemed calm. Relaxed even. But there was something about the man's eyes.

They were lifeless.

Cold.

They reached the back of the park and Scarface pushed Jack toward the fire exit, which was nothing more than a gate in the chain-link fence. On the side of the fence, parked in the grass alongside the park, was a black SUV. A bearded driver sat in the front seat, nervously puffing on a cigarette.

Scarface shoved the fire exit gate open.

To Jack's dismay, no alarm sounded.

The bearded driver got out of the SUV and opened the back door. A gun was in his waistband.

As a cop, Jack knew that a victim typically was taken from a crime scene to a murder scene. He had no doubt that if he went with them, he'd be a dead man.

"You there! Stop!" a man shouted behind them.

Renard and three policemen were jogging through the water park toward them.

The Frenchman turned and raised his gun.

Renard froze. He was out in the open with no cover, as good as dead.

Jack punched the Frenchman hard, catching the base of his jaw.

The Frenchman's gun fired.

Renard and the policemen scattered.

A blinding pain erupted at the back of Jack's head. His legs crumpled beneath him, and he slammed face down into the gravel.

The edge of Jack's vision blurred and dimmed. Jack looked up, hoping to see Alice, but she was nowhere in sight. Everything went black.

# 53

Alice stifled the scream in her throat as she watched from the shadows of a building as three men closed in on Jack. She had no weapon but she couldn't let them get to Jack. She inhaled, readying herself to sprint across the open ground, when a hand clamped over her mouth and a strong arm wrapped around her waist.

Lifted off her feet, she was pulled back into the shadows of the building.

Alice started kicking. Her heels hit bone and flesh, but the man tightened his grip.

Another man stepped in front of her. It was the man who attacked them at the shed. "You can't save your husband now."

Alice's eyes darted to Jack. The three men had caught up to him. One had taken the bag away from Jack and another held his arm against Jack's side.

Alice's eyes widened, as did her mouth, while she prepared to take a chunk of flesh out of the hand clamped over her.

"But you can save him if you listen to me," the man said. "I have people that will help. You need to trust me."

Alice looked back at Jack. The men were leading him toward the rear of the park.

"Those men all have guns," the man continued. "You took ours and I doubt you brought them with you because of the security. But the men who have your husband didn't have that problem."

Alice stopped fighting. What the man was saying made sense. Why he was helping them wasn't as important to her as the fact that he was helping. They saved Jack once. She needed their help to do it again.

She curtly nodded.

The man behind her set her down on the ground and took his hand off her mouth.

"You there! Stop!" someone shouted.

Renard and the other policemen were jogging toward Jack and the three men.

The thin man behind Jack turned, raised a gun and pointed it at Renard.

Renard froze.

Jack punched the thin man in the face.

The thin man's gun fired.

Renard and the policemen scattered.

The park erupted into chaos and parents raced to grab children and people everywhere ducked for cover or dashed shrieking for the exit.

The man behind Jack slammed his gun down on Jack's head.

Jack crumpled to the ground, and it took all her strength not to cry out and rush to his side.

The men grabbed Jack and stuffed him into the SUV as the police shouted at them to drop their weapons. The SUV's tires spun, kicking gravel into the air as it barreled out of sight.

"Move!" Alice pushed the man in front of her toward the now unguarded entrance. "Go while they're distracted." She ran and they followed. "Do you have a car?"

"You stole ours. We... *borrowed* another," the taller man said as the men sprinted beside her.

"You said you had people that will help," Alice said. "We need to go get them. Then we rescue my husband."

# 54

"What's up, buddy?" A familiar voice echoed in Jack's head. He hadn't heard the real voice in years, but he'd never forget it.

*Chandler.*

"You've really stepped in it this time."

Jack's eyes flicked open. He was sitting in a diner and his best friend was sitting across from him. It was a little breakfast-all-day restaurant that looked straight out of the fifties.

He knew it was a dream but whenever Chandler appeared in his dreams, he didn't want to wake up. And his foster brother always had something important to tell him.

Chandler chuckled and toasted Jack with his glass of orange juice. "Congratulations, bro! Your wedding was beautiful."

"I gave you a front-row seat."

"You liar. That was Alice." Chandler chuckled again. "But thanks. I'm humbled with how you honored me and Michelle like that." He drained the orange juice in one gulp. "But we need to have a little chat."

Jack looked down. There was a western omelet on a plate in front of him on the table and it looked and smelled delicious. He reached down for his fork but there were no utensils laid out.

"You can't eat now." Chandler shook his head. "You are seriously Jacked up." He laughed—a big laugh, deep and real.

Jack missed it. His chest hurt. So did his head. The memories of the last few days rushed back. His honeymoon. Diving. Ramon. Andres. The box ...

Jack tried to raise his arms but now he couldn't. He glanced down. He was tied to the booth in the diner.

"You mind untying me?" Jack asked.

Chandler's big shoulders bounced as he laughed. He clapped his hand to his forehead and ran it down his face. "You're dreaming, genius. I can't."

"Do something."

"I'm trying."

"Try harder, Casper."

Chandler leaned forward and wiped at his eyes. "Casper? The friendly ghost? Funny. You should try being nice to me if you want me to get you out of here."

"I'm sorry."

"No, you're not. You're smiling."

"It's a nervous habit."

"It's a wise-ass habit. Aunt Haddie always said so."

"Yeah, right. I can hear Aunt Haddie saying that now."

They both laughed.

"Seriously, Chandler. Can you do anything?"

"You need to listen to me and use that head on your shoulders while you still got it. Calm down."

"Calm down? These guys are going to kill me!"

"Not if you listen to me."

Jack shook his head. "They got the box. They have what they wanted. They don't need me."

"That's not what they wanted." Chandler leaned back and crossed his arms. "I can't believe I figured that out and you didn't."

"Figured what out?"

Chandler calmly took another bite of eggs.

"Tell me!" Jack's voice rose.

Other diners glanced over at them.

"Chill, man. I'm just trying to get you to think everything out. Andres said the box was proof they found the sub, right?"

"Yeah," Jack said. "I get that. And these other guys need something that's on the sub. That proves ... Hold the phone! The guys who grabbed me don't know *where* the sub is!"

Chandler raised a fresh glass of orange juice. "Congratulations, Sherlock. You've solved the case."

Jack tried to lean forward but he was still held in place by ropes. "One problem, Watson: I don't know where the sub is either."

"Bluff."

"Bluff?" Jack rolled his eyes. "That's why you sucked at poker. I don't have anything to bluff with. No ace up my sleeve. So, what if I tell them I know where the sub is, they'll realize I'm lying and then kill me. All that accomplishes is ..." A light finally went on in his head. "It buys me some time."

Chandler nodded again. "Good. I was worried that guy hit you too hard and knocked all the sense out of you. Are you gonna eat that?" He pointed at the omelet.

"Will you stop thinking about food!"

"Be nice. I'm trying to help you figure everything out. Do you want me to get you out of here or not?"

"You said you couldn't do anything."

"Technically I can't but I can still help—in a way." Chandler reached down and slid Jack's omelet over to himself. He took a big bite and smiled. "You didn't forget, did you? I told you I'd always have your back. I knew you'd never make it without me. That's why I got a Replacement to watch over you."

# 55

The Dyab stormed across the empty drawing room. His footsteps echoed off the walls. "Bashir!" he bellowed but only silence greeted him.

Had everyone left the villa?

All of his enforcers were gone. So were the servants.

"Bashir!" The Dyab held a black Uzi in his hands. The grip was slick with his sweat.

Running footsteps sounded down the hallway outside the middle of the room. A moment later, Bashir appeared.

He was covered in perspiration and panting for breath. In his hands was a bundle of wires.

"Where is everyone?" The Dyab tried unsuccessfully to mask the panic in his voice.

"They're gone," he said, holding out the pile of wires in his hand.

"Where?"

Bashir shrugged. "They fled after... the situation with the nun." He raised the pile of wires higher, holding them toward the Dyab like an offering.

"What *is* that?" he demanded, his voice rising.

"We've been breached," Bashir said. "The entire villa was bugged, except...one room."

The Dyab ground his teeth. "The Frenchman's!"

Bashir shook his head. "No. It was—"

Two loud pops rang out. Bashir arched his chest. The pile of wires in his hands tumbled to the floor. Bashir lurched forward two steps and collapsed.

The Dyab turned toward the hallway, raising the Uzi as he did.

Three more shots rang out.

Pain tore through his shoulder then his hip and stomach.

He attempted to pull the trigger of the machine gun, but his hand opened involuntarily and the weapon dropped with a loud clatter to the floor. Blood soaked his pants; higher, his insides burned. The bullet must have struck bone and ricocheted.

His legs wobbled. He stared at the open doors leading out to the hall.

Sister Angelica crossed over the threshold. A still-smoking Glock in her hand was aimed at his chest.

The Dyab stumbled backward. His back pressed against the wall and his legs gave out. He slid down to the floor. His legs were tucked beneath him at an odd angle.

"Is this your revenge for Sister Elizabeth?" The Dyab spat blood onto the floor. His 1911 pistol pressed into the small of his back. "Her death was an accident." He raised up his arms, his palms rising up.

Angelica smiled and shot him in the kneecap.

The Dyab screamed in pain.

"That is for Sister Elizabeth. She was a good woman." Angelica shifted her aim and shot his other kneecap. "And that is for my parents."

The Dyab thrashed on the floor. The pain so intense he could hardly see. "You said they died in an accident."

"You had them killed over a petty debt."

"You must forgive me, or you will not be forgiven! What about the vows to your order?"

"Did you really buy the whole innocent nun routine?"

Angelica's voice now had a hard edge. Her posture stiffened. She was poised. Powerful.

"You should have paid more attention to Sister Elizabeth's Bible lessons. The Devil's best disguise is to come as an Angel of light. For two years I've listened and watched you. I've learned all of your secrets and all of your flaws. But then came your great mistake."

"The submarine…"

"The government was already investigating you. You let Alaire run wild, and blood flowed in the streets. The net was closing in."

The Dyab slid onto his left elbow, his right arm now resting on his hip. If he leaned forward, he'd be able to grab the pistol stuck in his belt.

"Trying to sell the location of a nuclear sub was foolish."

The Dyab spat out another mouthful of blood. "You're doing the same thing. The money is too good to resist, isn't it? Forbidden fruit is the sweetest."

"I've already gifted the location of the sub to the authorities. That along with Alaire's arrest will go a long way."

"You gave away ten million dollars?"

"Short term sacrifices for long term gain. Now the government owes me. You neglected Sister Elizabeth's history lessons. Governments frequently deal with the Devil. Saddam

284 - CHRISTOPHER GREYSON

Hussein, North Korea, even Hitler. That is also why I gave Renard a book containing a small portion of your dealings. A necessary culling of the herd."

The Dyab scowled to hide the jealousy growing inside him. Her plan was genius, as should have been his.

"You're smart." The Dyab took the deepest breath he could and relaxed his right arm. He stretched his fingers out as he prepared to draw the gun. "I suggest a split. You don't know all of my tricks." He smiled confidently, his teeth coated in blood.

Angelica laughed. It was light and bright and infuriated him more than any sound he had ever heard.

The Dyab laughed too. But his was deep and tinged with hate. He reached for the gun on his back.

A bullet tore into his right shoulder. There was no pain now. He slumped sideways, gravity pulling him down in a twisted heap.

"There are still those loyal to me." The Dyab's voice had lost most of its bravado. "They will avenge me."

Angelica laughed again. She stepped forward and raised her gun. "No, they won't. That was your biggest mistake. People fear the unknown. The world should never truly know if there is a Devil or not. And they will never guess that a woman is now the Dyab. Nor will they ever come looking for her in a church."

Angelica pulled the trigger.

# 56

lice walked with the two men toward a car parked alongside the curb. Half a block away, emergency vehicles descended on the entrance to the water park.

The taller man reached for the back-door handle and Alice planted her feet.

"Hold on." She eyed the other man who had stepped off the curb as he headed for the driver's side. "Explain to me why I should get in this car with you. And let me be perfectly clear. You try anything and I'll scream so loud the police over there will come running, and by the time they get here, one or both of you will be missing some body parts."

The veins stood out along the shorter man's temples. He scowled down at her then glanced over at the growing crowd of police. "Not here. Too many police."

"Actually, it's just the right amount." Alice crossed her arms. "And taking my chances with going with the police sounds better than getting into a car with you two, if you don't tell me who you are."

The man took a step closer to Alice. Alice inhaled and opened her mouth.

"Vadik, enough," the taller man said, holding up his hand. "Fine. My name is Dimitri Ivanov. We are looking for the *Red Star*. It's a Soviet submarine that was lost in Bahamian waters many years ago."

"Why do you want it?"

"My father was the captain. Vadik here is the son of his first lieutenant. We need to find that sub to prove that our fathers were honorable men."

There was something about Dimitri that resonated with Alice. He spoke simply of a story that had haunted him. His eyes showed pain, anger, shame—she saw all the emotions burning there, but it was the way he said he *needed* to find the sub that truly touched her. She knew what he was feeling firsthand. She didn't know him or his character, but she believed him, and she felt his need—it was for the truth.

"We have to go," Vadik muttered. "We're drawing too many prying eyes."

Alice glanced at the entrance of the water park. A policeman was looking their way.

Dimitri opened the passenger door. "Come with us if you wish to save your husband. If you go to the police, both of you will die. Many are corrupt and working with the black market. That's how we know who you are, Alice."

Jack's voice rang in her ear. If he was here, the last thing he'd want was for her to get into the car. But if the roles were reversed and he had to rescue her, he wouldn't hesitate.

Alice got in the backseat and shut the door without looking back.

Vadik started the car and they slowly pulled away from the curb as another police car rushed to the scene.

Vadik leaned over and whispered to Dimitri in Russian.

"I'm sorry." Alice grabbed the seat and leaned forward. "I didn't get that."

Vadik glared in the rearview mirror. "Because I wasn't speaking to you." He looked at Dimitri and continued in English. "Bringing her with us is foolish. She knows nothing."

Dimitri scowled back. "I could not just leave her there. If the police grabbed her, they would hand her over to the black market."

"You both know I'm right here and can understand you." Alice's ire at being spoken about and not to was steadily rising.

"Do you know the location of the sub?" Vadik asked.

Alice shook her head.

"Then you're nothing but a scared girl that will get in our way." Vadik huffed. "You don't know where they've taken your husband, or the location of the sub. Like I said, you're of no use to us. Sit back like a good girl and shut up."

Alice pointed to Dimitri. "You're the one in charge, right?"

Dimitri turned slightly in his seat so he could look at Alice. He nodded.

"Let's get two things straight," Alice said. "I may need your help to rescue my husband but you need my help to find him so you can get whatever was in that box. I know exactly where my husband is. I'm tracking his location and they're headed for the dock." She held up her phone. "So, keep your Neanderthal friend on a leash and get it through your head we're in this together."

Dimitri laughed. "I understand."

"Good. Let's go get the rest of your men." Alice sat back in the seat and stared down at her phone. Jack's phone was still on, and he was moving. They were headed toward the coast. She closed her eyes.

*Hang on, babe. I'm coming for you.*

# 57

Jack woke up as someone slapped him hard across the face. He lifted his chin off his chest. He was in a seated position. When he tried to raise his arm to wipe his eyes, he was unable to. His arms were tied to a chair, as well as his legs.

The room looked to be a warehouse. Cement floor, with two walls of shelves stacked with boxes on his left and right. In front of him was a large, roll-up, corrugated metal door. There were only two men in the room with Jack. The Frenchman from the water park stood in front of a table set a few feet before the door, his hand resting on the hardwood surface.

And there was a thick man, who was extremely tan, looming over Jack. His arm was raised, and he appeared ready to slap Jack again.

"I'm awake. No need for you to risk hurting your hand," Jack said.

Scarface's brows knitted together.

"Enough." The Frenchman strode forward.

As he did, Jack noticed the bag on the table with the metal briefcase lying beside it. Next to the bag was Jack's phone. Jack had to fight down the urge to cheer when he saw it. Alice would surely be tracking him. He needed to stall long enough for her to reach him.

"Detective Stratton." The Frenchman stopped in front of Jack and stared down at him. "I need to ask you some questions."

Jack had sat across from many killers before. Hardened men and women who had taken a life for one reason or another. This man was different. He was a true, cold-blooded killer. Jack had seen that when he drew his gun and fired at Renard. But something about this man bothered Jack to his very soul.

The Frenchman reached for his back pocket.

"Hold on." Jack cleared his throat. "Before you start threatening me or smacking me around or whatever else you're planning to do, let me save you some trouble." Jack worked up a grin. "We both know it would be easy for you to put a bullet in my head," Jack continued. "But I have two things you want."

The Frenchman seemed to relax. He shifted his weight to his heels and crossed his hands behind his back. He studied Jack like they were playing cards and he was debating what Jack held.

"One, I'll take you to the location of the sub. Andres told me where the *Red Star* is. I'll tell you where it is."

The Frenchman leaned in so close, Jack could smell his cologne and the faint aroma of a rich cigar. "You're playing a dangerous game, Detective Stratton. And you're playing with your life."

Jack gave a slight shrug because of the tightness of the ropes. "Actually, I'm just leveling with you. It would be easy for you to kill me right now, if you wanted to."

"True." The Frenchman smiled. "So, tell me. Where is the *Red Star*?"

Sweat beaded on Jack's brow. The moment the cold-eyed man no longer needed him, Jack was dead. "I don't know the longitude and latitude of—"

"He's lying!" Scarface drew back his hand, ready to hit Jack again.

"I can't tell you where it is, but I can show you. We sailed right over it. Andres pointed it out."

The Frenchman thought for a moment. His lips pressed together into a thin line. "What is the second thing you believe I need?"

"Your freedom. I'm an American law enforcement officer on his honeymoon. You kill me and they'll never stop looking for you. After I show you where the sub is, and you let me go, no one will care that you grabbed me."

Jack knew the Frenchman had no intention of letting him live. But if he believed that Jack was willing to trade the location of the sub, he might pretend to go along with it. That could buy Alice the time she needed to get help and find him.

The Frenchman walked over to the corrugated, roll-up metal door. He banged twice and it rose. Two men were waiting outside. He spoke to them briefly, but Jack couldn't make out what he was saying.

Jack stared at the harbor outside the door. A fifty-foot boat was moored at a dock.

The two men followed the Frenchman over to Jack.

"You will come and show us where the sub is." The man's cold eyes sparkled. "If you lie to me, I will do things to you that will make you beg for death. And then I will go find your wife and do the same to her."

At the mention of hurting Alice, Jack resisted the urge to bite the man's nose off his face. Instead, he nodded stiffly.

The two men picked up the chair, lifting Jack still strapped to it. They began to carry Jack out to the boat.

The Frenchman picked up the briefcase but left the bag and Jack's phone on the table.

Jack's breath caught in his throat. Without that phone, Alice wouldn't be able to track him.

The Frenchman strode out the door and down the dock.

As the two men carried Jack out the door, his mind raced. What could he say to get them to take the phone without tipping them off? He craned his neck and glanced back.

As Scarface stomped by the table, his hand shot out, grabbed Jack's phone and stuffed it into his pocket.

*No honor among thieves.* Jack stared up at the stars and mouthed *thank you.*

The Frenchman didn't have to worry about finding Alice. She would be coming for him.

And if that guy thought he was scary, he'd never seen Alice mad.

# 58

Alice followed Dimitri and Vadik down the ramp and onto the dock. There was no missing their boat: it looked like something that belonged in a naval museum. As they neared the ship, the crew appeared alongside the railing.

Four men, two women.

Alice scanned their faces and her hope sunk. She had expected to see clones of Dimitri. Strong, hardened sailors who looked like they'd not only seen danger but enjoyed it. But Dimitri's crew looked to be the exact opposite. They could have been tourists. They looked like soft, out of shape mothers and fathers going for a Sunday sail.

They gave Alice friendly waves and bright smiles.

She stopped and stood staring back.

*How can middle-aged marshmallows rescue Jack from the black market?*

Dimitri glanced over his shoulder and raised a puzzled eyebrow.

Alice lowered her voice. "They're not able to take on the black market. We need to go to the police."

A short, bald man with a pot belly and large, thick glasses waved again and Alice returned the gesture.

"He looks like my dentist."

Dimitri grinned. "Peter is a dentist. And Kirill is an accountant." He pointed at one of the women. "Lara is a chemistry teacher. Annika owns a restaurant. They are the children of the crew of the *Red Star*. They have come to clear their fathers' names." His voice was filled with pride.

Alice's chest tightened. "That's very noble but... you saw the men in the black market. They're dangerous. If we go after Jack, your crew will get slaughtered."

Dimitri laughed. He turned toward the crew and spoke in Ukrainian. They laughed too.

"All of them are the children of soldiers. They can all shoot and handle weapons very well."

In spite of Dimitri's confidence, Alice was nowhere near as sure. The black market was more than willing to kill... She wanted to go to the police, but would they shoot first and ask questions later? More likely, they'd "arrest" them and turn them over to the black market.

Alice looked down at her phone. The green dot marking Jack's location was moving and it was heading out to sea.

# 59

The Frenchman's boat sliced through the water beneath a darkening sky. He sat in the front talking to Scarface, who drove while the two men who carried Jack sat together on the left side of the boat. Neither of those men spoke; nor did they look up. The longer Jack watched them, the more he was convinced that they were pressed into service. They looked too nervous to be a regular part of any criminal operation.

Jack's hands balled into fists, and he pulled slightly against his bonds. The rope was new and would never break but the wooden chair he was tied to creaked. He relaxed and let his head hang down to conceal the slight smile that pulled on the corner of his mouth.

The Frenchman rose.

The two men sitting huddled closer together. They kept their eyes focused on the deck and lowered their heads as the Frenchman strode to the back of the boat.

As Jack met the cold gaze of the man, he knew that he should be afraid too. Anyone in Jack's situation had the right to be scared, but Jack wasn't. He met the man's unflinching stare with open eyes and a crooked grin. It wasn't a macho thing. Nor was it very smart of him to do it. He was certain it was provoking the man. Every voice in his head from Alice's to his father's and Aunt Haddie's was screaming at him to at least pretend he was frightened but he couldn't.

He wasn't scared at all.

All he felt was rage.

It was an emotion that had been beaten into him. One of his earliest memories was the pain of being kicked so hard he couldn't breathe. His mother's pimp wanted to teach her a lesson. But she wasn't home, so he decided to use Jack as the example.

Jack was five but he'd never forget the pain. Or the fear. Lying there on the floor unable to defend himself alone in the apartment with a monster. He begged. He cried. But the beating continued. As Jack tried to crawl away, the pimp stepped on his hand until the bones cracked. Then he jerked him off the ground, holding Jack up by his throat.

As the pimp screamed and swore and shook Jack like a rag doll, something inside Jack snapped. It wasn't physical but a part of him died. The fear vanished.

With his teeth clacking together and his legs swinging a foot over the ground, Jack felt suddenly free. Like he was flying.

The pimp stopped shaking Jack and a puzzled look crossed his face.

Jack flashed him a bloody grin and a hoarse chuckle escaped his lips.

The pimp dropped him to the ground, but Jack didn't stop laughing. And when Jack stared up, he saw the man's confusion change. At first, he didn't know what expression was on the man's face. His eyes looked bigger, his brows were arched, and his lips pulled back. Then Jack placed it. He'd seen that look on his own face in the mirror so often—fear. For some reason, the pimp, staring at a bloody and beaten little boy laughing like a lunatic, made him afraid.

And that made Jack strong. He started screaming at the man. He didn't know what the words meant, but as loudly as his bruised voice box would let him, he shouted the pimp's own swears and curses back at him.

The pimp shoved Jack over backwards, but he continued yelling louder and added other words that he heard before to his chorus of threats and swears.

Calling him crazy, the pimp ran out the door.

In the silence that followed, Jack realized something he'd never forget—being afraid was a choice. Jack chose to fight the fear. He chose to beat the fear down and kill it.

The Frenchman stopped in front of Jack. He grabbed the railing as the boat rocketed across the sea. The well-dressed man stood there studying him. He raised his arm and pointed out to the left side of the boat. The sun was setting, and the sky was bathed in a red glow. "Do you know what's over there, Detective?" he shouted over the roar of the motors, causing the others to turn and look at him. "Florida. Your wife may have gotten away but if you are lying to me, I know where your parents live. And I would very much like to take a holiday to the sunshine state."

Jack forced his crooked grin to remain unchanged but inside he recoiled like the man had struck him. "I can save you the airfare. I'm taking you to the sub. Leave them and my wife alone."

The Frenchman smiled. "And what about you? Didn't you suggest earlier that I just let you... walk away?"

"There's no way you're going to let me go. I know that now." Jack hung his head. "But if I tell you where the sub is, there's no reason for you to hurt my wife, or my parents."

"That, my friend, is the only bargain you can make. And I accept. I'll give you one chance to tell me the truth. Are we going to the location of the sub? Because when we get there"—he pointed at the two men huddling together—"I'm sending those two divers down. If they don't find it, everyone you love dies."

Jack's shoulders slumped. "It's there."

"We'll see." The Frenchman walked to the front of the boat.

The veins in Jack's forearms pumped with blood as he strained slightly against the ropes. This time, the wooden chair cracked. The ropes around his chest had a slight bit of slack in them now.

Once they got to the site Jack picked, the two men would go into the water, leaving it a two-on-one fight. The Frenchman didn't stand a chance. He'd only be fighting for his own life.

Jack would be going to war for his family.

# 60

lice stood at the bow of the *Refute*, staring down at the phone in her hand and a map of the ocean. She'd lost Jack's signal ten minutes ago. Not surprising—there were no cell phone towers out here. She knew she would eventually lose it but still, her heart felt as if it stopped when the signal did.

She stared into the salty air as the ship plowed onward into the darkness. The sun had set and the sea was black.

But Jack was out there. She was certain. Trying to find that small boat in the vast sea...

*Please, Lord, you know where he is. Show me.*

Footsteps behind her made her turn around.

Dimitri strolled across the deck toward her. He walked slowly, and stopped next to her at the railing. "Do you have other family, Alice?"

The question made the knot in her stomach grow. "A foster mother."

Dimitri raised an eyebrow.

"My parents died when I was young," Alice explained.

"I was a boy when my father died. My mother passed three years after him."

"I'm sorry."

"We've both weathered similar storms, it seems." Dimitri's thumb rubbed the railing of the ship.

"My grandfather was in the military, too," Alice said. "General Andrew Kolisnyk."

Dimitri's thick brows pulled together. "Your parents were Ukrainian?"

"My mother."

Dimitri sighed. His lips pressed together in a sympathetic line. "Are you certain that you want us to stay on this heading, Alice?" His voice was surprising soft. "Vadik thinks we should follow the course Jack's boat had been traveling. They headed straight out to sea after leaving the harbor. We can change back onto that course. Say the word, I will give the order."

Alice inhaled. The sea air calmed her nerves even as the salt stung her eyes. "I know Jack. He would know that his phone signal would cut out too. He'd take them somewhere I know."

"But you don't know these waters."

"There's one place I do. The pink sand beaches of Eleuthera Island. Jack promised to take me there before the honeymoon was over."

Dimitri straightened up and clasped his hands in front of him. He looked like he was debating about listening to his first mate or her. Alice hoped he reached the right conclusion. But just in case he didn't, she had a plan for hijacking the boat.

"Dimitri!" Peter, the man who reminded Alice of her dentist, jogged up. He was out of breath but smiled. "Vadik needs to know if he should alter the course."

Dimitri gazed out to sea. The salt air tugged at his beard. "We follow her heart. Stay the course."

Peter turned back to the wheelhouse and waved both hands back and forth.

The boat's engine slowed and started, slowed and started. Everyone except Dimitri grabbed the railing.

"Vadik isn't happy," Peter muttered. "He's goosing the engine."

"But he is obeying. That is the important thing."

Alice stared out into the darkness. Her hope was fading with each passing minute.

Her phone beeped.

She glanced down. On the screen was a message asking if she wanted to join the Serve and Protect Network.

"Jack's close!" Alice forced herself not to scream. "My phone picked up his phone's signal!"

"Has it stopped? What kind of boat is it?" Dimitri asked as all three ran toward the wheelhouse.

"Kill the lights!" Alice pulled at Dimitri's elbow. "They'll see us!"

Dimitri turned to the wheelhouse and made a slashing motion across his throat. The engine quieted. Dimitri whistled softly and the lights on the ship shut off but several emergency lights still glowed.

Peter stripped off his shirt, stepped over to the light closest to them and covered it with the shirt before shattering it with his boot.

More muffled sounds of plastic and glass breaking popped from all over the ship and they were plunged into darkness.

Dimitri stopped inside the first door. "Peter, get the rifles and the goggles. Alice, give him a hand then meet me in the wheelhouse."

The hairs on Alice's neck rose as Dimitri hurried up the staircase but she followed Peter anyway. She had to give these men some trust if she was going to save Jack.

Peter hurried down a metal staircase and through the large room that served as the mess hall. The equipment room beyond was filled with gear but was incredibly organized. Peter rushed over to a locked cabinet and removed two rifles and a pistol. He fumbled with the weapons until Alice quickly grabbed one of the rifles.

"Thanks." He wiped his sweaty brow with a shaking hand. "I'm not used to all this excitement." His smile wavered and Alice saw the fear in his eyes.

"You're doing great." She tried to reassure him as she stepped to the side, gently turning the rifle in his hand toward the deck and away from pointing at her stomach.

"Sorry," Peter mumbled. "I forgot. Gun safety and all that, right?"

Alice nodded.

Peter started for the door.

"What about the goggles?" Alice asked.

Peter snapped his fingers. "I'd forget my head…" He rushed over to a shelf and unhooked a pair of military-looking goggles.

Alice followed him out of the room and through the mess hall. They climbed one level of stairs, dashed down the small hallway, then clambered up another set of stairs to the wheelhouse.

The rest of the crew were there. Vadik was driving and Dimitri was staring out to sea.

"Goggles." Dimitri held his arm back to them but didn't take his eyes off the light bobbing up and down on the water.

Peter handed Dimitri the goggles and collapsed into a chair, huffing and puffing.

Alice stood beside Dimitri gazing at the light on the water. It was still a ways off but she could tell by the outline it was a boat.

Dimitri swore in Russian.

"It's a Wave Cutter."

"That's a fast boat," Vadik said. "If they get underway, they can outrun us."

"Do you see Jack?" Alice asked.

Dimitri raised his hand and closed it in a fist.

Vadik pulled back the throttle and the boat immediately slowed to half speed.

"Five men. Jack is one of them." Dimitri nodded. "Two men are putting on scuba gear." He lifted the goggles up. "The wind is with us. It's coming directly to the bow so it's masking our engine noise. Lara, take the goggles and a rifle and go to the bow. Kirill, back her up with the other rifle. Annika, get to the spotlights and on my signal, you will light them up."

All three nodded curtly and left.

"What should I do?" Peter asked as he still tried to catch his breath.

"Stay here with us." Dimitri nodded. "I may need you to relay orders so catch your breath."

Vadik's hand reached for the throttle. "Continue ahead at half speed?"

"Nyet." Dimitri stared back at the boat bobbing on the water in the distance. "Once they are in place, full speed ahead."

# 61

Angelica stepped over the Dyab's body and walked over to the fireplace. She seized the long lighter then strolled from curtain to curtain, igniting the fabric as she passed. With the room burning behind her, she headed downstairs. Her heels clicked off the marble and her reflection smiled back at her from a gold framed mirror hanging in the hall.

All of this was hers now but she wouldn't take any of it—except the Dyab's computer records, and his financial accounts of course. She'd let the police find two bank accounts easily and a third from which, with a little effort, they could recover the money when the time was right. It would be twenty percent of his holdings, enough to convince them to stop looking.

The villa had to fall into the police's hands. She wouldn't even have to make a phone call. The fire department would alert the police when they found the bodies. A search of the villa would reveal the cellar and its captives—including herself.

They had all seen the Dyab, except Samuel of course, and would identify Sebastian.

*Fool.*

But his mistakes were her gain.

Taking out her phone, she called the last piece of the puzzle.

"Hello?" a man answered.

"Oliver Rolle?" The phone disguised her voice. "I know who you work for and what you are seeking. First, you need to rescue the Americans. I am texting you their location."

"Who are you?"

Angelica smiled. A hundred different responses came to mind but she settled on, "Who I am is of no importance. Doing the right thing, is. There is one more matter to deal with—the New Dawn. I will also be sending their location."

"What do you want for all of this help?"

"Nothing."

She hung up and laughed. The sprinkler system kicked on. The fire department would soon arrive and the next part of her plan would begin.

But for now, she'd relish her victory.

The Dyab was dead, and a new one had emerged from the ashes.

# 62

Jack stared at Eleuthera Island as it came into view on their right, bathed in the bright moonlight. A few days ago, he'd been hoping to walk along the pink sandy beach then make love to his bride beneath the stars. He promised to take her there. His phone signal must have long since died out so he was praying that she would figure out that's where he'd lead his kidnappers.

She was his only hope.

The two men in the back of the boat started silently putting on their scuba gear. They didn't speak, but from the intense looks they shared back and forth, Jack knew they were having a silent conversation. And from their expressions, he wondered if once they went into the water, they planned to just keep on swimming.

The moonlight reflected off the water, illuminating the far-off beach. It was hard to judge the distance to shore, but he doubted anyone could swim that far. Not in the open sea.

The thin man said something to the tan man driving and then turned to look at Jack.

The hair on Jack's arms rose. He'd seen the look before.

Alice was too late. The thin man was about to kill him.

Lights flickered on all around the edge of the diving boat as Jack silently prayed.

The thin man strode across the deck, the lights gleaming like torches in his cold eyes.

Jack worked up a grin. "You really *don't* want to kill me."

"No. I really *do*." The thin man smiled. "Besides, if you told the truth about the location of the sub, I no longer need you. And if you lied ..." He shrugged. "I can no longer trust you."

"You should never underestimate the power of having a hostage." Jack pulled his hands as close together as the ropes would allow. "Especially an American tourist who happens to be a detective. I'm pretty valuable."

"You aren't worth Jack. That is an American expression for worthless, is it not, Detective?" The Frenchman continued, "I think you lied about knowing the location of the *Red Star*. I had to at least look. But whether you did or not, I don't care. I'm going to hunt those you love and kill them anyway."

Alice's face filled Jack's memory. She was asleep. Smiling. It was right after they'd made love. And just as suddenly, the image was gone. Replaced by the image that haunted many of his nightmares. Alice in a white coffin. Her eyes open, the emerald green now cold and gray.

But this image was different.

Alice was pregnant.

After Jack's childhood he believed he was numb to grief and pain. Then Chandler died. And the war took more friends. Then Michelle.

The vision he just witnessed felt like someone tried to rip his soul out.

The Frenchman had just made a horrid mistake. He wanted Jack to fear. Maybe the technique worked on others but Jack didn't react to fear like normal people did. Jack had been beaten down by fear so much, it was different for him.

Fear was the key that unlocked all the memories of Jack's hate and hurt. And in that cage inside of him lived a beast.

Jack pulled against the ropes as hard as he could. The ropes tightened and cut into his skin. He didn't really feel it. All he could think of was tearing the Frenchman limb from limb. Adrenaline burned through his veins. Wood splintered and the chair broke into pieces beneath him.

Jack's hands were still tied behind his back but he was free.

The Frenchman's eyes widened. He reached behind his back.

Jack planted his foot and delivered a side thrust kick to the man's midsection.

The Frenchman flew backward, a pistol falling from his hand before he slammed into the back of Scarface.

The two divers looked at each other and dove over the side of the boat.

The odds just doubled in Jack's favor. He raced forward, lowering his shoulder. He slammed into the Frenchman, driving him and Scarface into the console.

Shoving the Frenchman off of him, Scarface grabbed Jack's shirt. He yanked Jack forward and off balance. They were now nose to scarred nose.

With Jack's hands tied behind him, he couldn't punch.

Scarface must have realized it too. He smiled at Jack.

Jack arched his back, then drove his forehead into the man's nose as hard as he could. Fireworks went off in Jack's eyes but the man shrieked in pain.

Scarface fell against the console. His hand landed on the throttle. At the stern of the boat, water shot high into the air. Scarface must have twisted the steering wheel because the boat was now making a tight circle.

Footsteps behind him made Jack spin around.

The Frenchman rushed him, a knife in his hand thrust forward like a spear.

Jack's hands might be tied but his legs weren't. He kicked for the man's head.

The Frenchman ducked.

Jack's eyes widened as the heel of his foot just missed the man's head.

Time slowed.

The lights of the boat gleamed off a piece of broken chair still attached to the rope that had bound Jack's right ankle to the chair. His foot may have missed the man's head but the broken piece of wood slammed off the side of the Frenchman's face like a policeman's nightstick, knocking him sideways.

Jack planted his foot and kicked again. Jack's lower leg struck the Frenchman in the ribs.

The man doubled over, dropping the knife.

Thick arms coiled around Jack's waist as Scarface tackled him from behind.

Jack landed hard on his side. Scarface pinned Jack to the deck. Jack struggled to roll out from under him but the man outweighed Jack by at least fifty pounds.

Clutching his stomach, the Frenchman moved to the back of the boat and toward the gun sliding around on the deck.

Jack kicked blindly. His legs struck something and the Frenchman tripped.

The three men were entwined in a pile, swearing, kicking and punching.

The boat rocked.

Scattered equipment slid into the men. The metal briefcase Ramon recovered from the *Red Star* came to rest against Jack's shin. He kicked the case into the gun, sending both objects out of the Frenchman's reach and to the stern of the boat.

A wave crashed over the side, sending salt water spraying over everything.

The dropped knife slid out from under a life preserver. Scarface grasped the handle.

Lying partially on top of the man, Jack pulled at the ropes tying his hands behind his back. He couldn't grab the knife.

But he wasn't defenseless.

Jack opened his mouth wide and clamped down on the man's forearm.

Scarface screamed and thrashed and let go of the weapon.

Jack rolled onto his back and brought his knees up tightly to his body. Skin scraped off his wrists as he pulled his bound hands down and over his feet.

The Frenchman grabbed the boat pike. The five-foot-long wooden pole ended in a metal pointed tip with a hook curling back down.

Jack's hands were now in front of him but they were still bound together and it was a two-on-one fight. They also had the advantage of reach and a weapon.

A wave rocked the boat violently. All three men swayed sideways but kept their footing. The knife skittered closer to Jack but the Frenchman could run him through before he could grab it.

Jack stepped toward the stern. His feet landed on the anchor chain. He was running out of boat.

Light from above and to the left suddenly flooded the boat. Above the noise of the sea, the fighting and the motor that was still making their boat travel in a circle, a louder rumble rose. It was an engine. And this one sounded huge.

Another wave buffered the ship. As his enemies grabbed the railing for balance, Jack seized the chain.

He began to swing it around his head.

The Frenchman stopped.

Jack stepped forward. He lashed out with the chain but the Frenchman ducked.

Scarface crouched low.

Jack started his circle again. Faster and faster the heavy chain whizzed above his head until he brought it down.

The Frenchman raised the pike.

The chain slammed into the wood, knocking the pole from the Frenchman's hands.

But the chain fell on the deck.

And Scarface scooped it up. He pulled the chain toward himself until it was taut.

Jack faced off against the stronger man in a life and death tug of war. And with Jack's hands in front of him, still bound, it was a war he was certain to lose.

Scarface coiled the chain around his beefy forearm. Once, twice, three times he wrapped it and seized it with both hands. He smiled at Jack.

Jack returned the grin. He spun to his left, grabbed the emergency release pin on the anchor winch and shoved.

The boat rocked as the heavy winch tumbled off the side and into the sea.

Metal clanked and clicked as the chain disappeared yard by yard over the railing. Scarface screamed as chain tightened around his flesh. Yanked off his feet, he rammed into the Frenchman, knocking him down, before Scarface hit the side of the boat. Up and over he went, shrieking, silenced by the splash, then down to the depths below.

Jack shuffled sideways and grabbed the knife on the deck with a reverse grip. He sliced off the ropes binding his wrists.

His hope of evening the odds was short lived. When he looked up, the Frenchman was holding his reclaimed gun and aiming at Jack's chest.

The roar of the approaching engine rose to a deafening level. A huge shadow passed over the boat. An enormous metal ship steered straight at them. And like a deer on the railroad tracks, they didn't stand a chance.

# 63

Dimitri rushed down to the bow as Alice watched the battle on the other ship from the wheelhouse. She felt like she was trapped in a nightmare. She could see her Jack fighting like a gladiator against two men, but there was nothing she could do.

"We're going to crash." Vadik reached for the throttle and pulled it back.

"Don't slow down!" Alice shouted but the Russian ignored her.

The engine of the boat Jack was in came to life, casting a spray of water high in the air.

"They're going to get away! Speed up!" Alice yelled.

"You don't give the orders!" Vadik scowled.

Alice's heart raced. She had to do something or her husband would die.

"Get back!" Alice pointed the pistol in her hand at Vadik's chest. "NOW!"

The Russian raised his hands and backed away.

"Alice…" Peter's voice rose high.

"Grab onto something," Alice warned as she shoved the throttle forward and steered toward the other ship. She aimed for the rear of the boat but knew there was no way she would just strike the engine of the other ship. She grabbed the handle for the fog horn and tugged down.

A blast of sound split the air.

Dimitri cast a puzzled look up to the wheelhouse. His eyes widened and he began shouting as he waved his arms back and forth.

Everyone on the deck braced themselves.

Alice pulled the horn again.

The ship shuddered. Fiberglass and metal shrieked as the large boat crushed the smaller craft.

Alice prayed that she could save Jack and didn't just kill him.

# 64

Jack stared at the gun pointed at his chest. The barrel swayed with the rocking of the boat.

The Frenchman's smug grin disappeared. His eyes rounded. The gun barrel drooped. "They're insane!" the Frenchman shouted, taking a step back.

A fog horn split the air and the blinding spotlight swept over them. A huge ship was on a collision course with their boat. The fog horn gave another deafening blast. The engine thundered. An enormous wake rushed in front of the huge ship; it rocked the little boat so hard, the Frenchman slid backward and slammed against the railing.

The gun fired. The bullet blew a hole into the fiberglass next to Jack's foot.

Another wave tipped the little boat almost completely on its side. Holding the railing with one hand he threw the knife as hard as he could.

He aimed for the Frenchman's chest but the handle of the weapon hit the thin man's hip. The shining blade spun upward and hit him in the face. Blood splattered his pale skin. The Frenchman screamed and dropped the gun.

The shadow of the bow of the other boat loomed above, and the impact was imminent.

The Frenchman dove overboard.

Jack grabbed the railing and was about to do the same—until he saw the briefcase lying on the deck in the stern. That was the key to proving their innocence.

He scrambled toward the back of the boat, his feet slipping on the shifting vessel. The bow of the other boat hit the smaller boat's side, lifting the boat upward.

Every loose item on the deck came sliding toward Jack. Like a football player scrambling to recover a fumbled ball, Jack kept his focus on the aluminum case, sparkling in the lights of the ship like a silver prize. He thrust his hand down. His fingers closed around metal.

Fiberglass splintered behind him. The front of the small boat was being sucked beneath the bow of the larger one. Jack grabbed the railing with his other hand and dove as far away as he could.

It felt like he'd just dived into the middle of a waterfall. Churning water sent him spinning end over end. His fingers tightened around the briefcase but the force of the water was so strong he was losing the battle.

Grabbing the case with both hands, he held the case against his body and started swimming down. Pieces of boat battered his already beaten body. The saltwater stung his rope-burned skin.

The sound of the small boat being smashed to smithereens was distorted by being underwater. Another noise rumbled louder than the destruction—the turning of the large ship's propeller.

# 65

Holding the case against his chest with his left arm, Jack kicked frantically and clawed his way down and away with his right arm. The thump of the propeller grew louder as the ship passed over him. With each turn of the shaft, the vibrations pulsated more strongly through him. It was as if some giant slapped his back with an enormous hand, then pulled him back only to do it again.

Suddenly, all his forward progress stopped. He was still swimming as hard as he could but he wasn't moving any longer.

The propeller began to pull him back toward the ship and its spinning blades.

The thought of being sucked into the huge blades and getting chopped to pieces like a carrot in a food processor sent a fresh surge of adrenaline coursing through him. He struggled as if the Devil was dragging him to hell.

Slowly, he started to pull away from the ship. The deafening noise of the propellers grew fainter and slowed.

Someone had stopped the engine.

The wave of relief running through him was short lived. His lungs burned. One danger had passed but how far was it to the surface?

Jack's long legs kicked furiously as he swam straight up. He rocketed toward the oxygen he desperately needed.

His head punched through a wave and he stared, blinking, at the night sky. Pieces of debris floated all about, illuminated by flashlights that swept the water.

Jack stifled his cry for help when he heard voices from the ship. They were speaking Russian.

Taking a deep breath, Jack surveyed his surroundings.

Grabbing a broken piece of Styrofoam, Jack used it to cover his head as he quietly paddled toward the ship.

He had assumed it was Alice who had tracked him out to sea but the Russians must have caught her and used her phone to follow him.

Praying Alice was aboard the ship, Jack swam toward the back of the boat.

From deck, many different voices were calling out. Ropes were cast over the side and flashlights swept the water.

"Help!" someone yelled from the sea near the bow of the boat.

All of the lights on the ship shifted to focus on the man in the water. Everyone on board the ship rushed in that direction.

Jack swam to the side of the ship, grabbed one of the ropes and pulled. It had been fastened to the railing. It was awkward and slow to pull himself up but he managed to make it onto the deck without losing the case.

The commotion at the front of the ship continued. There were over a half dozen people crowded around the railing. The two large Russians were easy to pick out. They hoisted one man out of the sea. From his size and clothes, it must have been

Scarface. Jack was surprised he freed himself from the anchor chain.

There was another shout and everyone turned to look overboard. More ropes were thrown out but Jack didn't wait to see who would be rescued next. He rushed over to the back of the cabin. Hanging next to the fire extinguisher was an ax and a machete. Jack used the machete to cut the ropes dangling from his wrist and legs.

Moving quickly, he slipped inside the cabin door. A staircase led up and another down. Jack headed upstairs toward the bridge. He was breathing heavily. Water dripped off his chin and faintly dinged off the blade of the machete as he crept upward.

He peered through the open doorway. The bridge was deserted. Everyone must be at the bow. Jack scanned the room. Lying across a table in the back was a long rifle with a scope. He grabbed the weapon, checked the full magazine and chambered a round.

Pressing his back against the wall, Jack peered down onto the deck.

Six crew members hovered over Scarface and one of the scuba divers lying on the deck. The large Russian was asking them questions.

Movement at the bow railing caught Jack's eye. Someone was still shining a flashlight on the ocean surface. They turned around and Jack swallowed.

*Alice.*

Jack shattered the large window with the butt of the rifle. "Let her go, or you die!" Jack bellowed as he set the large Russian's chest in the center of his sights.

"Jack!" Alice shouted. "No! No!" She frantically waved her arms and raced forward. "They're helping us!"

Dimitri kept his arms raised but smiled. "I'm very glad to see you alive, but this is a strange way to thank my crew and me for saving you and your wife's lives."

Alice covered her mouth, a sob escaping.

Jack lowered the gun and ran to her. He thundered down the stairs, turned the corner and Alice rushed into his arms.

Pain raced up his side but he ignored it. He held her; his strong arms wrapped around her.

Alice lifted her chin and stepped back. Her eyes were wet with tears. She raised a bloody hand toward his face.

"You're bleeding!" they both cried out at once.

"I don't think I am," Jack said. "Is it you?"

Alice reached out and touched his side.

Pain radiated along his right ribs. He winced and shied sideways. "Nope. It's me."

"Dimitri!" Alice shouted.

"It's not that bad," Jack protested.

Footsteps echoed off the metal grate. Dimitri grinned broadly. "Welcome aboard the *Refute.*"

"Jack's hurt." Alice's eyes brimmed with tears.

"I'm fine." Jack thrust out his hand. "I can't thank you enough for saving my wife."

Dimitri's eyes widened. He stared at the metal briefcase in Jack's hand. "Those are the records of the *Red Star.* My father's ship."

"It's also the proof that Alice and I are innocent." Jack's hand tightened on the case.

"I need to see what's inside of it."

"You earned that," Jack said. "But I'm taking it to the authorities after you do. Agreed?"

Dimitri nodded. "Why don't we take a look at that cut downstairs. They're bringing the prisoners down now."

"How many men did you rescue?"

"Two." Dimitri pointed at the door leading to the dock.

Four crew members marched Scarface and one of the scuba divers through the door and down the stairs. The two men were pale and trembled. When Scarface looked up and saw Jack, he threw up a large amount of water.

"There was another diver and a Frenchman. The Frenchman's dangerous. Very dangerous."

Dimitri nodded. "My men can handle them. We've contacted the authorities and will wait here until they arrive. Until then, let's get you patched up." His eyes shifted downward but he wasn't looking at Jack's wound—he was staring at the briefcase. He wiped his mouth with the back of his hand. His eyes had a far-off look to them.

Jack had seen the expression before but couldn't place it. Then he remembered his first drug bust. It was a former teacher who spiraled out of control from painkillers all the way to meth. He'd gone nuts in a local drug house and stabbed two people because he claimed they stole his last hit. When Jack had shown up for the call, the man was literally tearing down the walls of the room looking for it. Five cops were needed to get him under control, yet he wouldn't stop fighting.

Until he saw the little bag of meth under the couch. As he stared at the drugs, a calmness came over the man on the outside, but inside, Jack knew he was burning with desire. The man had lost everything, his wife, kids, job and now his freedom, but he stared at that meth like it was his savior.

Dimitri, staring at the briefcase in Jack's hand, had the same look on his face.

# 66

J ack lay on a table while Peter, one of Dimitri's crew, bandaged his side. The cut wasn't as bad as it looked, but his ribs felt like a mule had kicked him.

Scarface and the diver were lying on cots that had been set up for them. Both men's hands were bound but from the haggard expressions on their faces, Jack doubted they could put up much resistance.

Dimitri stood at a large wooden table. The metal briefcase lay closed in front of him. Dimitri leaned forward and stared at the case the way a bomb examiner would study an explosive.

Footsteps clanged on the staircase outside the mess hall.

Vadik and the rest of the crew marched in. "We haven't found the other two," Vadik said, walking over to Dimitri. "And no one has showed up."

Dimitri frowned. "We should call again."

"A word, Captain." Vadik motioned to the door.

The two men moved to talk just outside the doorway.

Alice squeezed Jack's hand.

He motioned her closer.

She leaned down and kissed his forehead.

He whispered in her ear, "How long has it been since you found me?"

She stiffened. "Forty-five minutes."

Jack wasn't certain about emergency response times on the water, but something wasn't right. A helicopter would have been here long ago, even a fast boat. And those emergency cutters were like jets on the sea.

Jack stared back at Dimitri. He was pointing at the briefcase. His jaw was set. The veins in his arms stood out.

Vadik stepped closer to Dimitri. "Nyet," he said loudly and lowered his voice, but from the way his teeth were bared, their conversation was quickly getting heated.

Peter stopped bandaging Jack's side and turned to look at the doorway.

"What about our fathers!" Dimitri bellowed.

"What about us!" Vadik screamed back. "Our fathers left our mothers and us at home while they chased their own foolish dreams. Do you think my father cared for me? And now I've got the chance to make something of my life and you're going to just give it away?"

"No one will give you money for the *Red Star!*" Dimitri loomed over Vadik.

"The Dyab will!"

"I will not sell our fathers' honor to the Devil." Dimitri turned his back on Vadik. He took a step forward and planted his foot.

Sadness replaced the fire in his eyes and his dark eyes cooled.

Vadik shoved him forward.

Dimitri stumbled into the mess hall and fell. He landed on his side, blood running down his back.

Vadik stood in the doorway. A dripping knife in his hand. "I will."

Jack leapt from the table.

Vadik slammed the door shut. A metal bar slid into place.

As Jack vainly tried the handle, Alice and Peter rushed to Dimitri.

"You don't know where the sub is!" Jack pounded on the door.

Behind the little glass portal, Vadik grinned. "You led me right to it."

"I was bluffing, you idiot!" Jack screamed. "I don't know where it is!"

Vadik laughed. "You're bluffing now. You Americans are all the same."

Annika ran over to the door. "Vadik. Please!"

Vadik swallowed and slowly shook his head. "You should have stayed on deck when I asked you to." He lifted his hand. He was holding some kind of controller.

Annika started to cry. "Don't do this! Please!"

Vadik pressed the button.

The ship shook violently. Somewhere in the stern a muffled explosion reverberated through the metal. The vibrations shot up Jack's legs and made his heart race.

Jack pushed his way past the crew and raced for the rear door of the mess hall.

"Jack!" Alice called out to him as she helped Peter with Dimitri.

Jack seized the rear door handle. It wouldn't budge. They were trapped in a steel box.

A siren sounded somewhere above. Emergency lights flashed.

Annika looked up. Her tear-stained face was ashen. "Vadik's scuttled the ship. He's condemned us to our fathers' fate."

# 67

The wound in Jack's side burned as he raised the fire ax high and brought it down against the door latch.

Metal clanged; the ax handle cracked but the thick latch didn't budge.

Kirill and Peter took turns bashing on the front door with a fire extinguisher and metal bar. But for all their effort, it was like trying to open a coconut with a plastic spoon.

The ship was listing heavily to the port side. Alarms continued to blare and the emergency lighting had kicked in.

Jack called to Kirill. "Can you get the hinges off the doors?"

"Impossible. We're trapped."

Alice dashed over. She'd been rooting around in the cabinets and closet looking for anything to use to get out. She held up a small propane torch. "What about this!" She shook it. "There's still some left. Maybe we could burn through the door."

"They're steel." Kirill shook his head. "You'd need my thermite to burn through them."

"You have thermite?!" Jack grabbed him by the shoulders. "Where?"

"The supply room." He pointed past the locked rear door. "It would work but we can't get to it."

Jack rushed over to the vent on the ceiling and pulled the cover off. The opening was too small for anyone to fit through, even Alice.

Scarface started laughing. "It looks like the Devil is going to claim you after all."

Jack turned to Dimitri. Peter and Alice had bandaged the stab wound and stopped the bleeding but he'd lost a great deal of blood. His face was pale and he lay on his back staring at the ceiling. The look on his face said it all—he'd given up.

"We need a way to get to the supply room!" Jack glared down at him. "You know this ship better than anyone."

Dimitri closed his eyes. "There is no way."

The ship shuddered and rocked. Slowly it dipped further down.

"Water!" Peter pointed at the rear door of the mess and the water now seeping underneath.

"You're the captain of this ship, Dimitri. Do you think your father just gave up? Think!" Jack shouted.

"Jack!" Alice stepped closer to him.

Jack leaned over so he could look Dimitri in the eyes but the Russian kept them closed.

Jack grabbed his shirt. "You said you wanted to prove your fathers weren't cowards. Maybe you should prove you're not one first!"

Dimitri's eyes flashed open. He grabbed Jack's wrist. There was strength in his grip. He met Jack's stare and his eyes widened. "Behind the stove! There's another vent. It connects to the main air distribution. It may be large enough."

Jack and Kirill raced over to the stove and yanked it away from the wall. They ripped the aluminum vent down, revealing a two-by-two-foot greasy opening.

Jack turned to look at the crew, but he already knew none of them were small enough to fit through. The only one who could—was Alice.

"You need thermite, right?" Alice asked Kirill. "Anything else?"

Kirill held up the torch Alice found earlier. "No. This will light it. It's in the cabinet on the far-left corner. Clearly labeled."

"You're not going." Jack said the words before he thought them through. He held up his hand. "I know you will, I just meant..."

She grabbed him, pulled him down and kissed him. "I love you too."

***

Alice slid through the greasy vent feeling like meat being stuff inside a sausage casing. It smelled like that anyway. It was maddeningly frustrating going. With all of the slime coating every inch of metal surface, she only inched forward.

But she was making progress. Light shone from a vent up ahead. When she reached it, she pushed against the metal but the grid didn't move.

She felt around the edge in the dark, hoping to located tabs or a latch. In the four corners, she touched the sharp ends of screws.

Alice swore.

Pressing her back against the wall, she pulled her legs up to her chest and pushed against the grate. It bulged out but didn't open.

Snarling and swearing, she started kicking. She concentrated on the lower right corner. It started to move. Slowly, more and more light showed through.

The corner gave way. She pushed and the metal bent. It wasn't that much, but she could fit through. The back of her shirt tore and the metal sliced into her skin as she pulled herself under the grate.

Her hands landed in four inches of water on the deck.

She dropped into the hallway. The ship was shifting onto its side fast now. Metal creaked and groaned like a wounded animal.

The door at the end of the hallway was closed. Vadik had sealed it shut with a padlock. There was no way of getting through.

Alice hurried forward. By the time she reached the supply room door, the water was above her knees. She pulled at the door but the pressure of the water made it hard to open. She managed to get her arm inside and pushed.

Water gushed from the room but the door swung open.

She sloshed her way over to the cabinet.

The lights overhead flickered.

Ripping the door open, her heart started pounding in her chest. Kirill was right. Everything was clearly labeled.

The problem was—it was all written in Russian.

Boxes, cans, and containers of all sizes sat on the shelf. Warning signs covered most of them. But three different containers had more warnings then all the others and they also had big stickers showing flames and explosions.

Alice grabbed a canvas tote off the wall and dumped out what was inside. She grabbed two plastic trash bags, wrapped up the three containers, one of which she prayed was thermite, then stuffed everything inside the tote and headed for the door.

The ship lurched.

Somewhere below, the sound of rushing water flowed. The lights flickered and died. So did the alarms.

Alice was plunged into darkness.

For a moment she froze. It wasn't in panic. She stood there with her eyes shut trying to picture the layout of the room with her mind's eye, and how far it was to the vent.

She opened her eyes but it was still so pitch black she might as well have kept them closed.

Water swept around her thighs. It was rising quickly.

She hurried forward moving her arms in an arc, feeling for the doorway. Her fingers touched the door frame. She reached out until her hand reached the wall then continued forward.

Rubbing her hand along the wall, she fought down her fears as the water rose higher. It was up to her waist when she reached the end of the hallway.

Where was the vent?

Alice turned back around. The water had risen so high she must have passed by it.

Lowering her hand into the water, she felt her way back down the way.

Her hand dipped inside the vent opening. The entire vent was now underwater.

Was the whole thing flooded? It was so slow going, how could she make it through underwater with the heavy tote?

Alice fought back a sob.

Then she pictured Jack's face. She remembered the first time she saw him. He ran into her on Auntie Haddie's porch when they were carrying groceries inside. He made her drop the bag she was holding and then gazed into her eyes.

Her heart was his then. He belonged to her and she to him. Somehow, she just knew it.

And there was no way she was going to let him die.

Stuffing the tote under the water, Alice took three gulps of air and pulled herself into the vent. She felt like she just climbed into a flooded casket. Her sneakers skidded on the grease and the heavy tote sagged back into her face. She pressed her arms against the sides and pushed.

She hardly moved.

Shoving the tote forward with her right arm, she pulled with her left hand and tried to push with her legs. She shot forward a few inches until the tote settled back down on her. She pushed and pulled again.

Forward progress was made but her lungs were burning.

She shoved the tote and it shot forward. Her hand broke through the surface of the water. Clawing at the metal like an animal trapped in a well, she lifted her head out of the water and gulped air.

Light flashed from above.

Something tapped against her cheek.

People were shouting but their words echoed off the walls.

"Shut up!" Jack's voice rose above the others. "Alice. Grab the rope."

She reached up and seized the cord that had brushed against her cheek. "Got it!"

The slack tightened and she started to rise up. The boat had to be at a steep angle for her to be this far below them.

Flashlights blinded her.

Someone took the tote out of her hands.

Jack swept her into his arms. He was kissing her and holding her.

"Yes!" Kirill held one of the containers up. "Everyone get back," he yelled as he sloshed to the door.

The water was now above even Jack's waist.

Peter was supporting Dimitri. The rest of the crew, the diver and Scarface moved against the wall.

Jack held Alice's hand. "Stay with me. When we get topside, the most important thing is to swim clear, got it?"

Alice nodded. With all that Jack had been through, it was a testament to his inner strength that he was still on his feet. But even he had limits. Once they got through that door, she had to make sure he made it off the ship.

# 68

The thermite burned through the lock, sending huge clouds of steam through the room. The acrid smell burned Jack's nose and the smoke stung his eyes but he forced himself to stare at the progress.

The water was rising faster now. The ship rolled even further on its side and the bow was lifting higher.

Kirill swung the steel bar grasped in his hands at the glowing door handle. Showers of sparks danced in the air. The handle sagged and fell into the water.

A huge cloud of steam filled the room.

"Calm," Dimitri shouted. "One by one—move."

In the light of the flashlight beams shining through the steam, Jack watched as Annika, the diver, Scarface and Kirill slipped through the open door. Alice stood by his side, holding his hand.

After everyone was through, Jack motioned Peter and Dimitri forward.

Dimitri shook his head.

Jack nodded and started moving.

"Stubborn man," Alice muttered. "Please don't tell me he's thinking about going down with his ship."

"He's not," Jack called back as he made his way down the hallway and toward the stairs rising up at an odd angle because of the listing of the ship. "He wants to know what's in that case as badly as I do. But he is going to be the last to leave. I respect that."

When they reached the deck above the mess deck, the boat rolled more on its side as the stern continued to dip lower. Jack held onto the handle on the wall with one hand and pulled Alice against his side with his other.

Even though most things on a boat are secured down, debris shifted dangerously as the ship pitched on the moving sea. They slammed into the wall for a moment, a loose fire extinguisher bouncing off the wall just in front of Jack's face.

Jack took a deep breath but before he could move, the ship did. Like a bucking horse trying to throw its rider, the bow of the ship rose up and shook back and forth.

Jack's grip tightened on the wall handle. His legs lifted off the ground. Alice screamed but clung to his arm and his belt.

Dimitri held onto the railing but Peter slammed head first into the wall and slumped to the deck.

The ship settled back down with a loud shudder.

"Come on!" Jack called back to Peter and Dimitri.

The large Russian was halfway up the twisted steps, the briefcase in one hand, his other trying to pull Peter up the stairs. The dentist was holding the side of his head. His glasses were gone and from the dazed look on his face, Jack knew he was in trouble.

Jack stared out at the deck. The bow was rising out of the water now at almost a sixty-degree angle.

"Let me go," Alice said. "You need to help them."

Jack nodded but held onto her hand as he made his way out the door. "My first priority is keeping you safe." He looked at the wall. There were still three life vests hanging there.

"I'm not going until you do."

"I love you, Alice." He slipped one vest over her head.

She pulled the straps tight and her eyes widened. "Don't even think about it!"

Jack lifted her up and took two steps toward the railing. "Swim as far away from the boat as you can."

"No way, Jack! I will punch you in the nose!" Alice's feet were kicking in protest. Her foot connected with Jack's side. He saw stars and let go.

She landed on the deck on her butt, and grabbed the railing. "Don't you—*DARE!*" she shouted. "And in case you didn't notice, they both need help. *OUR* help." She thrust out her chin, her green eyes blazing.

Jack winced as he straightened up. "Nice kick; glad you didn't punch me. And you're right."

Turning back to the doorway, Jack and Alice hurried back into the ship.

Dimitri and Peter were at the top of the stairs. Neither looked good.

Jack handed Dimitri a vest and Alice began helping Peter on with his.

"He's in shock," Dimitri said.

"Just need to lie down for a moment," Peter mumbled.

"Alice, stay with Peter," Jack said, as he grabbed the huge Russian around his waist.

"Follow me, Peter." Alice's voice was so calm that Peter nodded and smiled as Alice took him by the hand.

Jack waited until Alice made it through the doorway until he half dragged Dimitri out to the deck.

The four of them stood at the railing.

"Alice, you're first. I'll send Peter over next."

Alice stood up on the railing, kissed Jack's cheek and jumped. Peter's eyes widened and he gasped.

"Climb up." Jack helped the startled dentist onto the rail.

"Where's the captain?!" he shouted.

"Right behind us."

When Peter turned and saw Dimitri he calmed down. Pulling his legs onto the other side of the railing, his knuckles turned white. He looked at Jack and swallowed. "I can't swim."

"You have a life vest and Alice is waiting for you."

"I—"

Jack shoved him hard.

Dimitri laughed. "You would make a fine captain." His voice was weak.

"Stay with me, Dimitri." He went to grab the case from the Russian but Dimitri had tied it to his wrist.

"It stays with me," Dimitri mumbled.

Jack looked from the railing to the large Russian and gritted his teeth. He lowered his shoulder and hoisted the huge man across his shoulders in a fireman's carry. Taking one step toward the railing, he heaved.

The ship began moving again. Jack had expected it to tilt up but the bow dropped down, sending a huge wave high into the air.

Clutching the railing with both hands, Jack started to pull himself over the side. For a moment, he thought he was losing his mind. He wasn't staring at the churning sea, but metal.

Then he realized the boat was rolling over.

Like a log in water, the boat spun. And like a hamster in a wheel, Jack raced along with it. Salt spray filled the air along with the deep thrum of something that sounded like a wind turbine.

*The propeller is out of the water.*

The slick metal beneath his sneakers gave way to barnacles as the underside of the boat rolled out of the sea. Jack raced upward, running, slipping, grabbing and pulling himself on. He crested the hull but the boat was still turning.

Running was easier now because of the angle.

The metal beneath him buckled and the ship spun in the opposite direction.

Jack's legs continued to pump but his feet were hitting nothing but air.

He sailed out over the ocean in an arc. His feet struck the water and he landed face first into the sea.

Since he was a child, Jack had always been a risk taker. So when it came to jumping into a pond, there wasn't anything he hadn't tried. Rope swing, cliff, even bridges.

Many times, he'd landed wrong.

None of them prepared him for this belly flop.

But in spite of all the pain, he wanted to laugh. Like a good slap in the face, everything was now vividly clear. In spite of the ship rolling over, he could picture where Alice, Peter and Dimitri should be.

He just had to swim up and get them.

Jack's head broke the surface and he gulped in air as the *Refute* bobbed behind him, sending out waves that pushed him away from the wreckage.

"Alice!" Jack called out.

The propeller of the ship had stopped spinning but noise was everywhere.

"Alice!" Jack screamed again but she didn't answer.

Blinding light shone down in his face.

"There!" someone shouted.

The sound of a small motor rose above the other noises as an inflatable raft raced toward him.

"My wife!" Jack shouted. "She's in the water!"

"Alice is fine," a familiar voice called back. "Now let's get you taken care of."

The red skiff stopped beside Jack. Three men were aboard. One behind the wheel. One at the bow. And Oliver Rolle, who stood smiling down at Jack.

# 69

Jack lay on a gurney in the medical room of the Royal Bahamas Defense Force ship. Alice sat in the chair beside him while Peter lay sleeping on the other gurney.

"Did he say anything to you?" Alice asked. She was holding his right hand with her left hand; her other wrist was handcuffed to the chair.

"Besides the fact that everyone aboard the *Refute* had been rescued—nothing." Jack eyed his own handcuff, which was locked around the gurney.

The sound of the helicopter outside faded. "I bet they medevacked Dimitri out," Jack said.

"I hope so." Alice squeezed his hand.

Jack tried to turn a little to look at her. The metal chains around his ankles rattled and tightened. "I think the leg shackles were a little over the top."

"I wanted to ensure that you stuck around long enough for me to explain," Oliver said as he strolled into the room. His

English accent was even thicker now. "You do have a tendency to bugger off."

"And you've got a habit of lying." Jack sat up straight.

"How about we call a truce." Alice smiled.

Jack tried to cross his arms but couldn't with his handcuffed wrist.

"I'm amendable to that." Oliver pulled up a chair. "Oliver Rolle. Inspector in the service of Her Majesty the Queen."

Jack rolled his eyes. "You want to tell me that your spy name is the same as your real name?"

Olive chuckled. "I'm not a spy, although the movies do portray anyone working in Her Majesty's service as a James Bond-like character. Sorry to disappoint, but I'm a policeman. The Royal Bahamian Defense Force asked for some assistance in dealing with an undercover operation here. Since I'm originally from the Bahamas, it was decided we'd go with my own backstory. Less miscellaneous details for me to remember."

"So, you're a cop." Alice leaned forward. "You know we're innocent."

"We had to rule you out, of course." Oliver held up his hand. "Let me back up for a moment if you will and allow me to apologize. This whole situation became extremely sticky rather quickly."

"For you or for us?" Jack said.

"Both, actually. I was assigned to look into a situation dealing with the illegal activities on the docks, nothing rising to the level of a missing former Soviet Union submarine. A different department intercepted a phone call regarding that and looped us in. Unfortunately, I was on the lower end of the loop so my being able to confide in you was not an option."

Jack tried unsuccessfully to cross his arms again. "Can you take these stupid things off now?"

Oliver unlocked Alice's handcuff first. "You'll be please to know that both Andres and Irene Knowles are safe and sound."

"What about their baby?" Alice blurted, her pretty face etched with worry.

"It's a boy and he's doing well. His mum will need to remain on bed rest for a bit. He still has a lot of growing to do," Oliver said, grinning broadly.

"What a relief! Thank God!" Alice exclaimed.

"What about Vadik?" Jack asked.

"The search for him is still ongoing. Assuming he took a skiff from the *Refute*, he will not get far."

"And the Frenchman and other diver?"

Oliver's jaw clenched. The vein in his neck beat visibly. "No word."

Jack felt there was much more Oliver knew regarding the Frenchman but he didn't press him for the information. "And Dimitri? He was on the helicopter?"

"He's on his way to the mainland now." Oliver's eyes shifted to Alice. He didn't need to say more. The situation was grave.

"So where does that leave Alice and me?"

Oliver unlocked Jack's handcuff and shackles. "Still in a bit of a sticky situation I'm afraid. There's a lot of explaining that needs to be done and I'm certain that several different agencies wish to speak with you. This may take a while."

Alice stood up. "No, it won't. Please ask them to gather together tomorrow at noon and we'll give them their debriefing. After that, we're done."

Oliver chuckled dismissively. "I'm afraid you don't realize how these debriefings work, Alice. They're very complicated and quite time consuming."

Alice held up her phone. "I'm afraid you don't realize how I work, Ollie. We will do this simply and quickly as I have requested, so that Jack and I can salvage our honeymoon, or you will have a media storm on your hands that'll make Hurricane Axel look like a summer breeze. I will start a live stream and tell the entire world about the *Red Star*, the black market, the—"

Oliver cast a sidelong glance at Jack.

"She'll do it." Jack grinned proudly.

Oliver frowned. "All I can do is ask."

Alice looked into her phone and pressed record. "Hello! My name is Alice Stratton. I'm on my honeymoon—"

"Okay! All right!" Oliver stood and held up his hands. "I'll get it done."

"Thank you," Alice said.

"You two and your wild antics...." Oliver muttered as he headed for the door. "Each of you is a pistol, but the two of you together are actual dynamite!"

***

The next day, after almost six hours of testimony in front of a panel that Jack was certain was made up of organizations belonging to countries beyond both the Bahamas and England, he and Alice sat on a bench as Inspector Renard strode down the hallway.

The man came to attention and stuck his hand out to Alice then Jack. "Mr. and Mrs. Stratton. You have been cleared of any and all violations of Royal Bahama law." He reached into his suit pocket and handed them back their passports.

"Congratulations on solving your case, Inspector." Jack handed his passport to Alice for safekeeping.

"The snake actually devoured itself, in this instance." Renard smoothed an end of his mustache with his thumb. "But as the saying goes, more than one snake lives in the hole."

"I'm sure you'll catch them too," Alice said.

Renard shook his head. "I'm leaving that to others. My family and I are moving."

"Now? I'd have thought you'd get a promotion out of all of this," Jack said.

"One was offered. I declined." Renard looked at Alice and winked. "For some unknown reason, I came to realize how important it is to fight for your family."

Jack shook his hand and Alice gave him a hug.

As they watched him walk away, Jack squeezed Alice's hand. "It's hard being a policeman and having a family."

"You've told me that a hundred times, Mr. Stratton." Alice smiled up at him. "Marriage is hard in general. Aunt Haddie is the one who told me that. But we got this because we've got each other." She wrapped her arm around Jack's waist.

"They still haven't caught Vadik or the Frenchman," Jack said. "They won't even tell me who the guy was."

"It doesn't matter. Vadik doesn't know the real location of the *Red Star* and the Frenchman probably drowned. Either way, we'll never see them again."

Jack inhaled deeply. He wanted to believe her, but his gut was telling him something different.

"Now..." Alice's voice deepened. Her hand balled the fabric of his shirt and she pulled him close to her. "I'm going to make good on my promise and lock us away in the closest honeymoon suite I can find and not let you out for a week!"

"I'll race ya!" Jack wiggled his eyebrows and kissed her.

# EPILOGUE

Jack closed the suitcase on the bed and zipped it shut. The shower in the bathroom turned on. He was tempted to lie down and take a nap before they headed to the airport. He and Alice had spent a glorious week between the sheets. They'd made love twice today and it was still morning. He was exhausted. Very, very happy but he needed to get some rest. She was killing him.

*What a way to go.*

He smiled.

Someone knocked on the hotel door.

Jack quietly crossed the carpeted floor and stood to the side of the door. He listened then checked the peephole.

Dimitri stood in the hallway.

Jack opened the door but the huge Russian made no move to come in.

"Good to see you, Dimitri. I didn't expect you to be out of the hospital so soon," Jack said.

"It was just a flesh wound." Dimitri shrugged.

Nobody gets medevacked for a flesh wound. Jack had seen him stabbed and the amount of blood he'd lost firsthand; he knew Dimitri was minimizing his injuries but that was the kind of man he was. Humble.

"What was in the briefcase?" Jack asked.

"Vindication. The *Red Star*'s orders and the ship's log." A single tear ran down his cheek. He shot forward and hugged Jack with surprising strength. His voice was raw with emotion. "From my mother, my crew, their mothers and myself, I owe you a debt."

"You don't owe me anything." Jack thought back to his feelings about his own father's murder. He was glad he might have eased their pain.

Dimitri shook his head. "I pay my debts. Alice told me who her grandfather is. The name was familiar."

Jack stepped back. "Do want to come inside?"

Dimitri didn't move. "I've been looking for the *Red Star* for years. In doing so, I've met many... questionable contacts. I made inquiries among them. Alice's grandfather is a wanted man."

"I'm aware. The Ukrainian government thinks he took money."

"Others do too. There is a price on his head. A very sizeable sum. You both need to be careful. I don't want to scare your wife, but know this, Jack: the men after her grandfather are truly ruthless men."

Jack nodded. "I appreciate the warning. I'd also appreciate any other details you could find out."

Dimitri hugged him again and pounded his back. "I will, my friend. But don't take this threat lightly. One of them hunting for her grandfather is Anatoli Belilovski."

"I'm not familiar with the name. Who is he? The Russian Dyab?"

"No. He is a man even the Dyab would fear."

**THE GIRL WHO LIVED**

Ten years ago, four people were brutally murdered. One girl lived. As the anniversary of the murders approaches, Faith Winters is released from the psychiatric hospital and yanked back to the last spot on earth she wants to be— her hometown where the slayings took place. Wracked by the lingering echoes of survivor's guilt, Faith spirals into a black hole of alcoholism and wanton self-destruction. Finding no solace at the bottom of a bottle, Faith decides to track down her sister's killer— and then discovers that she's the one being hunted.

**Best Mystery-Thriller eBook of the Year** — *IPB Awards*
**Winner Best Thriller** — *National Indie Excellence Awards*
**Winner Best Thriller** — *Silver Falchion Award*
**Finalist eBook Fiction** — *Indie Book Awards*
**Silver Medal Suspense** — *Reader's Favorite Book Awards*

*How can one woman uncover the truth*
*when everyone's a suspect—including herself?*

*The Girl Who Lived* should come with a warning label: once you start reading, you won't be able to stop. Not since *Girl on the Train* and *Gone Girl* has a psychological thriller kept readers so addicted—and guessing right until the last page.

## ONE LITTLE LIE

### *A LIE IS A WELCOME MAT FOR THE DEVIL…*

Kate had high hopes when she moved to her husband's hometown, but her domestic bliss was short-lived. Blindsided by her spouse's public affair with his high school sweetheart, Kate's determined to hold onto custody of her kids and pull herself together. When Kate's struck in the head by a drone at her son's soccer game and face-plants in the grass, it's more than her self-esteem that's shattered. The drone's footage reveals that someone is stalking her. And though the handsome detective she's falling for vows to protect her, Kate knows to be wary of any man making vows.

With things spiraling out of control, she tells a lie. It was only *One Little Lie*, but her grandmother always said, a lie is a welcome mat for the devil, and with the one she told, Kate just rolled out the red carpet. Everything she worked for begins to unravel, along with her sanity. Confused, alone, and afraid, can Kate untangle the web of lies and unmask her stalker, or will she lose everything—including her life?

*One Little Lie* is a riveting suspense novel set in an idyllic town where money talks, gossip flows, and the court of public opinion rules. Jump on for a fun, fast-paced ride with a book you can't put down!

# DON'T MISS OUT ON ANY OF
# THE DETECTIVE JACK STRATTON SERIES!

The Detective Jack Stratton Mystery-Thriller Series, authored by *Wall Street Journal* bestselling writer Christopher Greyson, has 5,000+ five-star reviews and over a million readers and counting. If you'd love to read another page-turning thriller with mystery, humor, and a dash of romance, pick up the next book in the highly acclaimed series today:

**And Then She Was GONE**

A hometown hero with a heart of gold, Jack Stratton was raised in a whorehouse by his prostitute mother. When his foster mother asks him to look into a missing girl's disappearance, Jack quickly gets drawn into a baffling mystery. As Jack digs deeper, everyone becomes a suspect—including himself. Caught between the criminals and the cops, can Jack discover the truth in time to save the girl? Or will he become the next victim?

**GIRL JACKED**

Guilt has driven a wedge between Jack and the family he loves. When Jack, now a police officer, hears the news that his foster sister Michelle is missing, it cuts straight to his core. Forced to confront the demons from his past, Jack must take action, find Michelle, and bring her home... or die trying.

**JACK KNIFED**

Constant nightmares have forced Jack to seek answers about his rough childhood and the dark secrets hidden there. The mystery surrounding Jack's birth father leads Jack to investigate the twenty-seven-year-old murder case in Hope Falls.

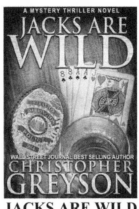

**JACKS ARE WILD**

When Jack's sexy old flame disappears, no one thinks it's suspicious except Jack and one unbalanced witness. He knows that Marisa has a past, and if it ever caught up with her—it would be deadly. The trail leads him into all sorts of trouble—landing him smack in the middle of an all-out mob war between the Italian Mafia and the Japanese Yakuza.

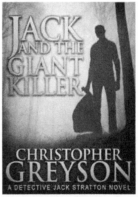

**JACK AND THE GIANT KILLER**

While recovering from a gunshot wound, Jack gets a seemingly harmless private investigation job—locate the owner of a lost dog—Jack begrudgingly assists. Little does he know it will place him directly in the crosshairs of a merciless serial killer.

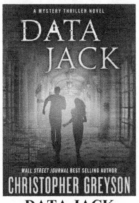

**DATA JACK**

When Replacement gets a job setting up a computer network for a jet-setting software tycoon things turn deadly for her and Jack. Can Jack and Alice stop a pack of ruthless criminals before they can Data Jack?

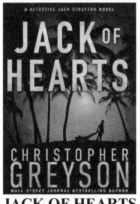

**JACK OF HEARTS**

Jack Stratton is heading south for some fun in the sun. Already nervous about introducing his girlfriend, Jack is still waiting for Alice's answer to his marriage proposal. Now, Jack finds it's up to him to stop a crazed killer, save his parents, and win the hand of the girl he loves—but if he survives, will it be Jack who ends up with a broken heart?

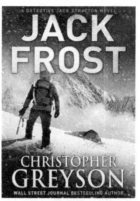

**JACK FROST**

Jack has a new assignment: to investigate the suspicious death of a soundman on the hit TV show *Planet Survival*. What started out as a game is now a deadly competition for survival. As the temperature drops and the body count rises, what will get them first? The mountain or the killer?

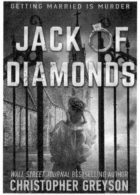

**JACK OF DIAMONDS**

All Jack Stratton wants to do is get married to the woman he loves—and make it through the wedding. As Jack and Alice fight a deadly killer, their long, happy future together seems like it's just inches from slipping away. This time, "till death do us part" might just be a bit too accurate.

Also available:

Epic Fantasy

**PURE OF HEART**

Orphaned and alone, rogue-teen Dean Walker has learned how to take care of himself on the rough city streets. Unjustly wanted by the police, he takes refuge within the shadows of the city. When Dean stumbles upon an old man being mugged, he tries to help— only to discover that the victim is anything but helpless and far more than he appears. Together with three friends, he sets out on an epic quest where only the pure of heart will prevail.

-----

-----

## INTRODUCING
### *THE ADVENTURES OF FINN AND ANNIE*

Finnian Church chased his boyhood dream of following in his father's law-enforcing footsteps by way of the United States Armed Forces. As soon as he finished his tour of duty, Finn planned to report to the police academy. But the winds of war have a way of changing a man's plans. Finn returned home a decorated war hero, but without a leg. Disillusioned but undaunted, it wasn't long before he discovered a way to keep his ambitions alive and earn a living as an insurance investigator.

Finn finds himself in need of a videographer to document the accident scenes. Into his orderly business and simple life walks Annie Summers. A lovely free spirit and single mother of two, Annie has a physical challenge of her own—she's been completely deaf since childhood.

Finn and Annie find themselves tested and growing in ways they never imagined. Join this unlikely duo as they investigate their way through murder, arson, theft, embezzlement, and maybe even love, seeking to distinguish between truth and lies, scammers and victims.

**Don't miss out, pickup the whole collection on Amazon today!**

# ACKNOWLEDGMENTS

I would like to thank all the wonderful readers out there. It is you who make the literary world what it is today—a place of dreams filled with tales of adventure! To all of you who have spread word of my novels via social media (Facebook and Twitter) and who have taken the time to go back and write a great review, I say THANK YOU! Your efforts keep the characters alive and give me the encouragement and time to keep writing. I can't thank YOU enough.

Word of mouth is crucial for any author to succeed. If you enjoyed the novel, please consider leaving a review at Amazon, even if it is only a line or two; it would make all the difference and I would appreciate it very much.

I would also like to thank my amazing wife for standing beside me every step of the way on this journey. My thanks also go out to my two awesome kids—Laura and Christopher, my dear mother and the rest of my family. Finally, thank you to my wonderful team, Anne Cherry, Maia McViney, Michael Mishoe, Charlie Wilson of Landmark Editorial, and the unbelievably helpful beta readers!

# ABOUT THE AUTHOR

My name is Christopher Greyson, and I am a storyteller.

Since I was a little boy, I have dreamt of what mystery was around the next corner, or what quest lay over the hill. If I couldn't find an adventure, one usually found me, and now I weave those tales into my stories. I am blessed to have written the bestselling Detective Jack Stratton Mystery-Thriller Series. The collection includes *And Then She Was GONE, Girl Jacked, Jack Knifed, Jacks Are Wild, Jack and the Giant Killer, Data Jack, Jack of Hearts, Jack Frost, Jack of Diamonds,* and coming soon *Captain Jack.* I have also penned the bestselling psychological thriller, *The Girl Who Lived* and a special collection of mysteries, *The Adventures of Finn and Annie.*

My love for tales of mystery and adventure began with my grandfather, a decorated World War I hero. I will never forget being introduced to his friend, a WWI pilot who flew across the skies at the same time as the feared, legendary Red Baron. My love of reading and storytelling eventually led me to write *Pure of Heart,* a young adult fantasy that I released in 2014.

I love to hear from my readers. Please visit ChristopherGreyson.com, where you can become a preferred reader and enjoy advanced notifications of book releases and more! Thank you for reading my novels. I hope my stories have brightened your day.

Sincerely,

Made in the USA
Monee, IL
18 October 2021